William Clark Russell

Jack's Courtship

A Sailor's Yarn of Love and Shipwreck. Vol 2

William Clark Russell

Jack's Courtship
A Sailor's Yarn of Love and Shipwreck. Vol 2

ISBN/EAN: 9783337327903

Printed in Europe, USA, Canada, Australia, Japan

Cover: Foto ©Andreas Hilbeck / pixelio.de

More available books at **www.hansebooks.com**

JACK'S COURTSHIP:

A SAILOR'S YARN OF LOVE AND SHIPWRECK.

BY

W. CLARK RUSSELL,

AUTHOR OF "THE 'LADY MAUD,'" "A SEA QUEEN," ETC.

IN THREE VOLUMES.
VOL. II.

LONDON:

SAMPSON LOW, MARSTON, SEARLE & RIVINGTON,
CROWN BUILDINGS, 188, FLEET STREET.
1884.

LONDON:
PRINTED BY WILLIAM CLOWES AND SONS, LIMITED,
STAMFORD STREET AND CHARING CROSS.

CONTENTS OF VOL. II.

JACK'S COURTSHIP.

CHAPTER I.

THE "STRATHMORE."

A GOOD proof of the interest my uncle took in my proposal to ship along with Florence and go to sea with her was in a letter I received next morning from him, enclosing a cheque for one hundred pounds. "My dear Jack," he wrote, "the accompanying money will enable you to pay your passage out, and lay in a stock of shirts and toothpicks for the voyage. Let us have no thanks —no nonsense. Just pay the draft into your bank, if you have one, and belay all jaw about it unless you want me to think you a swab, which is a term I think you object to. You'll be giving us a call soon, I hope. Yours, UNCLE."—There also arrived a long letter from Sophie in answer to the lamentations I had poured out to her two days before. The dear girl had evidently taken a great deal of trouble in writing this reply, for there were no less than seven quotations from five poets, whose works it must have been no joke to her to overhaul for the lines, all of which were very apt and bore fully upon the state of my heart; and moreover she was exceedingly poetical on her own account, as for example, when she assured me that love was a plant which tears were invented to keep green, and that if Florence and I were truly attached, Mr. Alphonso Hawke might cause all the seas of the world not only to roll between us but over us without washing away our affection. She gave me some news which was more interesting to me than the poetry, namely, that Mr. Hawke, his sister and daughters, had arrived at Clifton Lodge on the previous day, and that a Miss Booth had told her that Colonel Jones had said to her father that Mr. Hawke had told him that his daughter would be leaving Clifton for Australia in about three weeks' time. I say that this news was interesting to me because it proved that up to the present, at all events, no change had come over the spirit of Alphonso's intentions.

I wrote a few words of thanks to my uncle for his handsome gift, and a letter to Sophie, the production of which afflicted me with a lively sense of hypocrisy, as, in order not to excite suspicion, I had to write as if Florence's going rendered me inconsolable. However, if it is possible to conceive any sort of deception forgivable, I think mine was, ungrateful as it might appear, for it was practised at the request of my uncle, who very properly did not want his wife and daughter to have any knowledge of the blow I was aiming at old Hawke's schemes.

Two days after my chat with my uncle at the hotel, I determined to take a run down to the East India Docks and have a look at the *Strathmore*. But first I thought it advisable to call on my way at the offices of the Company, and ascertain if Aunt Damaris and Florence had booked their passage. Arrived at Fenchurch Street I entered the offices of Duncan, Golightly, & Co., and as I stood at the broad counter, behind which half a dozen of clerks were hard at work, the sense of my old life came up in me so strong that I felt as if my calling was still that of a sailor, and that I was here to obtain a berth. There was one old chap I remembered, the others were strangers. The old fellow looked at me through his spectacles, but did not recognize me, and went on with his work. A young man came to the counter, and I said, " You have a ship advertised to sail on the 28th ? "

" Yes, sir."

" Does she call at Plymouth ? "

" No. Passengers must embark at the Docks or Gravesend."

"I expect some friends will take cabins in that vessel, and if they go I shall accompany them. Is your cuddy full?"

"No, sir; there are still three cabins vacant."

"Give me the names of the people who have already booked, will you? I want to know if my friends are among them."

"What are their names, sir?"

"Miss Damaris Hawke and Miss Florence Hawke."

He looked at a pile of letters, and presently pulled out a sheet of paper, gilt-edged, adorned with Alphonso's old gander, and after glancing over it said, "Miss Damaris Hawke and Miss Florence Hawke, No. 6 cabin. The first-named lady arrived home in the vessel last voyage, and occupied the cabin she now applies for." He then laid a plan of the saloon before me with the cabins numbered. There was a row of six cabins of a side and two aft, the one on the port side being the captain's; the two forward berths facing each other and coming just under the break of the poop were occupied respectively by the first and second mates. "This, then," said I, putting my finger on No. 6 —that is, the one next the captain's, right aft— "is the cabin that has been taken by the two ladies you name. Which are the berths still to let?"

He indicated them.

" I'll go and have a look at the ship," said I.
" What's the charge for one of these cabins ? "

" Sixty-two pound ten."

" Do I get the cabin to myself for that ? " I
asked.   He answered that that would depend.
The company only guaranteed exclusive use on
payment of such and such a sum (I forget what
it was).   " I'll save my money and take my
chance," said I, " of there being more cabins than
passengers, in which case of course I shall have
the berth to myself ? "   He answered, " Yes,
certainly."

" Are the ladies sure of taking No. 6 ? "

" Sure," he replied.   " Half the passage money
was sent with the application."

My heart came into my throat when I heard
this.

" Tell me now," said I, " if the Captain
Thompson I see advertised as the commander of
the *Strathmore* is the Daniel Thompson who was
some years ago second mate of your ship the
Montrose."

He went to the clerk in the spectacles and
repeated my question.   The old fellow said " Yes,"
without looking up.

" Is he in London ? " I inquired.

" Yes, sir, and if you're going down to the docks
at once you'll probably find him about.   If you
like, I'll accompany you and show you the ship."

I thanked him and said I believed I could find
my way there without assistance, and so quitted
the office. I was in joyous spirits as I made my
way to the railway station in Fenchurch Street.
The fact of the cabin having been secured for Aunt
Damaris and Florence, and half the fare paid,
made me realize the meaning of the adventurous
job I was on to a degree I had not approached
before. For three months certain should I be
associated with my darling, week after week, day
after day, and my heart beat high in me as with
the rapidity of thought I drew a score of pictures
of our rapturous communion, in gales and calms,
in heat and cold, under skies of brass and nights
soft and sweet with moonlight and dew. And a
mighty vigorous imagination I must have had even
to come near to anything poetical in Fenchurch
Street Station. The roadway was filled with a
crowd of grimy fellows, turnpike sailors, loafing
scarecrows as bad as the worst specimens of the
ragamuffins I have seen shivering in shipping-
yards and scrawling their hatred of captains and
owners upon benches and whitewashed walls. It
took me back some years when I got upon the
platform and looked at the people who were
waiting for the train; mates in velvet waistcoats,
skippers with red faces and a consequential strut
smoking cigars, seamen of divers nationalities,
some with white bags, some with all they had in

the world wrapped up in a red or blue handkerchief; Dutchmen grunting like pigs, negroes with a bland grin on their black faces as they stared about them, and English Jack, drunk, shoving, and noisy. I say the sight took me back some years, and it wanted little to persuade me that my chest and bedding were aboard, and that I was bound along with the others for the "pier-head jump."

Presently a Blackwall train arrived, a lot of people tumbled out, and I took my seat in a first-class carriage that smelt like the parlour of a public-house after a night's orgy. Just as we were about to start, the door was flung open and a man bundled in. I was full of thought and hardly glanced at him. Presently he said, "Very genteel rolling stock they have on this line, sir. But I suppose anything's good enough for sailors. Do you object to my lighting a pipe to kill the fragrance in this atmosphere?"

"Not at all," said I, looking at him hard, struck by his voice, in which I fancied I could catch a note that was familiar to me.

He was a rather short squarely built man of about forty-five years of age, with reddish whiskers and beard that half circled his face as though you should cut a grummet of rope in half and pass it under your chin with the ends against your ears; his face was the reddest I ever saw on a man, and rendered peculiar by the colour lying in lines and blotches, so that when you took a close squint at him, his skin seemed to be covered with a red lace veil with the meshes thickened in places. He had fine honest laughing eyes and a heartily cheerful expression of countenance, and was in his way the completest figure of a merchant seaman one could imagine, dressed in dark blue cloth and a cap with a shovel-shaped peak to it. Finding me staring at him, he began to stare at me, meanwhile groping in his side pockets for his pipe and tobacco. At last I said, " Six years ago I was shipmate with a second mate aboard the *Montrose* named Daniel Thompson. If you are not he, then you are the devil."

"Daniel Thompson is my name," said he, " and six years ago I was second mate aboard the *Montrose*, and—why, heart alive oh! you're Jack Seymour!" and, with a sailor's warmth, he flung down his pipe and tobacco-pouch, jumped into the seat opposite me, and grasped both my hands. " Think of my not knowing you!" cried he. " But then you've grown a moustache and you're a foot taller, and who the blazes would recognize Jack Seymour in those shore-going duds ?"

"This is a strange meeting, Thompson," said I. "Will you believe it—I was actually bound in quest of you. I am going to the docks to have a look at your *Strathmore*. Do you know I am thinking of sailing with you ?"

"Sailing with me !" he exclaimed, letting go my

hands and returning to his pipe; "why, I heard that you had knocked off the sea some years ago—come into an estate—and was living up to the hammer somewhere or other."

"Oh!" said I, laughing, "don't suppose I'm going to sea with you as a sailor. I'm thinking of taking a cabin in your ship for a voyage to New South Wales. I saw your name in the advertisement as skipper, and just now called at the office of the Company to make sure of you. They told me I should find you aboard."

"I hope you'll come with me; I hope you'll come!" cried he in his hearty fashion. "We'll find many a yarn to spin together—many a talk over old days. But what in the name of Moses takes you to sea again, even as passenger? Didn't you get enough of salt water in your time? Only let somebody leave me an estate," said he, lighting his pipe, "and there's never a house agent in the United Kingdom who could find me a dwelling deep enough inland."

"I'll tell you presently why I am going to sea again," I replied. "But first let's hear of yourself. Are you married? are you saving money? how long have you been skipper?"

He answered these questions by a story that carried us to Blackwall, but though I kept on nodding and saying "Oh!" and "Really!" and "Indeed!" I am sure I did not give his yarn all the attention he believed it was receiving. The truth is, my mind was so busy with my own affairs that I could think of nothing else; though I took in enough of what he said to gather that he was married and had a couple of youngsters, that his wife had a trifle of money, and that he had commanded the *Strathmore* two years.

We sallied forth arm in arm, he jabbering incessantly, and, after walking a bit, came abreast of a ship whose name I did not need to inquire. I stopped to have a look. There in front of me lay the counterpart of the vessel in whose heart I had passed many a long month; whose mastheads I had watched swaying under stars which no northern dweller ever beholds, whose massive shrouds had shrieked back the refrain of the Cape Horn hurricane, whose topmost canvas had glimmered like dissolving wreaths of vapour amid the breathless gloom of the hushed tropical night.

"What are you stopping for?" shouted Thompson. "What do you see that you're staring aloft? Anything wrong there?"

"See!" cried I; "why, the picture of my old life, Daniel; the old business of the lonely watch, the streaming decks, the bunk under which I used to grope for my boots when the horrid shout of 'Eight bells!' awoke me from dreams of feather beds and soft tack and mutton-chops for breakfast. What a jolly life the sailor's is, Thompson! Why,

I'd rather be a rat in your lazarette than go through it again; and yet, hang me if the sight of that craft of yours don't infuse a sort of tenderness into me, too, though, for all I know, her iron ribs may be only one degree removed from the ore, and her timber planking as rotten as an old Stilton cheese."

"Don't you go and make any mistake of that kind, my young friend," exclaimed Thompson. "Rotten! Why, as a matter of strength, the Tower of London's a joke to that ship; and as to her angle frames being one degree removed from the ore, there's nothing wanting but a little grinding to convert them into the loveliest razors in the world. But come aboard, man, come aboard!" and we stepped along the plank over the side and sprang on to the deck.

A dock is to a ship what a dressing-room is to a lady, and you must expect dishevelment until she sallies forth into her ocean-world, when you will find her dressed in the latest fashion, painted and sparkling, and dropping many a handsome curtsey as she goes. The *Strathmore's* topgallant and royal yards were down, all her sails unbent, and the running gear unrove; the yards were braced fore and aft, there were lumpers at work in her hold, and grimy faces grinned at you over the combings of the main hatch; a crane alongside was slinging cases of merchandize into her, and her main deck was a surface of straw, dirt, wet, and what sailors call raffle. But just as a pretty wench with tousled hair, dirty face, befouled frock, and little toes peeping out of her yawning boots, preserves her prettiness and takes the eye in spite of her squalid attire, so did the *Strathmore* offer to the experienced gaze every point of a handsome, powerful clipper ship, notwithstanding her grimy decks, her disordered yards, the nakedness of her upper spars, her rigged-in jibboom. She was, as the advertisement about her said, a composite ship—that is, built of iron frames covered with wood. She was slightly longer than the *Portia*, with a trifle less of beam, and had the reputation of being a very fast sailer, though what is termed a wet ship. This indeed might have been guessed by looking at her bows, which were almost like a yacht's, with hardly any perceptible swell or " flairing." Her lower masts were painted white ; she had channels, though even then those appendages for spreading wide the lower rigging were going out of date, and chequered sides—a broad white band running the length of her, broken with painted ports, so that with her square stern decorated with a row of cabin windows, short royal mastheads, and exceedingly square yards, she might at a distance have passed for a frigate.

Thompson, however, gave me very little time to look about : for after taking a squint down the main hatchway and bawling out some question to the people below, he again seized my arm and walked me into the cuddy, as the saloon under the poop was formerly called. This was a fine sweep of cabin, most handsomely decorated, with maple panellings and stanchions cased in satinwood, superbly fluted and gilded, whilst as much as was revealed of the mizzenmast was cased so as to resemble a Corinthian column, abaft of which a pianoforte was secured. A very handsome staircase led into the steerage on the lower deck, and on either side were the cabins or berths; whilst overhead were two large skylights, racks full of glass for the tobles, globes for gold-fish, together with a row of brightly burnished swinging trays hanging over the tables, which were shaped like the letter T, one running athwartships atop and the other coming down nearly the whole length of the cuddy. I am no upholsterer or house decorator, and cannot talk to you about this interior in such a way as to make you understand what a radiant, breezy drawing-room of a place it was; but I often recall it and other passenger ship saloons I have peeped into when I hear of the splendours of the present age in that way, and wonder that there should be so much brag about us, really as though in magnificence of marine decoration we had gone leagues ahead, and clean out of sight of our ancestors: the truth being that many a long year before my time, in the days

of John Company's ships and the castle-like West
India traders, the cabins, hired by old Nabobs and
opulent planters at an immense cost, were a perfect
blaze of costly furniture, as let noble Tom Cringle
certify, who, in speaking of a vessel that he boarded
of five hundred tons, rattles away about panels fitted
with crimson cloth, edged with gold mouldings, and
superb damask hangings before the stern windows
and side berths, and plate-glass mirrors, and
brilliant swinging lamps, and a splendid grand
piano, and a rudder-case richly carved and gilded
to resemble a palm tree, "the stem painted
white and interlaced with golden fretwork, like
the lozenges of a pine-apple, while the leaves
spread up and abroad on the roof," and so on and
so on.   Faith, I often think there is a deal of the
swab in our natures: we barely allow our fore-
fathers the smallest merit, and, standing on tiptoe,
crow as if we bantams were the only Cochin-chinas
creation had produced.   Why, who shall swear
that at this moment some poor little creature is not
writing a book to prove that Trafalgar was a twopenny business, and that it would need the blue-
jackets of the present day to make a *battle* of that
job?   Is not Shakespeare overrated, and is there
no poet amongst us capable of better work?   Is
Wellington a patch upon the living splendid
generals whose breasts are one glorious constellation
of medals and orders?

But let me haul off from these distracting reflections before I lose my temper and grow personal; for hang me if I'm not already in the humour, mates, to give you an idea of what honest disgust sounds like! Well, as I have said, Daniel Thompson marched me through the cuddy, past the mizzen-mast, and the piano, and the stove, into his cabin, the door of which he closed, and overhauling a locker took from it a box of cigars and four fat bottles, and then producing some glasses, pointed to the cigar-box and afterwards to a chair, and said, "Now, Mr. Jack Seymour, make yourself at home, sir." This I did without parley, helping myself to a glass of excellent liquor and lighting a cigar. He did likewise, and in a few minutes we lay sprawling upon the lockers talking like brothers.

"This is the sort of cabin to go to sea in, Daniel," said I, casting my eyes round; "room to grope about in when something you want fetches away and gets lost, and a good view of the world out of those back windows. Is the cabin alongside just as roomy?"

"Just the same size," he answered.

"They told me at the office that it's taken by a Miss Damaris Hawke."

"Oho!" said he, "that's the lady that came home with us this time, and she's going out with us again, eh? She's a rum old fish; only wants a pea-jacket to make her a sailor. Coming on deck one night in the tropics she stepped aft and found the man at the wheel nodding, whereupon, hang me, Seymour, if she didn't take him by the arm and shake him, and ask him if he knew where he was going. The man fell to abusing her—he was a little Dane—and the shindy brought the second mate to them. I laughed till I cried when he told me the story, and ever after the hands called her Lady Damn-her-eyes, and put her into their songs. D'ye know her?" said he suddenly, as if struck by my face.

"Thompson," said I, "I'll tell you all about it—why I'm interested in Miss Damaris Hawke, why I'm going to Australia, why I choose this ship. But it's a profound secret, Daniel: a matter that concerns my very senses, for if I'm dished I shall go mad. On your honour as an old shipmate you'll stow what I'm about to tell you as deep down into your silence and confidence as it'll go?"

"Well," he replied, laughing, "so long as it don't involve any scuttling or stranding or firing job, you may trust me."

Thereupon, without any further preface I told him the whole story. How I had gone to Clifton on a visit to some relatives and fallen in love with Florence Hawke: how her father wanted her to marry another man named Reginald Morecombe, whose offer she had refused: how Aunt Damaris had arrived from Sydney and, as I supposed, recommended her brother to send Florence with her to Australia as a good way of getting rid of me: how, as I had no occupation, nothing in the world to do, I had made up my mind to go to Australia with her, and how my resolution had been completed by discovering that the ship whose name Florence had mentioned was commanded by an old shipmate and friend.

He listened as attentively and gravely as if I was talking to him on freights and bills of lading, and when I had done said, "I understand, Jack; but is the girl worth the trouble you are going to take?"

"Stop till you see her," said I.

"Is she fond of you?" he asked.

"I think she is," I replied.

"And I suppose," said he, "that you reckon upon getting her to promise to marry you on your arrival at Sydney."

I nodded, for there was no use in telling him that this voyage was only undertaken by me as part of a somewhat forlorn courtship.

"I'm afraid," said he, "you'll find the aunt a big mouthful as a pill. Does your sweetheart know you intend to join her?"

"No; nothing has been said—nobody but my uncle and you are aware of my intention. I'll get you to tell her I'm aboard when we're clear of the river."

He grinned and exclaimed, "I suppose you don't mind trusting me now that you know I have a wife. I wondered at your curiosity when you asked me if I was married; but I understand your fears. I was a very suspicious man myself when I was in love."

I laughed as I looked at his jolly bright-red face, and observed the self-complacency in it.

"But," continued he, "you're giving me, as skipper of this vessel, a rum commission. I hope when I've told her you're aboard you'll do the rest of the business yourself. I'm no hand at messages. I never could talk soft, and when I asked my girl to marry me, all I could find to say was, ' Susie, shall we get spliced? Say the word, and when you're ready there'll be a cab at the door with me in it.' After all," said he, "plain talk is better than romancing. A woman knows what you mean when you sheer alongside of her, and would much rather you should speak out than humbug with her hands and keep her waiting."

"Your views are very correct," said I. "But every man has not your sense. Daniel, there's one thing I shall have to do. I wish it were not necessary, but I don't see my way without it."

" What ? " he asked.

" I shall have to ship under an assumed name. I'll tell you why. Aunt Damaris has never seen me; but she would instantly guess who I am if she were to hear of me as Jack Seymour; and if she's a person capable of giving a seaman a talking to, you may depend on it she would furnish me with even less opportunity of being with my darling than I should find if we all remained at Bristol."

"That's quite true," said he. "If you ship as Brown or Jones, you can talk and walk with your sweetheart without exciting the aunt's suspicions— unless, indeed, you pile on your attentions too thick."

"I'll not do that," said I; "at all events, whilst she's looking."

"There's no reason," said he, "why you shouldn't take an alias. It's the usual thing with murderers, and forgers, and thieves, and why not with lovers? But I say, Seymour, whatever surname you take, please stick to your Christian handle, for I'm sure to call you Jack when I'm not thinking, and if you ship as Alfred or William, the slip will be awkward."

"Let's settle a name at once," said I. "Give me something that'll come easy to you."

"Anything in two syllables will do for me," he answered; "what do you think of Johnson?'

"Too common," I replied. "If Aunt Damaris resemble her brother, she respects blood—you know what blood is, don't you, Daniel?"

"I've heard of it," he replied. "It belongs to

the upper circles, don't it, and is rarely to be found
in anything much lower than a squire."

"As I was saying, if the aunt respects blood it'll
be worth while to impress her.   I wish you'd allow
me three syllables, Daniel."

"Well, I don't mind three," said he; "but whatever it is, let it be pronounced as it's spelt.   We
brought home a man last voyage called Majori-
banks.   When I saw the name written, dash my
wig if I didn't think he was in the army, and I
kept calling him Major Banks until, growing
annoyed, he rounded on me with, 'Excuse me,
Captain, my name is Marchbanks.'   No doubt the
correct thing to do with a major is to make him
march," said he, grinning from ear to ear over his
vile pun, "but if major's to be called march, why
isn't it spelt march?"

"What do you think of Trevelyan?" said I.
He reflected, and said he doubted if he should be
able to remember it, and asked me to give him
something in the nautical line.   But nothing that
I could think of as belonging to a ship or the sea
would satisfy me; so, after a number of sugges-
tions, we fixed upon Egerton, as having an aristocratic sound and being easy to pronounce.

On the whole, my friend did not seem so much
astonished by my scheme as I had expected; but
this might be because sailors see so many strange
things, and pass through so many curious adven-

tures, that the faculty of being amazed is soon worn out in them. We continued for some time talking about the voyage and Miss Damaris Hawke and other matters; and I then went to look at the unlet cabins, and, after peering and considering, decided upon taking No. 4, it being the roomiest of those which remained unhired, and for that reason safe to choose on the chance of some fellow sharing it with me.

"Will you come aboard in the docks or at Gravesend?" asked Thompson.

"In the docks," I replied. "If the Hawkes don't join you at Gravesend, we may take it that they are not going to Australia in the *Strathmore*."

"Ay," he replied, "for when we leave Gravesend we go clean away to Australia, I hope. You may certainly take it as you say, that if they don't join the ship at Gravesend they've either postponed the voyage or abandoned it."

"Then, of course, I shall go ashore again," said I.

"What!" cried he, "forfeit your passage-money and the delight of eighty or ninety days of sea and my society!"

I laughed and said, "But there's no use supposing they won't come. Hawke's not a man to send your Company a cheque unless he meant to get something for it."

"If it is to depend upon the aunt," he said,

" you need not fear of being disappointed. She likes the ship and she likes me, and I now recollect that when we were in the Channel she asked me if there was any chance of my taking the same mates and stewards next time, as she thought the former very *safe* gentlemen to sail with, and the stewards she considered extremely attentive. That looks as if she had made up her mind even then. Depend upon it, she'll come if she can."

I asked who the mates were, but he gave me names which were unknown to me. I then took a turn over the vessel, and having spent pretty nearly two hours aboard, I bade my old shipmate good-bye, begging him as he valued my happiness and prospects to behave with extreme circumspection when I joined the vessel; never on any account to let it be supposed that I had been at sea as a sailor, but to let the passengers imagine that he called me Jack because we had known each other as boys; and I wound up by asking him to come and spend a day with me at the West End. But this he said he could not manage, as his wife and children were in the country, and he meant to pass a few days with them, and when he returned his hands would be too full of business for visiting.

CHAPTER II.

HOODWINKING.

I WILL spare you an account of the thoughts with which I beguiled my ride home and the various reflections which kept me as restless as a buoy in a seaway. So far everything had been plain sailing; Daniel Thompson had proved to be my old shipmate, and the man of all others whom I would have chosen to go to sea with on such an errand as mine; a berth had been secured by Aunt Damaris and Florence, and half the passage-money paid; and the only fly in this pleasant pot of ointment with which I was greasing the *ways* of my courtship was the fear that at the last moment Hawke might change his mind and keep Florence at home.

However, my business was to go on steering a straight course and take my chance of the wind holding steady; and accordingly, on my return home from the docks, I forwarded the necessary deposit money to Duncan, Golightly, & Co. for cabin No. 4, and signed myself " John Egerton," feeling a trifle uncomfortable perhaps as I did so, though surely my conscience was needlessly sensitive, for I was as guiltless of all wrongdoing in assuming a name as an actor who puts on a wig and runs upon the stage and calls himself the Duke of Gloucester.

A few days after I had visited the *Strathmore* I went down to Clifton. Hearty as was my respect for my uncle's character, I never could think of him as a man capable of holding his peace, and I was in constant fear that he would betray my project to his wife, and that the news would reach Florence, and perhaps old Hawke. But I was mistaken; he was as secret as the grave. He had not only not given his wife or daughters the least hint of the truth, but he assured me that he had done his best to dismiss the thing from his own mind, that he might humbug his conscience into believing that he was as ignorant as the others.

" I want," says he, " to be able not only to look but to *feel* innocent when the truth comes out, so that should Mr. Hawke call upon me or send me an impertinent letter, I shall be able to talk to him with the sense of being an injured man."

This policy in him suited me perfectly, and I begged him to ask me no more questions about my schemes, " for the more I talk," said I, " the more you are obliged to know; whereas if nothing be said you cannot be sure, even whilst we now converse, that I am still bent on going to Australia."

"You're right," he replied, "and so we'll confine ourselves to Punch and Judy or the weather;" though for all that his curiosity was so sharp set that I believe he would have been glad to take his chance of his conscience had I offered him the least encouragement to make inquiries.

However, as I have said, it answered my purpose very well to keep him silent and ignorant. I was a bachelor, but I knew what married people are, and how if a wife comes to suspect that her husband is hiding anything from her she will never rest till she has it out of him. But I had a very difficult part to play with Sophie; so difficult that it drove me back to London next day and determined me to visit them no more this side my voyage, though but for that I should have been glad to eke out the time that remained by spending a week at Clifton, where I could have kept myself posted in all the latest news about the Hawkes' movements. The fact is, both Sophie and Amelia expected to find me miserably disconsolate, and I reckoned that Florence would either suspect my sincerity as a lover or guess that I had some scheme on hand if I was not reported to her by my cousins as being broken down. Consequently I had to put on the air of a man whose heart is bleeding, and no harder job did I ever undertake, especially whenever my uncle, who saw into my motive, was looking, for there would be a grin in the cock of his eye that made a sentimental countenance an enormous achievement.

Yet somehow I managed so well that my cousins honestly believed I was in a wretched state of mind, and Sophie did all she could to cheer me. She told me (the moment she had an opportunity of speaking to me alone) that she had met Florence soon after her return from the North in company with her sister, who was in a Bath chair, and had walked with her for nearly half an hour, scarcely noticing Emily, who was very cool, and talking to Florence in order to get all the news she could for me.

"I hope you told her," said I, in my most melancholy manner, "that her going to Australia was an awful blow to me."

"I did, Jack," she replied. "I said that if your heart was not broken outright it was because you believed that separation would not alter her, and that she would bring back the same loving loyal heart she took with her and renew your chance of proving your devotion. 'Before I come back,' said she, 'I dare say he will have found out that he mistook his feelings; he is very young, Sophie. And indeed,' said she, sighing *so* prettily, Jack, 'he ought not to wait nor give me a thought when I am gone, for who knows whether I shall ever return?'"

I groaned so heavily at this that for the moment

I was afraid from the look Sophie gave me that she considered it almost too full of anguish to be honest. But an uneasy conscience is always putting wrong constructions upon things.

"I answered," continued Sophie, "that though you were young you were old enough to be staunch, and I begged her not to leave England without giving me some token for you to remember her by—something for you to go on wearing until she came back."

"What did she say to that?" I asked.

"Why, that she would send me something for you; it hasn't come yet, but the moment it arrives you shall have it."

This moved me to a degree that made the tremor in my voice real enough. Indeed I was as much touched by this proof of Sophie's fidelity to me as I was stirred and affected by Florence's promise as an indication that I had made greater progress into the darling's heart than I had dared to hope. I squeezed my cousin's hand and thanked her tenderly for her suggestion to Florence, and then asked if there was any chance of Mr. Hawke changing his mind and keeping his daughter at home. No; she was afraid that there was no chance at all. Florence had told her that every preparation was being made for the voyage, their cabin was secured and they would join the ship at Gravesend. She said that Florence could not make head nor tail of her father's resolution; she never remembered speaking about me or behaving in any way to account for such an extreme step as sending her all the way to Australia. The suggestion came from Aunt Damaris, and was immediately seized by Mr. Hawke; and she could not account for his conduct, for his willingness to lose her society at home and subject her to the risk of a long voyage, unless something more than Mr. Jack Seymour was at the bottom of her father's reasons for sending her away.

"Did she give you any idea of what that something more might be?" I asked very anxiously.

"No, she has no suspicion. For my part, I believe her father's sole motive is to separate her from you. She declares that she has never said anything about you to him to account for his alarm. But how does she know? Feelings will leak out insensibly; her father may see more than she herself suspects she shows or even possesses. The wonder to me is that Florence should make no stand; that she shouldn't bluntly refuse to be driven to the other end of the world. But I suppose she is sincere when she says she likes the idea of revisiting Sydney, and no doubt she is not very happy at home just now: and then, again, she shows proper dignity in coldly and uncomplainingly obeying her papa and accompanying her aunt. And who knows, Jack, that she would not be willing to go to the North Pole if by making such a journey she could get rid of that worrying, fortune-hunting creature Morecombe?"

At this point we were interrupted and had to break off; nor was I sorry, for it was desperately hard to maintain an air of misery when alone with Sophie, whose sympathy was bound to render her uncommonly shrewd: and besides, conjectures as to Hawke's intentions were exceedingly unprofitable, seeing that all I required to be satisfied upon was, that Aunt Damaris and Florence meant to sail to Sydney in the *Strathmore*.

Well, lads, as I have said, I returned to London next day, because I was but a clumsy hand at masquerading, and was sure that my cousins would find me out if I did not look sharp and haul off. Sophie seemed a good deal struck by my impatience to be gone, and expressed her surprise that I did not stay, if only for the chance of seeing Florence before she left England.

"Do you think," cried I, "that I could say goodbye to my darling who leaves with a misgiving that we may never meet again? Sophie, I could not control myself—the trial would be too much for me. No! tell her, should you meet, why I hurried away: and above all let me have whatever she desires me to remember her by when you get it."

Whether this satisfied Sophie I did not trouble

myself to find out. I knew that whatever might be her thoughts I should right myself when she came to hear that I had sailed with Florence in the *Strathmore*, and meanwhile my business was to keep my plan secret. So before leaving my relations I told my uncle not to expect to see me at Clifton again, as the obligation to play a hypocritical part was altogether too hard, and I felt that every sham sigh I heaved was an outrage upon Sophie's affectionate, faithful nature.

"All right, my boy, do as you please," said he; "but I hope you'll send us a letter from Gravesend to let us know you're gone."

"Certainly," I answered.

"And, on reflection," he continued, "I think you had better address your letter to *me*, telling *me* your motive in going, and so on, as though I knew nothing about it. It will be something to flourish before old Hawke should he trouble me; and it will throw your aunt off the scent, for I don't want her to know that I was all along in your confidence."

This I promised to be sure to do, and then as we were alone I bade him good-bye, for unless he came to see me in London we should not meet again before I sailed. I had never said farewell to my father when I started on a voyage with more emotion than I felt as I held my uncle's hand. And yet so far as words went it came, between us, to no more than a brief "God bless you." Nevertheless I had to linger awhile to recover myself before seeking my aunt and cousins; and though there was little apparent significance in my manner as I took my leave of them, I assure you it was a bitter wrench to say good-bye to Sophie lightly, as though we were to see each other soon, when, could I have had my way, I should have hugged her, and told her we might not meet for months, and perhaps years, and thanked her again and yet again for all that she had done for me, for all she would like to do for me, for her loyal good wishes and sisterly pride in me.

And now, having got back to London, nothing remained but to lay in a stock of such articles as I required for the voyage, and wait for the 28th of the month to arrive. I had not many arrangements to make: indeed, the list was completed when I had bought a good box upon which I had "John Egerton" painted, and put my clothes and purchases in it, and when I had given notice to quit my lodgings to the landlady. And note here: it took me over half an hour to persuade the woman that I was in earnest, and bound to the other end of the world. I was so much a part of her house that she had come to look upon me as she did her front door and staircase, and when she understood that I was in earnest and really going, she sat down upon the floor and wept there.

It was on this day that the post brought me a small parcel, which on opening I found to contain a little square box and a letter. In the box was a locket with a wisp of gold-brown hair coiled up in it, and the letter was from Sophie telling me that the locket was my sweetheart's parting gift. "I may tell you," wrote Sophie, "that Florence quite implied she would have liked to give you this herself, by which you may judge she is not a little disappointed, and perhaps *pained*, by what I had to call your ' incapacity' to bid her good-bye. However, if she understands your reason and you are satisfied, it is not for me to lecture you, though I may as well declare, if I were going to Australia and my lover had not the heart to say farewell to me, I should leave with the feeling that if I chose to fall in love with somebody else across the sea, I might do so safely."

This was a snub to my tremendous young sincerity that set me gaping to speak out, but I restrained myself on reflecting that in a very few days both she and Florence would know the truth. So all that I did was to acknowledge the receipt of the locket in a few lines, saying that my heart was too full to write at length, and that the only answer I could return to her reference to my incapacity to say good-bye to Florence was to ask her to wait until my darling girl came home, and then judge whether I had remained staunch, and whether my behaviour was of a kind to justify Florence in falling in love with anybody else.

This letter being posted, I purchased a riband for the locket, and hid the little keepsake away under my waistcoat, so proud and happy in the possession of this thing that I cannot recall my delight without sorrowfully reflecting that before I could ever again enjoy pleasure so pure my boyish heart must return to me, and I must be loving my first love as I loved her then, when the morning of life was around and the shadows upon the dew leaned into the west.

CHAPTER III.

I EMBARK.

Monday, September 28, 18—. This was the day
fixed for the sailing of the *Strathmore*, and I had
ascertained from the owners, to whom I had forwarded the balance of the passage money, that if I
meant to join the ship in the docks I must be on
board not later than eleven o'clock in the morning.
I had sent my luggage down on the previous
Friday, and, Monday being arrived, I bade my
landlady farewell, and, armed with a large carpet-
bag, in which were stowed the few conveniences I
immediately required, I jumped into a cab and
was driven to Fenchurch Street Station. I had
had so much time in which to thoroughly think
over the resolution I had formed to accompany
Florence to Sydney, taking my chance of what
might follow when we were landed on Australian
soil, that, now that the hour I had so long looked
forward to was arrived and I had practically embarked, as I may say, on my wild and singular

undertaking, I set about the job of joining the ship with the same cool deliberateness of mind I should have possessed had I been going in her as mate for seven or eight pounds a month, or as a passenger bound on some commercial errand.

It was about half-past ten o'clock when I reached the ship, and the scene of life raised up in me such a flavour of my old calling that I felt as if I had no business to be going leisurely aboard, but ought to be tumbling about the decks, shouting out orders, and seeing all ready for hauling out of dock. The *Strathmore* was now in regular sea-going trim, loaded down to well above the line of her yellow sheathing, all yards across and the sails bent, the long-boat full of live-stock, the hen-coops along the poop crammed with poultry; huge squares of compressed hay (which flung a farmyard smell upon the air), secured near the main rigging, blue peter floating lazily at the fore, the Company's house flag at the main, and the English ensign at the peak. The main deck was full of people, steerage and 'tween-deck passengers and their friends conversing in groups, and waiting for the inevitable signal for separating. The scene was a familiar one to me, and yet I found myself, as I stepped over the gangway, glancing with perfectly fresh interest at the old picture of here a young woman silently crying; there a family of father, mother, and little children gathered round the aged couple who had made a weary journey to see the poor hearts off, and who would find the return home wearier still; yonder an ill-clad man standing with his arms folded, looking at the ships which lay around, his haggard face giving you a good image of the dejected, doubting, harassed mind inside him. The *Strathmore* was not an emigrant ship, but she had accommodation in her 'tween decks, between the steerage bulkhead and the mainmast, for a few poor people who were charged emigrants' fares and went out as emigrants; and, consequently, her deck on this day presented all the interest of an emigrant vessel: and I don't know whether in all this world there is any sight to equal the scene a ship bound on a long voyage offers just before the steam-tug lays hold of her, and whilst passengers and their friends are mingled on her decks. There are the little children gaping about them full of wonder; there are relatives holding on to one another's hand in a grasp that once relaxed may never again be felt; you hear sounds of sobbing and the painful echo of laughter between, the hoarse voices of men, the sharp feverish chatter of women striving to put as much talk as might fill up a day into these last ten minutes; and dock officials yell directions to Jack who is sprawling about on the forecastle, drunk, and singing and grinning and lurching here and there, with a kind of defiant rolling, as if he would have you take notice that he for one doesn't mean to make a blubbering job of this leave-taking; whilst overhead the great spars and masts tower into the dusty blue and look ponderous pieces of furniture now that all the sea-gear is rove and the sails bent and rolled up; and they set you thinking of the pallid heights of canvas they will be presently uprearing, and of the night that shall come down by-and-by upon the distant sea, amid which this same ship will be heaving slowly, with never a sound rising from her heart wherein those men and women and childen shall be slumbering, with a thousand fathoms of water betwixt them and the bottom of the black profound whose surface is full of starlight.

I ran my eye along the poop, but did not see Captain Thompson, and as the mates were strangers to me, I thought I could not do better than turn to and set my cabin in order, and write a letter to my uncle ready for posting at Gravesend. There was nobody at that moment in the cuddy, though I could hear a stir in the steerage, the sounds coming very plainly up the hatchway. I stood a moment looking along and, thought I, "If I could see one of the stewards now, I would ask him if the Hawkes' luggage was in their cabin;" then I said to myself, "Better not ask questions, Jack, for you never can tell what may not set Aunt Damaris putting two and two together. Look for yourself."

Whereupon, putting my bag upon the table, I marched to No. 6 cabin, knocked, received no answer, tried the handle, found the door unlocked, and peeped in.

A single glance was enough: one side of the cabin was full of boxes, parcels, etc., with Miss D. Hawke and Miss F. Hawke plainly painted or written on them. The sight of these traps was the same as seeing the owners, so far as the certainty of their sailing in the *Strathmore* was concerned; and closing the door, I came away, picked up my bag, and entered my own cabin.

The light was feeble, owing to the scuttle or window being in the shadow of the quay wall, but, nevertheless, I was able to see that I was not to have the cabin to myself. Luggage that did not belong to me stood near my box, and in the bunk under mine was a collection of articles including a waterproof coat, a gun-case, a bundle consisting of an umbrella, a walking-stick, a sword-stick, etc. I was a good deal disappointed, as I had reckoned upon being alone. Evidently the *Strathmore* was taking out a full complement of passengers. The consideration now was, what sort of companion was I to have? A cheerful, amiable fellow, whose society would be a pleasure, or a sea-sick growling old hunks whose company would be a perpetual affliction?

I peered at the things in the bunk, and then

noticing a name painted on the top of a box somewhat resembling mine, I bent down to see what it was, and read in large white letters:

"Reginald Morecombe, Esq.,
    Cabin Passenger.   Per *Strathmore*."

I could hardly credit my senses.   I stood up and stared around me, then took another squint at the card, and, lost in amazement, looked at the traps in the bunk, and came once more to the card. "Reginald Morecombe!"   There it was plain enough, and I stood erect, absolutely dumbfounded. But, stop! how was I to be sure without seeing the fellow that *this* Reginald Morecombe was Florence's admirer?   Might there not be another man of that name among the millions who populate Great Britain, and through the operation of one of those strange conjunctions of circumstances which sometimes happen in this life, might not he have chosen the *Strathmore* to sail to Australia in, and had the half of my cabin allotted to him?   I examined the boxes, but not being able to see inside them, I found nothing more suggestive than the name.   I then overhauled the traps in the bunk, but there was nothing to be learnt by looking at the gun-case and the macintosh.   Nevertheless, though I could not have taken my oath that my companion would prove Mr. Hawke's young friend, I was so perfectly convinced in my own mind he was nobody else, that I was as much confounded, annoyed, and nonplussed as if I had entered the cabin and found the man in bed in it.

Was this the explanation of Hawke's singular willingness to send his daughter away on a long voyage? Did he hope by boxing up her and Morecombe for three or four months in a ship that the young fellow would succeed in worrying the girl into accepting him? Was it Aunt Damaris' scheme? *She* would be here, at all events, to help the youth, and her house would be open to him at Sydney. And did Florence know he was to accompany them? If not, why there would be positive *baseness* in her father's scheme to make the *Strathmore* a mere trap for her. But if, on the other hand, she knew all about it, why did she keep the news from Sophie? Why had she sent me a keepsake to remember her by, and messages to cherish, when all the time she was aware that she was going to Australia in company with the man whom her father had chosen for her to marry?

I sat on my box with my forehead in my hand and my mind in a whirl. Voices were bawling on deck, feet were stamping overhead, people were moving about in the cuddy. I knew by the cries which reached me that we should be warping out of dock in a few minutes, and such was the state of bewilderment into which I had been flung by the conviction that my cabin-mate was to be no other than Hawke's young friend, by the astonishing pertinacity old Hawke was exhibiting, by the determination of Mr. Morecombe, who was going to abandon society for sea-sickness and a long voyage in the hope of winning Florence, and by the fear that the girl had all along known he was to join her and her aunt, that I declare for some moments it was just the spin of a coin whether I should jump on shore, send for my traps at Gravesend, and drop all thoughts of Florence as completely as I abandoned the voyage.

This was my mood, when, casting my eyes towards the bunks, which were built one above the other, the absurdity of the situation in which Morecombe and I would be placed by occupying one cabin and sleeping one atop of the other, struck me; I burst into a fit of laughter and roared so lustily that I came very near to choking. And nothing, I believe, could have done me more good; the flood of merriment seemed to cleanse my mind and leave room for the old devil-may-care spirit to assert itself again.

Without more ado I opened my box, bundled such things as I required to have at hand into one of the two small chests of drawers with which that cabin was furnished, and then, pulling out a writing-case, began a letter to my uncle. When it came, however, to using a pen and collecting my thoughts, I found I was rather too agitated to say much. I opened by telling him I was going to Australia, and why, as though he had known nothing of my intentions, and then went on to say that I was on board, that the Hawkes' luggage was in their cabin, and that some baggage labelled "Reginald Morecombe" was in *my* cabin. I could not yet positively declare that this Reginald Morecombe was Hawke's friend, but I would let him know in a postscript when the man came aboard at Gravesend. "If he proves to be Florence's admirer," said I, "you will understand, and especially Sophie appreciate, the profound cunning old Hawke exhibits by this manœuvre. I only hope that Florence is ignorant of the plot: unhappily I shall not be able to tell you how this is, for I am not likely to see her until we have been some time under way. If in my postscript I inform you that my cabin companion is *the* Reginald Morecombe, please take the earliest opportunity of letting old Hawke know that I have sailed in the *Strathmore.*" I then wound up by thanking him for his kindness, and begging him to ask Sophie's forgiveness of me for concealing from her my intention to accompany Florence, and brought my letter to an end with a proper sentimental flourish.

Having finished that job, leaving the envelope open for the postscript I had promised, I put on my hat and shoved my head out of the cabin-door to see who might be about before boldly issuing forth, since for all I could tell Florence might have come aboard whilst I was below. True, I had understood she was to join the ship at Gravesend, but her aunt might have changed her mind and chosen to start from the dock: anyhow, I could not be sure, and the very last thing I wanted was to plump up against the darling unawares, and frighten her before her aunt or anybody else into a betrayal of our being " auld acquaintance "; and so, I say, I peered out cautiously, saw a group of persons talking near the companion steps, and an under-steward in a camlet jacket rubbing the table. But there was nobody I knew in sight; I therefore walked on to the main-deck, and found to my surprise that we were out of the dock and in the river, and that a tug had got hold of us and was canting our head towards midstream.

I walked a short distance forward so as to be able to see who was on the poop before going there. Most of the 'tween-deck and steerage folks were below, but a few had clambered on to the bulwarks, and a knot of them stood on the forecastle waving their hats and handkerchiefs to their friends who stood on the walls and pierheads watching the noble ship start. I took a good look aft, and seeing nothing but strange faces, saving Dan Thompson, who stood alone listening to the bawling of the mud pilot, and watching, without of course taking any part in the busy scene, I mounted the poop ladder and went up to my friend.

"Hallo, Jack!" said he, gripping my fingers heartily; "I was only just now thinking of you and wondering whether you were aboard. When did you come?" I told him. "Whisper," says he, "what's the name I am to call you by? Confound me if I can recollect it; something to do with edge, hadn't it?"

"Egerton—Jack Egerton," I replied; "and for heaven's sake, Daniel, don't go and forget it. Think of edging down; that's nautical, you can't forget that."

"No, no, Egerton—Jack Egerton—I have it now," said he. "Be easy; Egerton's the word."

"Since I've been aboard," said I, "I've been rendered doubly anxious by one of the most bothersome things happening that ever you could imagine. I was in hope of getting a cabin to myself, and I find I'm to have a companion."

"Well, and what does that mean?" cried he, with a broad grin on his jolly nautical red face; "merely that Dan Thompson's a mighty popular skipper, beloved of ladies and gentlemen. Would you have me sail with unlet cabins? And besides, how many bunks does an old lobscouser like you want to sleep in?"

"That's not it," I replied; "I don't object to a companion. But guess who he is to be?"

"Pooh, pooh! out with it, man; how the dickens can *I* guess?"

"When I spoke to you of the business that's bringing me on this voyage, did I tell you," said I, "that there was a young chap named Morecombe wanted by my sweetheart's father as a husband for my pet."

"Did you?—may be, may be. And what then?"

" Why, smother him, Daniel, his luggage is in my cabin—he's to be—not my bedfellow, thank heaven, but he is to lie in the bunk under me. The old man has hoped to make a rat-trap of your ship for his girl. He's planned the voyage for her, that young Morecombe may be in her company all the while you keep at sea and after you've set us ashore. And if that's not enough," cried I, savagely dwelling upon the baseness of the plot (as if I, lads, were the most innocent of beings, and not in the smallest degree working out a very much more audacious scheme), "he's to share my cabin and I'm to have the privilege of hearing him snorting under me in his sleep for seventy or eighty days."

Daniel burst into a loud laugh. " What'll you do, Jack?" he exclaimed, "since he's to be under you, will you contrive to smother him one night? Your bunk-planks are movable, you know, and there's nothing to prevent you coming down upon him. Pity your mattress isn't a feather bed;" and he broke into another long guffaw.

At this moment the pilot roared out an order to the wheel, and my friend ran to the rail to peer at something ahead, and there he stood, clean forgetting all about my troubles and thinking only of his ship. It was scarcely the right moment to bother him, though I was determined, before we brought up at Gravesend, to have my way with him in something I required him to do. So I hauled off and went and sat on the edge of the after skylight to think a bit, and to have a look at what was going on. And plenty there was to see, as there always is on the Thames, which is the noblest river in the world to my mind. I have been upon African and Indian and South American rivers, and beheld a thousand strange and shining beauties, and in China have slept on a rushing stream amid a crowd of wobbling and straining junks, with a glimpse of temples beyond the outlandish trees, and a soft wind sighing under the sharp hard blue of the sky, and smells about as aromatic as the materials which go to the making of a plum-pudding. But the scenery of the Thames is the work of human hands, and that's the impressive part of the noble old stream. Gaze along it in an atmosphere of yellow light, when magnitude and vagueness are given to the leagues of waterside structures, and when objects

gloom upon the dun horizon and cheat you with
the idea of immensity by the remoteness they
take. The *Strathmore's* flying-jibboom was looking
right over the elliptical stern of the tug, and we
were swarming down the bend which bears the
polite name of Bugsby's Reach. And hereabouts
was no lack of life on that day; there were half
a score of big vessels in this Reach coming or
going, whilst lighters crept by broadside on, tugs
sped along in quest of towage jobs, passenger
steamers drove through the steel-coloured water,
with a glancing of silver at their keen stems, and
a whirl of snow slucing in a broad current from
under their counters. I took notice of a big India
steamship leisurely making for Gravesend, trim as
a man-of-war, her sides and funnel spotless, her
scuttles winking like stars in her as she coiled
her ebony length along the southern sunshine and
rounded eastwards into Woolwich Reach, whilst,
towing past her for London, there came a small
full-rigged ship from the other side of the world,
her brave little hull covered with scars of the conflicts she had fought in distant seas, her canvas
clumsily rolled up, her gear grey from constant
wetting and drying, and the crew on the forecastle
pointing out to one another the familiar scenes
ashore.

This is one of the contrasts the noble river gives
you. And look yonder at the familiar Thames

wherry, with the old waterman resting on his oars and squinting over his shoulder at the passing tug in whose tumble, as the steamer rushes past, the little boat flounders and wallops, and sets the old chap's oars flourishing like a pair of knitting-needles in a woman's hand, whilst his hat shortens and enlarges with the reeling as if he wanted to show all observers what an optical illusion was like. And hark now to the panting of that little screw tug that heads up river with a chain of deeply-laden coal barges in her wake, and see the lazy grimy villain atop of the dirty heaps, in shirt sleeves, a pipe in his mouth, and his sooty face to the sky.

Our voyage was begun on a fine bright day, if so be the hauling out of dock for Gravesend can be called the beginning. We were too near London for the azure overhead to be rich, but there was a gay autumn tone in it, with a lightening of the blue into a kind of silver over the furthest reaches of the south shore, against which every tree, house, and curve of land took a delicate black outline like a sketch in ink. The sunshine poured full upon our ship and put fiery lines into the yellow top-masts and topgallantmasts, and notched the sky-lights and the brasswork with flashing white stars; and the soft wind that followed carried the smoke of the tug along with us for a space until we rounded into Galleons Reach, when the dark coil floated away in a bluish shadow over Plumstead Marshes. There was a constant coming and going of figures upon the main deck, with sad-hearted faces overhanging the rail watching the passing land, and some drunken horseplay of sailors upon the forecastle, where stood the chief mate of the ship ready to echo the pilot's orders to the tug.

A few of the cuddy passengers had joined the vessel in the docks and sauntered about the poop. I took notice of what was unmistakably a newly-married pair; they kept together arm in arm, and the husband showed his wife the card in the binnacle, the pump for washing down betwixt the mizzenmast and the skylight, the quarter boats and the captain's gig over the stern, with the air of a man who meant to get his honeymoon out of everything that came in his road. There was an elderly gentleman of a stern cast of countenance, who walked about with his hands behind him, and every now and again he would come to a stand and cast a look aloft in a manner that made me suspect he knew the difference between the head-pump and the poop-downhaul. I afterwards found him to be Captain Jackson, R.N., going to Sydney, with his wife, on some government business. There were other persons standing about the poop and looking at the brilliant river-show, but I did not give them much attention, having more interesting subjects to occupy my mind with. And do you ask me if there was any yearning in my bowels after the old city we were leaving in our wake, and the soil that was dropping astern fathom by fathom as the tug hauled us onwards? Not an atom, my lads. Had I been leaving a wife or a mother, or some one dear to me, why then of course my face would have been as melancholy as the longest and yellowest of the visages among the third-class passengers. But I was outward bound, in the vessel that was to carry the darling of my heart to Australia. I was going for a sail around the world, not as a poor devil who had to haul upon ropes or keep a look-out with his eye against a snow-squall, but as a cuddy passenger who was to eat the best that was in the ship, sleep in all night, and go below when it rained. If I was thoughtful, it was because I was puzzled and worried by the discovery that young Morecombe was going to make one of our happy family, not because I was leaving England, or because I was afraid of being sea-sick.

Well, by-and-by we were abreast of Erith, floating pleasantly along, the sky hollowing over our mastheads into a deeper tint, and the ship making a noble show upon the broadening stream, with a certain rugged heavy appearance aloft that handsomely fitted her deep trim and the appearance of the men and women who stared over her bulwarks. An outward-bounder she was from the vane above the truck to the line of white water which the wheels of the tug swept under her glittering figure-head and along her glossy bends, and I sat looking at the massive yards lying square upon the towering masts, and at the fretwork of shadows cast by the fore shrouds upon the galley and the longboat, and thought of one day when the North-east Trades had breezed up into half a gale of wind, and when I leaned over the jibboom with my hand upon the outer jibstay and saw such another vessel as this rushing at me under a maintopgallant sail set over a single-reefed topsail, sending the surges boiling far ahead of me with every downward crash of the shearing cutwater and flinging a continuous roll of thunder upon the gale out of the iron-hard hollows of her white canvas.

Thompson had been talking to a middle-aged lady with an Irish accent, and when they separated I went up to my friend and said, "Daniel, can you listen to me for three minutes?"

"Certainly," he answered; "I must apologize for interrupting you just now, but didn't you notice the dumb-barge right in the road of the tug? Those things are the curse of the river. Captains' lives are made up of nothing but actions brought against them by barge owners. What is it you have to say, Seymour?"

"Egerton, man—Egerton! Didn't I exhort you not to mistake?" cried I.

"Look here, Jack," says he, "Egerton be blowed! I shall never be able to remember it, and therefore to make sure I must call you Jack and nothing else. You can say I'm a cousin, if you like, a foundling adopted by your parents, a foster-brother, half a twin, anything you choose. But I'll bungle Egerton as sure as your name's Seymour; so Jack it must be between us, and I'll leave you to account for the familiarity."

"If you can't call me, Egerton, then I must be Jack," said I; "there's no familiarity, and consequently any accounting for it would be a mistake. And now I am going to ask you to do me a favour. When we reach Gravesend and I catch sight of Miss Hawke coming aboard, I must go and hide, for fear that, should she see me, her astonishment might lead her to suspect who I am."

"But don't the aunt know you?" asked Thompson, who had evidently forgotten the story I had given him in the docks.

"No," I answered, "she has never seen me nor have I ever set eyes on her. Morecombe I once caught sight of, but I am unknown to him."

"And does Miss Hawke know you?" said he.

"Why, hang it all, my good Daniel," cried I, "didn't I tell you that she was half in love with me, that I was passionately in love with her, and making this voyage for the sake of being with her and in the hope of inducing her to marry me?"

"Yes, yes, I remember now," he added; "and what is it you want me to do? You said something about hiding."

"I said that when Miss Hawke heaves in sight I must go below. You must take the very first opportunity you can find to tell her privately that I am on board and beg her not to show any astonishment when I appear, and that you will introduce me to her as though I was a stranger."

"What sort of a girl is she? I'm willing to oblige you," said he, "but hang it, Jack, you're now asking me to take liberties. What will she think when I beg her not to be astonished?"

"Do you think, Daniel," said I, "that I am likely to place an old friend like you in a false position? She will think that you are behaving very kindly to us both in cautioning her against allowing her surprise to betray me to her aunt."

He took a few short turns up and down in front of me, with his good-natured red face working as though he was rehearsing the thing, and then said, "Well, there can be no harm; I'll do this. When she arrives, and a chance comes, I'll say, ' There's an old friend of mine aboard—an old shipmate— named Jack Seymour!' She is sure to sing out,

'What, Jack Seymour!' and I'll answer 'Yes.
He tells me he has the honour of your acquaintance, and has asked me to let you know he's
aboard, in order that when he turns up you mayn't
be frightened.'"

"Not frightened, Daniel," said I; "surprised.
All the rest will do capitally."

"Surprised, then," he continued. "And then
I'll say, 'for reasons I've not troubled myself to
ask, he tells me he's shipped under the name
of Egerton, but as I can't reckon upon always
remembering that name, I shall call him Jack.
It's not my business,' I'll say, 'to inquire into
names. All I've got to do is to carry my ship and
the people in her safely across the ocean.' I'll
say that, Jack, to satisfy my own mind; no harm
in it, I hope?"

"None whatever."

"And what else is there to do?" said he.

"Why," I replied, "you can tell her that I've
asked you to introduce me to her."

I saw he did not like that, but instead of
declining he said, "What d'ye want to be introduced for? Go plump to her and ask her what
she thinks of the weather. People don't stand on
shore-going ceremonies at sea. You ought to
know that, Jack."

"Never mind that part of the job, Daniel. If
you'll just tell her I'm aboard, and let me know

when you have given her the news, I shall be eternally obliged to you."

"All right, my lad, I'll do that," said he, clapping me on the shoulder and laughing in my face; and then, taking a look round, he said something to the pilot and went below.

CHAPTER IV.

NIGHT IN THE RIVER.

I COULD not help wondering at my impudence in thrusting my love business on the mind of a sea captain, full of the responsibility of a big ship crowded with 'passengers and loaded down to her chain-plate bolts with valuable merchandise. However, I had calculated upon his help and was not going to be cheated out of it; and, besides, there would be a freemasonry between us which few landsmen could fully understand. We had been old shipmates, had had many a frolic together ashore under Southern and Eastern skies, were fast friends whilst professionally associated, and consequently he would act and speak before me privately without any of the reserve he would think necessary to maintain for the preservation of his dignity in the presence of others. What sort of captain he made I could not yet tell, but I remembered him as a smart, exceedingly intelligent seaman as second mate; a man who had made his position by hard work and close attention to his duties; who, if he had not crept aboard through the hawsepipe, had not gained admittance by the cabin window, but as apprentice, had worked his way up out of the slush-pot into command of one of the finest ships which then traded to Australia.

Lunch was on the table and I went into the cuddy to take my first meal aboard the *Strathmore*. Only two or three of the passengers came to the table, among them being Captain Jackson. He talked in a loud voice to Thompson, who sat at the head of the table; and I remember the navy man inquiring if the ship was not uncommonly deep in the water, to which Thompson replied that her height of side was an inch more than she had last voyage.

"Well," says Captain Jackson, "it's my ignorance of merchant vessels that makes me ask the question. I was brought up in frigates and line-of-battle ships, sir, and am used to a dip of twenty feet, and when I required to judge our pace of sailing by looking over the side, I had to peer a long way down before I came to water."

"You're going to alter all that in the navy, I hear," says Thompson; "hulls are to be flush with the water, aren't they? and nothing's to show but the things you point your guns out of?"

"Oh," cried Captain Jackson scornfully,

"what's going to be altered in the navy I'm sure I don't know. I'm sorry, but I can't help the change, sir. Iron and steam are the curse of the country, sir; they have robbed us of our ships and of our sailors. What's a man-of-war in these times? An immense floating kettle, sir, with fire inside it and steam blowing out of the spout; and how can they call the men who man those monstrous utensils sailors? What could Nelson have done with a parcel of fellows brought up in floating saucepans, where there are no yards to brace about, where a bolt of canvas would furnish all the sail needed, and where the helm is worked by a steam engine?"

Thompson tipped me a wink as the prejudiced old fellow stopped his chatter by filling his mouth. This specimen of the gallant captain's opinions made me glad to think that he was to be one of us, as I might reckon upon a deal of amusement. No humorist equals the man who passes his closing years in pointing to the past with one hand and pulling the nose of the present with the other, and I never tire of hearing such people and encouraging them to talk.

He began again about the *Strathmore* being overloaded, and his wife, a large stout lady with a cast in her port eye, who sat next him, said she was sorry to hear that he had misgivings on that subject, for nobody could imagine how deeply her

husband was versed in all nautical matters, being
the author not only of a marine dictionary, but of
a work on the management of boats at sea. On
this the Irish lady, Mrs. O'Brien, who was seated
near Thompson, said to him, "Captain, if the
gentleman knows all about it and says the ship is
too deep, then she must be unsafe, and I hope ye'll
have her lightened before we get among the waves,
which they tell me roll mountains high in the Bay
of Biscay."

How Daniel eased their minds I don't know,
for, having finished lunch and suspecting that
Gravesend would not be far off, I left the table
and went on deck to look about me, thinking as I
mounted the companion-steps, and hearing my
friend blandly jabbering about free-board and
tonnage (soul-sickening subjects), that the old
navy man would give him some trouble with his
prejudices if he did not mind his eye.

It was half-past one or later yet, and we were in
Northfleet Hope, as the stretch of water betwixt
Grays and Tilburyness is called, and by squinting
over the port bow I could see where Gravesend lay
by the colour of the sky there. The wind had
freshened and the water was trembling and running
in a stress of little waves under it; the smoke from
the tug's funnel fled away flat from the orifice and
blew down upon the water; a couple of yachts with
the tacks of their mainsails triced up were passing

us in a smother of foam, through which their greenish copper flashed like a shark's body in the boiling and seething white of a ship's wake, an old black collier, with the clews of her square foresail stretched on a boom, was staggering along within pistol-shot of a lovely slope of mud on the Tilbury side; and a tug was dragging a fine Yankee barque up the river, hands aloft unbending the sails, and the stripes and stars making a brilliant spot of colour against the sky, under which a flight of windy-looking clouds were speeding with a ragged look in their tails as if they had been torn out of some solid body of vapour that would not be long in coming.

Now that Gravesend was almost within hail I grew desperately nervous and agitated, and seemed to realize with a deeper sense of it than had yet come to me the resolution old Hawke was illustrating by his stratagem of sending Florence and Morecombe away together on a long voyage. Evidently my cousins were perfectly right when they had said that the young fellow was not to be got rid of by a plain refusal. The worry in me was rendered livelier by my anxiety to make sure that the man who was to share my cabin was the fellow I feared he would prove. I stood watching the passing shore as we opened Gravesend Reach, and then presently the old town which I knew so well as a point of departure and arrival—for I had always sailed out of the port of London—hove in view, its bits of piers forking out into a squadron of wherries that danced around them, and I saw the windows of the Falcon Hotel sparkling in the light (may be Florence was at that moment watching the approaching ship from one of them, and it was her eyes I mistook for the sunshine in the window panes), and the lumber of houses that huddled close to the river's edge ; while far away down the Hope, shining like marble in the fitful radiance of the cloud-swept sun, were the white heights of Cliffe, crowning the visible confines of a stretch of water that was full at that hour of shipping, at rest or under way, and gay with the windy streaming of scores of flags.

It was three o'clock by the time the ship was moored to a buoy, very nearly abreast of Gravesend, and, armed with a pipe and a small but powerful telescope of my own, I went forward on to the forecastle, where I could watch the passengers come aboard without being noticed myself. There was a squally look in the sky, and it was blowing a fresh north-east wind with an edge of winter in it that made the pilot cloth coat I wore a very acceptable garment. The women and children on the main deck, and the rather squalid-looking gentry who paced the forecastle or hung about the galley for the warmth and shelter down there, gave, I am bound to say, a somewhat slum-like look to the ship in that part of her which they were permitted to use. But when I glanced at the clear quarter-deck, with the shining windows in the cuddy front and the brasswork and painting there, then at the long sweep of poop which ran with a very clear white surface into the sky that was pouring past in clouds, and then turned my eyes aloft where the house flag, dwarfed by height, was rattling like a peal of musketry at the main royal masthead, and looked at the grand spread of yards, and noticed the frigate-like pose of the masts, stayed to a hair, every sail with a bunt as smooth as a pillow, the ratlines ruling the shrouds as straight and square as the shear poles, all the braces hauled taut, and the wind giving a curve to every slack line it met and rushing away out of the topmast rigging with a kind of angry hiss in its wild humming, I thought that if Florence was viewing the *Strathmore* from yonder hotel or any other land point, she would be thinking her a noble-looking craft for her class and character, and not the less fitted to ride the stormy seas of the Atlantic and Southern Oceans because Captain Jackson, R.N., found her deeper than he thought good.

Well, mates, after I had been keeping a look-out for about twenty minutes I spied a boat shove off from the steps behind the pier, and bringing my glass to bear I noticed that the waterman headed for us and that there was a man sitting in the sternsheets.　I kept the little telescope upon this last, and presently made out a large moustache, a white billycock, an eye-glass, stick-up collar, and a figure dressed in a grey coat with a cape, and a rug over his arm and a black portmanteau alongside of him.　I had only seen Mr. Morecombe once, as you know, but the moment my glass gave me the face of the fellow in the sternsheets of that boat so that I could clearly see the features of it, all doubts as to the man who was to share my cabin vanished. Reginald Morecombe it was as certain as that it was I who was watching him.　The name on the luggage below ought to have convinced me, but though I had been pretty sure I was not so sure as I was now, and such was the effect of this confirmatory and conclusive evidence upon me that, though God knows I should have reckoned myself in anything but a merry mood, I burst into a wild laugh, shaken to the heart by the absurdity of us two taking this voyage for the same purpose, coming together without the least suspicion of each other's intention, and actually sharing the same cabin, and sleeping one atop of the other !

However, if there was any comfort at all to be got out of the fact of this man coming aboard it lay in his arriving alone, for that looked to me very much as if Florence knew nothing of the plot that had been devised, and I might count upon good results following her disgust if it turned out that she was ignorant of the conspiracy between Hawke and Aunt Damaris and Morecombe. I went on to the quarter-deck as his boat sheered alongside, and watched him come up the gangway ladder. He knew very little about ships, I took it, and was boarding the *Strathmore* for the first time I suspected by the way he halted and stared, as if he didn't know which end of the vessel belonged to him ; and I dare say he would be puzzled by the crowd of 'tween-deck passengers who stood by to see him arrive and by the appearance of the main-deck, which with its rows of scuttle-butts, spare booms, hatchway gratings, coils of rigging upon pins, and the dirt and confusion which third-class passengers have a happy knack in bringing along with them as a part of their luggage, must have presented to the entirely shore-going eye a very complicated appearance.

He paid the waterman and took up his bag, and seeing him looking around in quest of some one to inform him what was next to be done, I stepped up to him and said, " Excuse me, sir ; are you Mr. Reginald Morecombe ? "

He bowed and said " Yaas," and looked at me gladly as if thankful to heaven that some one knew him amid this wilderness of ropes, live-stock, and frowsy passengers.

" It was a mere conjecture of mine," said I. " A Mr. Reginald Morecombe is to share my cabin, and if you are the gentleman, I shall be happy to show you where it is."

"Oh, thur-thur-ank you, thank you," said he with his stammer, following me. "How deyvelish confusing a ship is. This vessel looks vewy dirty. Who are all those fellahs outside?" meaning the people on the main deck, for we were now in the cuddy.

"'Tween-deck passengers," said I. "This is the cabin we are to share,"—bundling into it. "I found these traps in the lower bunk and supposed you had chosen it. But top or bottom is the same to me. You can have which you like."

He peered with his glass in his eye and said, "Oh, thur-thur-anks; I·think the under one will suit me best. I am a wetched sailaw," grinning palely, "and the one beneath is the easiest to enter. What vewy queear beds for fellahs to lie in! But I suppose a man gets used to this sort of thing in time."

I was in the act of leaving the cabin, being anxious to watch for the arrival of Florence and her aunt, when he said, pulling his moustaches and smiling with tremendous politeness, "I baig your pardon, as we are to be companions in this—aw—this woom, might I be allowed to ask your name?"

I was within an ace of answering that it was Seymour—the word was trembling on my lips when I suddenly remembered, and stammered, "John

Egerton—Mr. John Egerton. You'll see it on that box there," and I swung hastily out into the cuddy that he might not perceive the conscience-stricken look which I could feel as hot as fire in my face. I stopped a moment to pull out the letter I had addressed to my uncle and scribbled with a pencil the following postscript : " The Reginald Morecombe who is to share my cabin is *Mr. Hawke's young friend.* Endeavour to let the old man know as early as possible that I am accompanying his daughter to Australia. I want to have the full benefit of his fears and rage, and the sooner he is told the longer he will suffer. Would any man have conceived the pompous old chap capable of such an underhand stroke as this ? God bless you all." This being written, I closed the envelope, and gave the letter to one of the stewards to put into the bag which would be cleared or sent ashore before the ship sailed, and then went on to the maindeck in order to take another spell of watching on the forecastle, but just as I was stepping out of the cuddy some people came over the gangway, the sight of whom sent me backing and cowering under the starboard poop ladder for fear that Florence might be among the party. They proved to be five cuddy passengers, and when I found that my darling was not one of them I made my way to the forecastle and resumed my seat there.

You will have seen, my lads, that much had not

passed between Mr. Morecombe and myself; but little as it was, there was enough of it to convince me that my relatives were perfectly right in saying that the man was a fool. I may make his words look as much like his pronunciation of them as I can; but there's no art that I'm master of to represent the dawdling, affected tone of his voice, the foolishness of his smile, the astounding good opinion of himself that he managed somehow to convey. Part and parcel of the man his conceit must have been to strike me as it did at a time when he was so bothered by the novelty of his surroundings that even an actor would have been natural under the circumstances. Not that I found him less good-looking than I thought him that day when I caught a glimpse of him at Bristol seated in old Hawke's carriage; but for all that, the few sentences he had let fall, and above everything his smile, persuaded me that there was a world of truth in what my aunt had told me about his good looks disappearing in his stupidness when you got close to him in talk; and when I thought of how Florence had spoken of him as a fool, and remembered that she had refused his offer of marriage, why, I began to consider that after all perhaps nothing better could have happened for me than that Morecombe should have fallen into Hawke's scheme (for Hawke's it was, if it was not the devil's), since what was more likely to complete her disgust of the young fellow than being placed in the one situation of all others in which she would be unable to keep clear of his unwelcome company unless she imprisoned herself in her cabin?

Full of these agreeable reflections, I sat with a grin upon my face poising my telescope ready to level it at the first boat that should come away from Gravesend. The wind was strong and cold; no rain had fallen as yet, but the clouds were full of wet and I guessed that we should have a sopping night. Only a few of the crew were about, the rest being, as I might suppose from experience, too drunk to be of use. I was near the scuttle and could hear the fellows jabbering and breaking into songs that sounded as if all hands were sea-sick. Queer it was to me to feel as I looked around me, and spied the first mate stumping the break of the poop athwartships, an ordinary seaman in the maintop at work on some job up there, the second mate in the waist singing out to a hand in the foretopmast crosstrees, and so on, that I had nothing to do with the ship, could go where I liked, use the weather side of the poop whenever I chose, and enjoy more liberty than even my friend Daniel. I suppose most men who have knocked off the sea as a profession have felt what I am describing when they have taken a voyage as passenger whilst their memory of sea discipline and work was fresh.

At last I began to get rather tired of the

Strathmore's forecastle, and above all of the wind that was whistling nippingly into my starboard ear, and was wondering if it was to fall dark before Florence and her aunt came aboard. As I was in the act of rising to stretch my legs and take a final squint at the flight of steps near the pier before going aft, I spied a boat draw out from the other wherries. I waited, but would not seem to look too inquisitively, for just then I noticed young Morecombe posted near the port-quarter boat holding the ship's telescope—which he would have found on brackets under the companion hood—with his face turned my way. Presently he rested the glass on the rail and aimed it at the approaching boat; this was my chance to take a hurried squint myself, and the moment the faces of the persons in the sternsheets of the boat entered the field of the lenses my heart gave a mighty throb. Ay, boys, she was coming at last! I had seen her darling face, the trembling of the feather of her hat in the strong wind, and thrusting the little telescope into my pocket, I went and posted myself before—or as landsmen might say *behind*—the forecastle capstan, so that it might screen me from observation as she came over the side.

Morecombe had made her out, too, by this time, and after looking at the boat through his eyeglass for a few moments, he turned tail and disappeared down the companion steps. I looked to see him reappear on the main deck, making sure he would receive the ladies, but he did not show up again. His manner of leaving the deck suggested to me that he was doing precisely what I was—hiding. But I did not give the matter very much thought, being fully occupied in watching the boat, whose approach filled me with extraordinary agitation and excitement. If ever a fear had risen in me that something might, at the last moment, stop my pet from coming, it was ended now. There she was, nearing the ship as fast as a couple of watermen could row her; in a few minutes she would be in the vessel, for many a long week to be my adorable shipmate; no more need of twopenny lodgings, of imploring Sophie's help, of day after day passing without giving me a sight of her. No wonder my heart beat fast and rapturously. I had attempted a bold adventure, but so far all had gone as if ordered by my own wishes; and now my darling and I were to be together until Australia was reached; and of what was to follow then I had so little doubt, that had she been coming to me as my bride my spirits could not have been more triumphantly joyous.

The wind had raised a middling stiff wobble on the water, and the boat jumped and tumbled in a very lively manner as she came along. Every moment the spray would fly over her like a hatful of feathers tossed on the breeze, and I would notice Aunt Damaris, who, of course, would be Florence's companion, duck and curtsey as the shower blew along. She wore a thick greyish-coloured veil and a hat resembling a man's wideawake, and as I watched her bobbing in the sternsheets of that boat I thought to myself, "What would be your ideas, my old beauty, were you to know whose eyes were gazing at you from the *Strathmore's* forecastle?" Presently the boat came alongside, and in a few moments Florence and her aunt stepped over the gangway and immediately went into the cuddy, followed by one of the under-stewards with an armful of odds and ends belonging to them. I went on to the main deck and posted myself between the foremast and the galley, out of sight of the poop and quarter-deck, whilst I considered what I had best do. I had made up my mind not to let Florence see me until the news of my being aboard had been given her by Thompson (who by the way had gone ashore). I was not going to run risks. It was not for a moment to be doubted that if Aunt Damaris got to know I was in the *Strathmore* she would abandon the voyage by that vessel and carry Florence away, with Morecombe, of course, in their wake. Consequently, even Florence herself ought not to know that I was to be one of the vessel's passengers until we were well afloat and the nearest port a long distance astern.

These being my considerations, I stood debating
what I should do. I had no excuse to stick to my
cabin for the rest of the afternoon and evening,
for we were not at sea, and I could not sham
sickness, nor, indeed, did I relish the notion of a
long spell of solitary confinement. Dinner would be
served at half-past five or six, and of course I could
not take my place at the table. My best plan clearly
was not to go aft at all until it was time to turn in,
at which hour I might take it Florence and her aunt
would have stowed themselves away in their cabin.
I had half a mind to walk into the forecastle and
see if there were any faces about that I remembered,
and then reflecting that there was rather too
much drunkenness there to make a visit agreeable,
I was turning my attention to the 'tween-decks and
planning a voyage into those regions for the
shelter of them and the secure hiding-place they
would make for me, when my eye caught sight of a
figure in the boatswain's berth sitting upon a chest
and drinking tea out of a pannikin which he held
in one hand whilst he flourished a lump of soft
tack in the other. This berth or cabin was bulk-
headed off from the rest of the forecastle and
formed a kind of wing on the port side of the deck,
a corresponding structure facing it on the starboard
side. The boatswain and carpenter of the *Portia*
had shared a similar bedroom in that ship, and
the same arrangement would be found, I supposed,

in this sister vessel. I stepped over to the door of this cabin, meaning to ask the man, whoever he might be, if he knew at what hour we were to get under way in the morning, when, struck by his appearance, I looked at him attentively and exclaimed, "What, Jimmy Shilling! After all these years—still alive oh! Surely you remember me!"

He took a kind of slow long look at me over his pannikin and then put it down and stood up. "Mr. Seymour!" he exclaimed. "Well, I'm blowed! how are you, sir?"

This man had been boatswain's mate in the *Portia,* and fours years ago he had looked ten years younger than he did now, so scurvily does the sea use her children; but his grizzled beard, the weather-ploughed look of his leathery skin, and the knots which hauling and pulling and swearing and piping had tied up around his eyes and over his temples did not disguise him from me. I gave him a hearty handshake and sat down, bidding him not mind me, but to go on with his supper, or whatever the snack he was working at might be styled.

At that moment in steps the carpenter, a hairy, wiry sea-dog, with a beard like a worn-out scrubbing-brush upon his chin, and strange pale eyes, as if they had lost their colour by looking too much to windward in wet weather. The boatswain politely introduced me to him, whereupon he pulled off his fur cap as a salutation, and pitched it into his bunk, and then hauling forth a short black pipe from his breeches pocket, he filled it out of a well-worn brass box, and began very gravely to smoke.

"You don't mean to say, Mr. Seymour," said the boatswain, "that you've come to sea again?"

"No, Shilling," said I, "not as a sailor man. I'm going to Australia along with you—as the old chantey says, 'I've embarked into a ship which her topsails is let fall, and all unto an ileyand where we never will go home,' but not to soil my hands with your filthy grease and tar. No, Shilling; no more keeping a look-out, no more hauling and slaving for this child. You may pipe your whistle and be hanged; you'll never get me to dance to it. I'm a cuddy passenger, my lively hearty, taking a sail round what the negro calls dis circumnabular globe for the fun of watching others do what I've had to do myself, and don't mean to do again."

The carpenter grinned broadly behind his pipe, and the boatswain exclaimed, "Cuddy passenger, eh? Shingles," addressing the carpenter, "ain't the cuddy a place under the poop where the ladies live, and were ye may find by looking nothing but fust-class eatin' knocking about?"

"If it ain't there, it ain't forrards," answered the carpenter; "leastways in this vessel."

"And a good job too," said I. "Mr. Shingles,

would you have ladies to live among the drunken Dutchmen you may hear snorting like hogs, if you'll put your ear to the forescuttle."

"You're right, Mr. Seymour," exclaimed the boatswain. "Hogs they are, and it's animals after that there pattern to which sailors have reduced themselves. Sailors do I call 'em! Why, I'd swallow that pannikin, Shingles—bolt it afore ye whilst you sit looking on—if out of this ship's company ye'll be able to pick me one man that hasn't more to learn of his calling than an apprentice, when I first went to sea, would ha' needed teaching after he had been six months sailoring."

"Right you are, mate," replied the carpenter, smoking thoughtfully; "but there's no use grumbling. A man must take things as they come. If ye can't get first-class seamen, then ye must put up with middlin' sailors; and if *they're* not to be got, then ye must be content with sojers and scaramouches and turnpike men. My argument is, what's the use of cussin' and swearin'? Will you have a pipe of tobacco, Mr. Seymour, sir?" and he fumbled about for his brass box.

I took a pinch for company's sake and put it into my pipe, and then all at once bethinking myself that these fellows were calling me Mr. Seymour—and, mind you, in no uncertain notes, for the boatswain had the most roaring voice that ever human being used in calling upon sailors to quit their beds of down and mount the masts, whilst there was the true deep-sea rumble in the carpenter's pipes—I said, "Jimmy, and you, Mr. Shingles, my name aboard the *Strathmore* is not Seymour but Egerton. Will you try to think of that, my friends? There are some passengers aft who mustn't on any account know I'm here. And they can only find out that I *am* here, even when I am sitting among them, and they are looking at me, by learning my name. So I'm Mr. Egerton, Jimmy, and you Mr. Shingles; and in some second dog-watch, when everything's quiet aloft and the sailors are at prayers, I'll tell you why I've come to sea in your ship, and give you both such a yarn that you'll never afterwards want to use curling-irons for your hair again so long as you live."

"All right, sir," said the boatswain; "Hegerton's the word, and Hegerton it is."

"Same here," warbled Chips.

Note in this the beautiful gentlemanly spirit of the sailor. Had a landsman heard me say that I had changed my name, then—unless I had explained that property was the cause—he would straightway have suspected me of arson, forgery, or murder, and that I was flying to Australia to escape British justice. On the other hand, these two shell-backs asked no questions, suspected nothing, simply said "Hegerton it is," and so made an end of the matter. Having gone so far with them, I thought I would go farther yet, and I told them that as my friend Daniel Thompson, their skipper, was ashore, and unable therefore to let a certain passenger know that I was in the ship, and as I did not want to meet that passenger until she had been informed that I was aboard, I desired to keep forward, or somewhere out of sight, until bedtime, and asked leave to use their cabin.

"To be sure you may, Mr. *He*gerton," said the boatswain, with a grin, as he put a gale of wind into the aspirate to let me know how completely he had mastered the word; "and if ye'd like to sleep here, there's my bunk and welcome."

This hospitable offer I declined, but I told him if he'd get me a pannikin of tea from the galley, and a piece of bread, I should feel very much obliged to him, and these things he at once procured; so that, seated on his chest, with the fumes of the strong cavendish cake-tobacco that sailors smoke mingling in my nostrils with the steam of the galley tea, and the wind making a rushing noise in the rigging outside, I felt as if I were once more a sailor, and only waiting for the order to turn to to bundle out with the others and fall to work. I had a pleasant talk with these men about the ship and the skipper (whom they had both sailed with before, and spoke of in high terms), and amongst us we revived some old and pleasant memories; and then, having duties to attend to on deck, they left me alone. It was now raining, with a promise of a dark foul night, and the wind was screeching in squalls overhead. I poked my nose out and looked along the decks; a couple of brass-bound apprentices (the *Strathmore* carried five of these "young gentlemen") were lurking about the head of one of the poop ladders, swathed in oilskins, and the second mate, similarly attired, was rambling about in solitary dignity in the neighbourhood of the wheel. Not one of the passengers of any description was to be seen; and the deserted dark wet decks, the rain flying in clouds of drizzle past the masts, the streaming rigging, and the gloomy sky, which the shadow of the approaching night was fast darkening, made a truly miserable and depressing picture. I wondered what Morecombe was doing; whether he was with Aunt Damaris and Florence. But there was no use wondering. My present business was to kill the evening, and so I lighted a pipe, and on looking at the carpenter's bunk spied a book at the foot of it which proved to be a collection of tales of shipwreck, and several of these yarns I read to the hoarse accompaniment of the wind groaning and roaring outside.

The dinner bell rang, the evening gathered, and, by and by, on taking another look aft, I saw the cuddy lamps alight, and the passengers eating their first dinner aboard the *Strathmore*. It was no joke peering through the wet from the grim and rude interior of the boatswain's cabin at that brilliant cuddy, as though I were a 'tween-deck passenger and could only peep and envy. The tea and bread I had eaten had, it is true, plugged my appetite, still I felt as if there was enough hunger leaking out to qualify me to give an opinion on old Drainings' cookery; and above all, this skulking was extremely disagreeable, as tending to make me reckon that my courtship was to consist altogether of hiding and seeking. However, it was clearly not my policy to go and rise up before my darling as if I was a ghost, and frighten her, as I was bound to do, if my presence was not gently made known to her; and so comforting myself with the reflection that the necessity of skulking would soon be over, I once more picked up the book of shipwrecks and went on reading until Jimmy and the carpenter came into the cabin.

No company do I like better than sailors', and the conversation of these two men was a real entertainment. It was evening, the anchor-watch had been set, a riding light was burning on the forestay, and, there being nothing more to do until the tug came alongside in the morning, the carpenter and boatswain were at liberty to yarn and smoke as long as they pleased, and then turn in. Threshold impressions, memories which belong to the first step of any momentous matter, are always lively and lasting, and that, no doubt, is why I recall the picture of that berth more vividly than I can see anything else in that vanished ship: the oil-lamp like a coffee-pot hanging overhead; the two bunks with their rough furniture of coarse blankets and mattresses which looked as old as Captain Cook's time, and as if they had been making voyages round the world ever since; the flap table against the ship's side; the battered sea chests upon which many a pound of stick tobacco must have been cut, to judge from the web-like notchings along the edges of the lids; the oilskins and sou'westers hanging on nails up in a corner, looking like seamen who had committed suicide. The lamp cast a narrow stream of light through the sliding door on the deck, throwing out upon the darkness a few links of the huge chain cable that was stretched along from the windlass, and a coil of gear upon a belaying pin at the foot of the fore-mast, and such things.   It was strange to hear the rushing noise of the wind and the seething of rain swept through shrouds and stays, and yet feel no motion in the hull, for the night was so black and the sound aloft so ocean-like that it was almost impossible at times to realize that we were on the smooth Thames, and Gravesend pretty nearly within musket-shot.

Not choosing to go supperless to bed, and yet not

caring to make the steward wonder by asking him
for something to eat, I partook of a bit of fresh
beef which the boatswain brought out of a shelf,
and one bell (half-past eight) having been struck
on the quarter-deck I relieved my entertainers of
my company, knowing very well that the poor
tired fellows would turn in and fall fast asleep the
moment my back was turned. The rain had
ceased, but the sky had a wild look, and the decks
were full of water for the want of a list to carry
the wet through the scupper holes. I made my
way aft and came to a stand opposite the cuddy
front, through the windows of which I could command a view of the interior without being seen.
Dinner had been cleared away a long while before.
The place looked to me to be full of people, and I
noticed the newly-married couple (whose name I
afterwards heard was Mr. and Mrs. Marmaduke
Mortimer), Captain Jackson, R.N., and his wife, a
young gentleman named Thompson Tucker, Mrs.
O'Brien, one or two other ladies, and at the
thwartship table, at the end, Florence, Aunt
Damaris, and Mr. Morecombe! When I saw that
fellow talking to the aunt, and Florence sitting
quietly alongside, my old miserable misgiving
returned. It looked almost certain that she must
have known Morecombe intended to accompany her,
otherwise, could I suppose, if he had sneaked on
board as I had, that he would have had the courage

to discover himself within an hour or two of her arrival? Just as I was sure, if the aunt learnt that I was on board she would forthwith carry her niece ashore, might not he in the same way have feared that if Florence knew that he was going to make the voyage in the ship, she would insist upon leaving the vessel? Of course he enjoyed an immense advantage over me by having Aunt Damaris on his side, and he might presume upon that to make his presence know to Florence. Nevertheless, it rendered me extremely unhappy to see him there in that warm, comfortable, brilliant cuddy, close to Florence and chatting with the aunt, and not to be able to satisfy my mind that his voyage had been arranged without the girl's knowledge.

The better to see her I went on to the poop, for they were all three of them sitting well within the range of the after skylight. A figure was walking up and down—one of the mates, no doubt—but it was too dark to see which of them it was. The wind was mighty keen, having grown more northerly and coming very fresh. I walked to the after skylight and looked down, and there under me was the beautiful face of the girl for whom I was taking all this desperate trouble and heaping discomforts upon my head. Had she been alone, the sight that skylight framed would have been like a vision, for the blackness stood all around the illuminated glass, and the deck was dark too, so that the radiance of the lamps, and the face and glittering hair of Florence, and the swell of her lovely bosom rounding above the table on which she rested her elbow with her white hand under her chin, were all contained in a kind of luminous square; but unfortunately for the beauty of that irradiated night-piece, Aunt Damaris was in it and so was Morecombe. There they were, all three of them, and I watched them. For ten minutes I stood overhanging that skylight, but during that time I never could detect that Florence spoke once, neither did I observe that she ever turned her face towards Mr. Morecombe. It would be hard to tell her exact expression in that light: the glass was wet and the moisture made its transparency treacherous, but if there was not a look of coldness and offended pride in her face, then I am blessed if I can tell you what other sort of appearance it presented. I took, as you may suppose, a prolonged squint at Aunt Damaris. One glimpse I had caught of her, as you will remember I told you, at Bristol, but the impression left was exceedingly small, and what I now saw therefore was quite fresh and new to me. She seemed about sixty years old: very sharp features, a long narrow nose, a wide mouth with thin lips, and small restless black eyes. Her hair was grey, and she was very bald about the parting. She wore two old-fashioned sausage-shaped curls in front of the ear. She looked to be dressed in black satin, for the stuff gleamed whenever she moved : her cap was large, with plenty of riband in it, and around her neck was a stretch of lace * or something of that kind, with the ends hanging down in front of her. She had the appearance, I am bound to say, of a respectable, well-to-do old lady.

Well, whilst I was staring down at them, I saw Florence lean towards her aunt, say something, and then rise. The old woman lifted her eyes to her and seemed to expostulate ; then, apparently thinking better of it, she got up too, and shook hands with Mr. Morecombe, but Florence gave him such a chilly bow that the sight of it brought my two hands together in a rapturous squeeze, and then in a breath there was nothing left of the picture the skylight had framed but the bare table. I turned to go below by the cuddy front entrance and found the person I had noticed stumping the deck at my elbow and peering at me.

"Are you a cuddy passenger ? " said he.

"I am," I replied.

"Oh, I beg your pardon," said he. "May I ask what name ? "

"Mr. John Egerton," I answered.

"My name is Thornton," said he, "and I'm the chief officer. I did not notice you at dinner.

* The right name is *fichu*, Florence has since told me.—JACK.

I don't think I have seen you in this vessel before; when did you come aboard, sir?"

"In the docks."

He continued to peer at me as though he could not make up his mind as to whether I was an Irish assassin or the latest English forger, but when, in reply to the question, I gave him the number of my cabin and the name of the person who was to share it with me, he exclaimed, "Oh, it's all right, sir, of course," and resumed his walk. This matter, trifling as it was, nevertheless hugely disgusted and annoyed me, and I was never more disposed to curse myself for a fool for putting myself into situations full of mortifications, misconstructions, and the obligation of sneaking and skulking. I lingered a few minutes on the poop, not choosing that the mate should flatter himself that he had hastened my departure. There was no rain, but the darkness was thickened with a rolling and eddying mist that sometimes drove past the illuminated skylights like bursts of steam. The lights at Gravesend twinkled wildly, and the loom of the high land behind was visible in a deeper blackness above the winking flickering sparks. The river from the light abreast of Northfleet away down as far as the Hope looked as if a galaxy of stars were hovering over its glooming waters; how many vessels those lanterns represented I could not imagine, but anyone might easily suppose, from the appearance of the multitudinous shining, that an immense fleet had brought up in Gravesend Reach. Most of the lights were stationary, but here and there you would see one reeling and staggering with a sweeping movement upon the darkness, denoting some small craft tossing upon the little sea which the strong wind had raised in the river, whilst close at hand over the side the water glimmered amid the deep night-shadow in dull flashes of pallid froth, and washed in a crunching sound along the bends of our motionless vessel, making the rudder jar now and again with a faint rattling of the tiller chains in the leading-sheaves. Aloft, the noise of the wind was like the shearing of a gale through a forest, but many a wild note there was in addition twanged on the harp-like rigging, and you could not have stood and listened for five minutes, with the sobbing of the water to help your fancy, without believing that a world of phantoms had come down on the wings of the wind and alighted on those darkling spars and faintly glimmering yards— ghosts of mothers singing to wailing babies, ghosts of ruined men groaning in their misery, ghosts of madwomen shrieking in torment. A strange chorus, mates, as you all know, for what sailor's thoughts have not run to it? though, to find a meaning in such spirit-crying, there should be no shore-lights about, you must be leagues and leagues away out at sea, on the forecastle, say, where you may be alone—for aft there are the helmsman and the officer of the watch to keep you company—with a composant burning at the foreyard arm, and the ocean a wild and hurling shadow around you, with the desolate glint of foam under the bows and trailing in a line astern, making the deep as sad as a winter landscape with a sweep of blown snow lying on the black land under the blacker sky.

A few minutes of this were as much as satisfied me. I went on to the quarter-deck, and looked through the cuddy windows. Florence and Aunt Damaris had withdrawn to their cabin ; indeed, all the ladies had retired, and the only occupants of the cuddy were a group of three or four men, Morecombe amongst them, sipping grog at that part of the table which was nearest the stove.

Seeing the road clear I entered, walked straight into my cabin and went to bed.

CHAPTER V.

MR. MORECOMBE IS SEA-SICK.

HAD I been a sailor just turned in after having been twenty-four hours on deck, I could not have fallen asleep more quickly nor slept more soundly. At what hour Mr. Morecombe came to bed I do not know; I never heard him, though he was the first thing I remembered in the morning when I awoke and found the autumn sunshine standing like a wall of silver against the thick glass of the large scuttle or circular window. I put my head over the side of the bunk and saw him underneath; he was wide awake, and instantly sang out, "Hallo! good morning."

"Good morning," I answered.

"I say," cried he, "can you tell me the time? My old turnip has stopped, and hang me—aw—if I know whether I ought to get up or not."

I looked at my watch that was in my waistcoat, slung within reach. "A quarter to eight," said I.

"At what hour do we bweakfast, do you know?"

said he, forking his legs out of bed and looking about him for his smallclothes.

" I really can't say. If you'll put your head out the steward will tell you, if he's in sight," I replied, debating within myself whether to get up or sham indisposition and have breakfast in my cabin. I decided upon the latter, and accordingly lay down again, drawing a long face as I turned my nose up to the deck above. The ship was on a level keel, but there was the tremor of passing water in the light outside, and I might easily guess that we were in the wake of a towing tug. It was pretty plain, however, that we had not long been under way; fine as the weather might be now, there was too much weight in last night's wind to leave the water calm in the river's mouth where the Channel swell would be, and I reckoned by the feel in the hull that, even if we had passed the Nore, Prince's Channel was still some distance ahead.

Morecombe put on his drawers and boots, and, opening the cabin door, peered out, and catching sight of one of the stewards, ascertained the breakfast hour, and then said to me, " We bweakfast at a quarter to nine. Would you like to get up ? because if so I'll go to bed until you've done dwessing. It's a dayvlish tight fit for two," says he, looking around him, " and wot me if it isn't too cold for tubbing. Suppose there's a bathwoom somewhere ?"

"I shan't get up," said I; "I don't feel very well."

"Not sea-sick, are you?" he exclaimed. "Oh, hang it all, you can't be sea-sick *yet*. Why, the ship isn't moving!"

"It's not the movement, it's the smell," said I. "It's what they call the bilge water. Sniff strongly, and you'll see what I mean," and I gave a bit of a grunt.

"Wot me if I'm going to sniff," says he. "Don't smell anything wong natuwally, and don't want to fancy things. I say, didn't you tell me your name was Egerton?"

"You'll see it on that box there," I replied, pretending to speak with an effort.

"Any welation," says he, lathering himself for a shave, "to the Tatton Egertons?"

"No," I replied, knowing that the fellow had a lot of titled connections, and that I must mind my eye.

"Oulton-Park Egertons, pwaps?" said he, flourishing a razor and squinting at himself in the looking-glass.

"Nothing to do with them," I answered.

"Is it the Ellesmere family then—or pwaps it's Wilton?" said he, awaiting my answer before applying his razor.

"It's a Kentish family," said I in a faint manner. "There were five of us, counting my parents, and I am the only one surviving."

His mind went to work upon this answer whilst he shaved, but he didn't appear to make much of it. When that job was over he said, " What's taking you to Austwalia—hailth ? "

" That's it," said I. " Lord, isn't the ship heaving ! or can it be the bilge water ? "

" Dayvlish odd ! " cried he. " Deck's as steady as land, and whatever bilge water may be, dooce take me if I can smell anything wong."

" Oh," said I, " perhaps you're an old sailor; if so, it's not fair to laugh at me."

" Old sailor," cried he ; " well, I've done a bit of yachting with my uncle, Lord Alchester. Know him ? " I wagged my head. " But I'm as ignowant of the water and of—aw—ships of this kind— haw—by gad, as I am of tailoring. More so, dooce take me, Mr. Egerton, for, look heeah; a man can't live long without finding out that tailors are fwightful thieves and beastly bill-discounters. Glad to think that old Hebwew, Madox of Bond Street—— Know him ? " I replied that I did not. " Madox isn't his wight name," continued he ; " can't say what it is, and curse me if I care. Glad to feel I owe him thwee hundwed pounds, though. He can't take a boat and follow me, you know ; ha ! ha ! Ever been to Austwalia before ? "

I made a sound that might pass for yes or no.

" Vulgar people the Austwalians, I heah ; but,

poor dayvils, they can't help it. If we send out convicts there, why, dooce seize it, it's too much to expect their descendants to be gentlemen. Had a little blood gone wong and they'd twansported it, why, then you know, you might expect to find a bit of polish hecah and there-ah. I know an old Austwalian cock—shan't tell you where he lives—who's got so much money that this cabin wouldn't hold it in sovewins. Of all the old snobs—— Why, he sports a crest with as much assuwance as if it had come to him from the Conquewor ; whereas I'd bet any man half a dozen hats that he stole or invented it since he awived in England. A fellow can't help spwinging from nothing, you know, but it's a doocid piece of impertinence when he not only imitates his bettaws, but twies to pass himself off as one of them."

His reference to Alphonso—for what other old Australian cock should he mean ?—as a cad was extremely agreeable to me. " Little you wot, my aristocratic friend," thought I, as I watched him combing his hair and putting on his high stick-up collar, " how all that you say is being taken down against you." Why, I never should have dreamt that the creature was such a chatterbox nor such a consummate ass as his conversation proved him to be. Was it very surprising that Florence should think him a fool and despise him and reject him ? How should such an ape make love ? Even his good looks, as I now began to perceive, were effective only on the first impression. I had thought him handsome, as you know, when I saw him in Bristol—and handsome he was; but as I lay with my eyes upon him now, I reckoned that the girl he married would need to be as great an idiot as he not to find his beauty mighty insipid after a month or two.

In handling this fellow I am annoyed to feel that I can't put him before you with the right kind of colour to make the picture true to life. He had a sort of stammer impossible to express in words; he garnished his language with a variety of oaths—of the most approved and modish kind, no doubt, and quite in keeping with the character of a young swell—but which I am obliged to soften or omit, and so sacrifice a characteristic I remembered him by: and he said aw and haw just as Sophie had described (indeed, I fancied I could detect the source of Hawke's aristocratic pronunciation and hesitation), but in a manner so peculiar, that were he in the next room and you heard one of those aws you would be able to put a perfect image of the man before you merely from catching the conceit, the imbecility, the impudent suggestion of condescension, and I know not what other things which the sound conveyed.

Having finished dressing, he said, putting on his hat, " If we haven't left Gravesend, curse me if I don't go ashore and have a look at the place. Had scarcely time to do more yesterday than get a fit of indigestion. Since I have the bore of twavelling I may as well see all I can, and as Gwavesend's a place where the common people go and eat shwimps in the summer, I ought to be able, when I wetuen, to tell my friends that I've been over it."

I did not undeceive the man, and, as he was leaving the cabin, I asked him to be good enough to send the steward to me. This seemed to astonish him, for he said, "'Stwardinawy you should feel sea-sick! If you're ill now, by George, what'll you do when we get out upon the sea?" He then went away, and presently the steward arrived—a smart little man in a round jacket and bow legs, named Hay.

"When breakfast is ready, let me have a cup of tea and something to eat here, will you?" said I.

"Yes, sir."

"Where are we now, steward?"

"In the Warp, sir," he answered, naming the well-known stretch of river betwixt the Nore and the Oaze Deep.

"Is the captain on deck?"

"He's just gone into his cabin," replied Hay.

"Please go at once and tell him, with my compliments, that his friend, Mr. Jack Egerton, will breakfast in his cabin, and that he hopes to be able to go on deck during the afternoon."

I knew that Daniel would understand my meaning: for you see, on recalling his short memory I was afraid that he would forget to tell Florence I was aboard unless I employed some means to remind him of his promise. However, I was speedily eased of that fear by the steward returning. "The captain's compliments to you, sir, and he certainly hopes you will be well enough to come on deck this afternoon, and perhaps before. He'll look in upon you, sir, after breakfast."

Well, there I lay in my bunk, sometimes laughing to myself until I was like to split, when I thought of Morecombe and the wonderful absurdity of our sharing the same cabin, and then falling as grave as a judge and feeling a kind of tremble running through me when I turned my mind to Florence and wondered how she would receive the news of my being in the ship and what sort of greeting she would give me when Daniel "introduced" us. I pulled out her locket, which, you may reckon, boys, I wore day and night, and found a sort of strength in kissing it, for after all I considered she must like me a deal more than a little bit to have sent me that keepsake, and she surely would not like me less for following her to the world's end, as I was literally doing. Anyhow, she could not use me worse than she had treated Morecombe, if there was any meaning in the manner I spied in her when I peered through the skylight last night; and when I recalled the bit of behaviour I had taken notice of, it surprised me that the man should be able to carry himself so easily as he did in his imbecile conversation with me; for knowing how her coldness would affect *me*, I found it mighty hard to understand his indifference, for so it seemed, even when I had made the most liberal allowance for him as a conceited fool who was cock-sure in his own mind of winning the girl sooner or later, and was only astonished that such a killing, lovely, highly-connected creature should not have been instantly accepted.

The first breakfast bell was rung, and half-an-hour later I could hear all the passengers at table, a regular hum of voices, broken by the clattering of plates and now and again the loud distinct tones of Captain Jackson and Mrs. O'Brien. I strained my ear to catch the only notes which would fall sweetly upon it, and sometimes fancied I could detect the rich bell-like music of my darling's voice; but fancy it was, of course, and I wished it to be so, for it pleased me best to think of her as cold and silent, and averting her beautiful face from the eye-glass that I might reckon would be peering at her hard by, with a puppy's eye behind it.

The steward came into my cabin with a well-stocked tray, in the inspiration of which methought I could trace my friend Daniel; and glad was I to fall to, for the aroma of the good things on the cuddy table stealing in through the venetian-like panelling of the door had excited a lively hunger in me. I speedily cleared the tray, tumbled out of my bunk, shaved and dressed myself, and then, opening the scuttle and finding it to leeward, I lighted a pipe and smoked it with my face in the aperture, so that no smell of the tobacco should pass into the cuddy. It was like looking through a telescope without the magnification. Only a small view was to be got through the open port, but what there was of it was all sunshine and streaming waters, a kind of trembling white radiance, with the lines of the breeze-swept river-surface shining like ribs of polished steel through it, and a glimpse across the Kentish flats of the Whitstable and Herne Bay coast, looking like a stretch of blue haze. The tug was towing bravely, and the noise of the seething of the foam from her paddles washing past beneath me came up like the sound of a fountain; but I would now and again hear an ominous creak, a significant strain of timber or bulwark, and note that the horizon would take a slight slant first toward the bows and then towards the stern, as if it were the central portion of some gigantic see-saw. If, thought I we are beginning to feel the swell *here*, we should be finding a pleasant tumble further on.

Another half-hour passed. The motion was growing more defined, the creaking busier, and I was beginning to feel mighty tired of my cabin and to pine for the sunshine, and the breeze, and the leg-stretching space of poop. What! already? Somebody was sick in the next cabin. The groaning was as that of a monk wrestling with Beelzebub. There was no periodical explosion, no hopeful and soothing blow-up, but a steady grumbling, and now and again a slight roar. On a sudden a tap fell on my door, and in walked Daniel Thompson. His red face was illuminated by a broad grin, whilst he snuffed and exclaimed in a sepulchral voice, "Hallo! who's been smoking here?"

"It's that box," said I, pointing to Morecombe's; "it's full of tobacco. How are you, Daniel, and what news have you brought me?"

"Well, I've done your business," he answered. "It's all right. She knows you're aboard. You can clear out of this."

"Have you really explained already?" cried I. "What did she say? For heaven's sake, speak out, Daniel; I thought you were coming to see me after breakfast to arrange what to say to her?"

"I'm not going to make a long yarn of it," he replied. "I have other things to do. See here,

Jack, it was after breakfast: she and her aunt and Mr. Morecombe were on the poop. Hallo! what's that noise?"

"Somebody sick next door," I replied. "Heave ahead, Thompson."

"Well, they were on the poop. Presently the aunt goes below, young Morecombe having previously stepped over to Mrs. O'Brien to answer some question she had sung out to him. I saw my chance and went up to the girl, and after manœuvring a bit, as nervous as a stammering chap in a witness-box, and wishing you at Jericho for putting me on such a job, I told her plump that you had asked me to say you were aboard under some name which I couldn't for the moment recollect."

"Well?"

"Well—she just turned the colour of the ship's ensign. Split me, Jack, if ever I saw a girl blush so heavily before," said he. "A red Indian wouldn't have been in it alongside her. I'd have sheered off right away for fear that the others might twig the rosy look, and suspect I was making love to her, if I hadn't been more afraid, if they saw me go off in a hurry, that they'd imagine I had insulted her. But I say, my friend —she's a real beauty. You have a correct taste. She's a fine girl. I don't know that I ever saw a handsomer eye in a female. 'I'm an old friend of his,' said I, 'and I undertake this job merely to oblige him, and, I hope, you too,' said I. 'He declines to show up until I've informed you he's in the ship, and the next business, I think,' said I, 'he wants me to undertake, is to introduce him to you as if you were strangers, which, when done, will complete all that my friend Jack expects of me.'"

"Was that all that passed?" said I.

"That's all," he answered.

I thanked him heartily for his kindness, assuring him that as a friend in need he was the best of all friends, and I begged him to believe that I appreciated his friendliness all the more for knowing how the sense of his being skipper would bother him in his willingness to lend me a hand.

"What will you do now?" said he. "There's no need to keep below, is there? I think you told me the aunt don't know you?"

I answered that I would go forward, where I could command the poop; if Florence was alone I would come aft, but I explained that it would not be advisable to introduce me in the presence of the aunt, as Florence's manner, on our first meeting, might betray us.

"All right," said he; "but you'll understand, Jack, after I've introduced you to her you must go on making love alone. I'll have nothing more to do with it; and I hope you'll tell her never on any account in the future to speak of the part I have played, for though it might make my fortune among the girls it would ruin me among the fathers, who, after all, are the people who choose ships and pay the passage money."

I promised him in the most solemn manner that not a syllable concerning him should ever escape Miss Hawke or me, and he then went away.

I was in the act of struggling into a top coat, when the door was violently flung open and Mr. Morecombe bolted in. He was deadly pale, and his chest hollowed and swelled out like a pair of bellows, whilst his face had a twist in it as though he was strangling. He stood in the middle of the cabin glaring around him whilst a man might have counted ten, and his eyes then lighting on the wash-basin, he rushed up to it and vomited in the most dreadful manner that ever I beheld. No doubt I was right in suspecting that he had felt sick for some time, but had been fighting with his qualms on deck, and had rushed below to be ill out of sight of Miss Hawke. I tell you, his sufferings seemed dreadful, and he raised such an outcry as he hung over the basin, with both hands grasping his waistcoat, the perspiration streaming down his face, and first one leg and then the other giving a wild kick up astern of him as he roared, that I had not the heart to leave him until his paroxysm was over.

"Let me give you a hand into your bunk," said
I. "You can't do better than lie down, and I will
send the steward to you."

Well, I bundled him into his bunk, and never
did a more woebegone face embellish a pillow.
Ladies, you should have seen this good-looking
fellow! I pulled open his shirt-collars, which were
choking him, and hauled off his boots and put the
basin alongside of him. He lay groaning and
moaning like a wounded man, and the noise he
made appeared to have started off the person in
the next cabin afresh, for in the intervals of Morecombe's ramblings I could hear the muffled notes
of similar sounds beyond the bulkhead. I quitted
the cabin, and calling to the steward, told him
to look after the gentleman in number 4, and then
went on to the main-deck, watched with some
surprise by the little bow-legged fellow, who would
scarcely know what to make of a man that was one
moment too ill to leave his bed for the breakfast
table, and the next was stepping along the deck
with the deep sea-roll that comes like an instinct
the moment the trained leg feels the heave of
a deck-plank.

CHAPTER VI.

A NOBLE morning it was, streaming and shining, a light blue sky and a crescent of mares' tails over the mastheads and a flock of steam-coloured clouds scattering on the lee horizon, where the land was a greenish film on our starboard bow. To windward the pale green water ran into the whitish sky, and all that way there was nothing to be seen but a deep collier swarming along stiff as a church, with her yards hard against the lee rigging. The black smoke of the tug blew away from our flying jibboom end, and our ship followed with every stay-sail upon her hoisted, a crowd of passengers on the forecastle sunning themselves and standing black against the white cloths of the jibs, a blue vein breaking from the galley chimney, the gay decks glittering like sand, and a sweep of blue heaven deepening and lightening beyond the curve of the bows, which rose and sank upon the ruffled folds of the swell that was rolling out of the

Channel into which we were heading. I stepped as far as the main-hatch and then took a squint aft. The pilot was walking athwart the poop close to the brass rail, taking a sharp look ahead and around at every turn, but I had to go a little further to see as much as I needed of the poop, and when abreast of the galley I stopped again and saw Florence near the mizzenmast talking to some children.

Three or four only of the passengers were about, and Aunt Damaris was certainly not one of them. Thompson stood right aft near the wheel, and the idea coming into my head that he was waiting there to "introduce" me, and might be wondering what on earth was keeping me below, I pulled myself together and stepped without further ado on to the poop. He spied me the moment my head was above the ladder, and advanced to meet me.

"Jack," said he, "there's the lady, but you don't want me to introduce you, do ye? Hang it, there's nobody looking. Give me as little to do in this job as you can, mate."

"Let's carry the programme through," I replied, my heart thumping under my coat. "You told her you would introduce me." (This was not quite true, by the way). "Some confounded eye that we don't suspect may be on us; so take me up to her, will you?"

Florence had her back upon us, and pointed to the collier. whilst she talked to the children.

"Come along, then," said Thompson. "If it *must* be done, let's get it over;" and, leaving me to follow, he went up to Florence, who, in turning to him, saw me. Nobody but the nurse who had charge of the children was near enough to notice what was going on, and she called the youngsters away when we advanced; and lucky it was that nobody paid attention, for the abrupt manner in which Daniel had walked up to my darling and the extraordinary flourish he made over the business of introducing me must have set any observer wondering.

"Allow me, Miss Hawke," said he, contorting himself into the queerest of nautical bows, and waving his hands as though he were motioning to the man at the wheel, "to have the pleasure of introducing my friend Jack Edge—Edgy—hum! Mr. Jack Edgymore to you. Mr. Edgymore—Miss Hawke. Nice weather, Miss Hawke. The tug will be dropping us presently, and then we shall make sail, you know. Ahem! yes, that will be it;" and he fixed a bewildered eye on me as if he should say, "Must I go on talking a bit, or walk off at once?"

I raised my hat, and Florence, not being able to help herself, bowed, though one glance into each other's eyes was enough to satisfy us that we both equally felt the absurdity of this situation. But trying in its way as it was, let me tell you, lads, that *her* composure and self-possession could not have been completer had this been really our first introduction. A bright colour had flashed into her cheeks when she turned and saw me, but it was gone before Daniel had ended his speech, and looking at me with a faint, nervous, twitching smile upon her lips, she said in her sweet quiet voice through which ran a kind of tremble, "I was very much surprised when Captain Thompson told me that you were on board the *Strathmore* and going to Australia, Mr. Seymour."

When she pronounced my name Daniel laughed, and then appearing to find something deeply interesting in the sky to windward, he crossed the deck.

"I hope you are not angry with me," I began, scarcely knowing what to say, and hardly able to realize that I was alongside her *at last*, talking to her, looking into her beautiful eyes, and that this was just the very beginning of many weeks of constant association.

"Indeed I have not had time to find out," she replied. "I am too much astonished. I had no idea you would take such a step. If Sophie knew your intention, she should have told me."

"I assure you she knew nothing whatever about it," I replied. "I dared not trust her for fear of my project reaching your ears, and perhaps your father's. She wrote to tell me she wondered that I did not try to see you before you left, which made my secret the harder for me to keep from her, but her surprise will end when she gets my letter. Did you think I could endure to be separated from you? You sent me this to remember you by," said I, hauling out the locket, " but did you believe it would suffice? There is only one thing in this world that will satisfy me as a keepsake—and that is yourself."

She bent her eyes downwards, quietly smiling. Thompson was talking to the pilot; Mrs. O'Brien had got hold of the children and was amusing them; Captain Jackson and his wife stumped the other side of the poop arm in arm; everybody else belonging aft was below.

"Of *course* you know, Mr. Seymour, that my aunt is with me?" said she, after a pause.

"Yes," I replied. "She is the reason why I have shipped as Jack Egerton? Will you call me Egerton? If you address me as Seymour she will guess who I am."

"Ought I to say I will?" she answered, smiling. "It will be so difficult." And then with an uneasy look coming into her face she said, "Are you fair in asking me to be deceitful? I wish you had not come."

"Don't for heaven's sake, say so!" cried I.

" If my presence annoys you, I'll shift my quarters into the 'tween decks yonder, and never approach this part of the vessel for the rest of the voyage. It will be something, at all events, to feel that I am in the same ship with you. When I made up my mind to follow you I never feared that you would wish I had not come. It's true that I did not dare hope you would be glad to see me, but I counted upon your not being angry, for it is for love of you, and only for that, Florence, that I have followed you."

" I am not angry, Mr. Sey—, Mr. Edg—, Mr.— Oh, what am I to call you ? " she exclaimed, colouring and stammering. " I do not want you to leave this part of the ship; I—I—" The darling broke down, looking away with her sweet eyes over the sea, with a trembling of the lovely lashes as though tears were not far off; and then rallying a bit she said in her gentle way, with a quiver in the lower notes of her voice: " The deceitfulness is the only part I dislike. I shall never be able to address you as Mr. Egerton without feeling that I am telling a story."

" Then," said I, peeping round into her face, " if you can't help feeling that it will be wrong to call me Mr. Egerton, say Jack when we are alone —that will be enough; there's no need to address me by any name when others are present."

Here came another pause, and then said she—

" Do you know that Mr. Reginald Morecombe is in this ship ? "

" Perfectly well," I replied. " He shares my cabin ; and I have just left him horribly sea-sick, after stowing him away in his bunk."

" What ! does *he* know you are here ? " she cried, with her eyes wide open with wonder.

" He knows that Mr. Egerton is here—that's all," I answered.

" But have you never met before ? "

" I caught a glimpse of him once at Bristol, but he did not see me, and does not know me from Adam."

She raised her hands with a gesture of astonishment, and then I suppose the absurdity of his sharing my cabin—indeed, the ridiculousness of the position we were all of us in—struck her ; she broke into a short semi-hysterical laugh, though she grew very soon grave again, and turned a glance now and then at the companion hatch which caused me to ask her if she expected her aunt to come on deck.

" I don't think she will come," she answered. " She complained of feeling a little sick, and went to her cabin to lie down."

" Does not this motion inconvenience you ? "

" Not in the least," she replied ; and indeed I had already noticed how easily she poised her beautiful figure to the heave of the deck. Looking

at her closely whilst we conversed, and better able
to observe points in her now that my agitation was
gone, I took notice of a certain careworn expression
in her face—a sorrowful appearance that would
have passed with me as the grief she would feel
in saying good-bye to her home, were it not that
it looked too old to belong to the date of her farewell. She caught me watching her wistfully, and
I at once said—

"I am afraid they have been making you unhappy on my account. You haven't the healthful,
happy looks I remember, Florence; though, please
God, they'll be coming back to you now."

She did not answer me; whether or not she
liked me calling her Florence, there was no rebuke
in her face when I said the word.

"I heard from Sophie," said I, "that you were
a good deal worried when in Scotland. Did you
know that Mr. Morecombe was to be one of the
Strathmore's passengers?"

"How can you ask me?" she answered quickly,
with a sparkle like a tear in her eyes, and the cold
look I had noticed when peering at her through
the skylight on the previous evening coming into
her face. "I should not be here if I *had* known."

"Ah!" said I, "I see how the coast lies now.
What a mean wretch he must be to pursue you in
this fashion after your flat rejection of him. The
instant I entered my cabin and spied the fellow's

traps I saw the plot. How could your father have the heart to subject you to this sort of thing? What opinion can he have of you not to guess that the more Mr. Morecombe worries you the more you will hate him!"

She could not help smiling at this, dejected as she looked and was, and said—

"The idea of the voyage is Aunt Damaris', not papa's," as though she would apologize for her father.

"And was it Miss Damaris Hawke who suggested the notion of Mr. Morecombe's voyaging to Australia with you?"

"I cannot tell you, Mr. Sey—, Mr.——"

"Jack—say Jack, Florence," I exclaimed. "If you will not think of me as myself, think of me as Sophie's cousin, and you'll not find Jack hard to pronounce. If you do not mind me calling you Florence, why should you hesitate to call me Jack?"

"You call me Florence without asking my leave —how do you know I don't mind?" she answered.

Well, it was early times to press this matter of Jack, so I went back to my question as to what share Aunt Damaris had in the plot that had brought young Morecombe into the *Strathmore*. She replied that she could not say, as until she came aboard at Gravesend she did not know that Mr. Morecombe meant to sail in the ship. She

said that shortly after their arrival in Scotland
Aunt Damaris had asked her if she would like to
return to Sydney with her in September, and stop
a few months there.   She answered yes, the
voyage would amuse her, and she would be glad to
see Sydney again.   A little later her father talked
to her on the same matter, and made her see he
wished her to go with her aunt; so then she took
the thing in earnest, and wrote to Sophie about it,
but she had not the least idea that the voyage was
a plan to bring her and Morecombe together; she
never thought when she left England to see the
youth again, otherwise, though she was quite
willing to go to Australia, she never would have
sailed in that ship with him. She told me this in a
very quiet way, speaking softly and often looking at
me anxiously as if she feared I might distrust any
portion of her narrative. She did not utter a word
against her father or her aunt, nevertheless she
contrived somehow or other to make me see that
ever since she had met me she had led an uncomfortable, if not an unhappy life at her home; and
that being so, then there was very little to wonder
at in her willingness to leave it for a spell.   I
noticed that as we continued conversing the embarrassment she had first shown passed away, she
warmed up, glancing at me with a sort of pleasure
in her eyes as if she was beginning to thoroughly
realize that I was on board.   And, my lads, even if

this girl thought of me then as no more than a friend, there would be a pleasantness when she looked along the ship and saw the crowd of strange people on the main deck and forecastle and then over the bows and beheld the leagues of heaving sea there, in remembering that I was on board, with a face that brought up pleasant memories of Clifton, and Bristol Cathedral, and Sophie, and the like; for though, to be sure, her aunt was in the ship, the feeling that the old woman sided with her brother and had meanly played into his hands would so qualify the sense of companionship as to make the girl feel, when she looked around the sea, that she was hardly less alone than the loneliest of the 'tween-deck passengers. So I believe that she would have been glad to know that I was on board, even had I been merely a friend; but it would not do to pretend that I was no more than that to her. There were memories between us which rose in me as sweet as the recollection of kisses, and her nervousness and wonder at my presence being past, she could not view the ocean towards which we were towing, nor reflect that these were the first hours of a voyage that was to last for some months, without guessing that it must be something deeper than a boyish whim that had brought me alongside of her to take my chance of what she might think and how she might treat me.

I was much too earnest and absorbed in talk

with her to take notice of what was passing around. The swell of the sea was growing longer and heavier, and the funnel of the tug waved handsomely athwart our hawse as the great ship curtsied solemnly in her wake. Mrs. O'Brien, the nurse, and the children had gone below, and the only persons now on the poop besides ourselves were the pilot, the captain, the second mate, who stood to leeward near the mizzen rigging, and Captain Jackson and his wife. I should have said, had I been asked to forecast this adventure, that it would have taken me some time to reconcile Florence to my presence; that the sense that her father, were he to know that I was on board, would command her to have nothing to do with me, would weigh upon her as a heavy obligation; and that consequently it would cost me a long struggle to bring her heart nearer to mine—though if I had ever doubted of accomplishing this, never of course would I have undertaken the voyage. But whether it was that she liked me better than I should have dared to believe, or that her indignation at finding this voyage nothing but a trap set by her father and aunt for Morecombe to catch her in made her defiant, I found after the first five or ten minutes of uneasiness that she talked to me freely and gladly. She never appeared to give herself any trouble as to Aunt Damaris' movements, and, instead of thinking we had conversed long enough, and that she ought to go to her aunt in the cabin, she immediately joined me in patrolling the deck when I proposed walking for fear that she would feel the cold by standing. I caught Thompson grinning away like clockwork as we faced round on reaching the taffrail. What there was in us to tickle his fancy I do not know and did not care. I was passionately proud, happy beyond expression, triumphantly joyous at having my darling with me, keeping me company, talking with a lighter note in her dear voice, and letting me see, though without an atom of coquetry, that her first alarm at sight of me was false to her deeper feelings, and that she was welcoming me now—not perhaps as a man whom she loved, but as a man whom she knew devotedly loved her. She talked to me as if it did her good to open her mind, and although you may think that she ought to have found Mr. Morecombe a delicate subject to discuss with me, I assure you she spoke out about him with great frankness, and seemed to be amazed at his hardihood in taking this voyage with her after her refusal of him.

"Oh, but he's such a fool," said I ; "so ludicrously self-conceited that he won't believe you're in earnest. He supposes, I dare say, you don't know him well enough, but that you'll have found him out before you get to Sydney, and allow yourself to be vanquished."

She smiled disdainfully. "At all events," said she, "I've made up my mind to return in this ship. I have said nothing to Aunt Damaris, nor shall I for some time to come, but if Mr. Morecombe intends to remain in Sydney, that place will not be big enough to contain me too, and I shall go home with your friend Captain Thompson."

As she said this, my mind went to the fellow groaning and writhing on his back in the cabin, and I said, "If he's going to continue as sea-sick as he's begun he'll have more than he wants of the voyage before we are out of the Channel."

"Why," asked she suddenly, "do you insist upon calling yourself Egerton?"

"Because," I replied, "if your aunt finds out who I am she will not allow you to speak to me."

Here eyes took a brighter light as she exclaimed, "Do not you think I have any will of my own? There is no *harm* in your speaking to me, Mr. Seymour, and if I choose to let you do so I do not think that my aunt would object."

There was a perfect revelation to me in these few words. Sweet and tender and gloriously lovable I always knew her to be, but never should I have believed that with the adorable qualities of her heart she combined real force of character. And yet, upon my word, I had only to remember how she had refused Morecombe in defiance of all the influence her father could bring to bear upon her, and how loyally she had stuck to my cousins, and with what a brave, uncomplaining soul she embarked on this long voyage, to wonder that I should have needed a speech from her to find out that she had a high spirit. I hardly knew what answer to make her.

"I don't wish to influence you," she continued, "but if you have assumed a name only for my sake, let me assure you the disguise is unnecessary. You are quite right in supposing that my aunt would be very vexed to find you on board, but why should I study other people's feelings when I see how little mine are considered. I'm not responsible for your being here, but my aunt *is* answerable for Mr. Morecombe's presence, and she came to the ship at Gravesend expecting to find him in her, as I could see by the way they met. Aunt Damaris doesn't mind humiliating me by this plot, as you might call it, and since you *are* on board, Mr. Seymour, I do not know why she should not be told who you are."

There was no anger in her manner, but she spoke as a woman would who is deeply offended, with a flush in her cheek and a sparkling in her eyes and a trembling of the lips.

"I will do whatever you wish," I replied, "and I feel the truth of all that you say, believe me. But as my name is down as Egerton, as the stewards and others know me by that name,

and as it is on my luggage, it would be rather
awkward to alter it. And then," said I, " think of
the effect of the discovery upon Mr. Morecombe,
who, you must know, sleeps in the bunk under
mine. We should end our days like the Kilkenny
cats. If Sydney would not be big enough to hold
you and him, I am sure this ship would not be large
enough to hold him and me if once I discovered
that he knew who I was."

She broke into one of her old merry laughs, and
said, " You will do as you like, I suppose, but I
shall never be able to speak or think of you as Mr.
Egerton, aristocratic as the name is."

" I want you to think of me as Jack and call me
so—not of course before others, but when we are
alone. Will you ? " I asked.

" I can't tell you now," she replied, coming to a
stand at the companion ; and putting her foot upon
the step, she looked a few moments at the haze of
land on the starboard beam with a shadow of
melancholy on her beautiful eyes, and then saying,
" There is no chance of our not meeting again soon
now," she went below.

CHAPTER VII.

THE moment Florence was gone, Daniel came up to me. I should have been glad of a spell of solitude, if merely to enjoy the luxury of thinking over this meeting and conversation with my darling girl, and the noble hope that had come to me ; but my friend was not to be put off.

"You have had a longish bout of it, Jack," said he. "How have you enjoyed yourself? By thunder, she has a proper face and figure! Does she use her heels or her toes when she walks? Never saw such a floating movement in a woman on a rolling deck. Will not she be a fine dancer now, eh? How have you got on?"

"Pretty much as you did when you were courting, Daniel. I'm greatly obliged to you for your friendly offices."

"Not at all. Glad to have been able to steer you; but you're on your own hook now, my lad ; well out of my pilotage district, and must shift for yourself. But that I think you know how to do. How does she relish you under that confounded name of yours, which I never can remember?"

I made him some kind of answer, and changed the subject by asking where the tug was to drop us. "Abreast of the Foreland," he replied. "Yonder's Margate," and he pointed to the land which, owing to the haziness, loomed faintly in the distance, as though it were leagues away.

The wind had freshened, and was blowing a steady breeze with weight enough in it to give a heel to the ship, though she was under fore and aft canvas only. The swell came along from the north and east with a regular Channel roll, and a bit of a sea on top that hissed sharply in small green surges, and made an eager glancing under the sun that sailed fast among the squadrons of windy clouds which swarmed along the pale autumn blue. The swell was nearly ahead, and the ship pitched slowly as she went, smothering a broad space of water around her with a surface of blowing and winking and shining foam at every crushing and shearing blow of the powerful bows and cutwater; and the tug ahead sometimes rolled sponsons under as she dragged at us, now and again hoisting one or the other of her wheels almost bodily out of water into the air, where you could see it spin round like a circle of bright steel sparkling wet in the sun, and dipping her head in the smother she

raised until the sea-line beyond stood. as high as
the bridge, and then slackening the great hawser
into a bight as her stern swooped into the snow
under her counter and gave us a clear view of her
deck. Some of the steerage passengers overhung
our forecastle rail or main deck bulwarks, very
sick. The chief officer was forward standing by
for the tug to let go, and the crew lounged about
waiting for the order to make sail. It was a
moment full of interest and excitement. The little
steamer ahead was the final link that connected us
with home, and she would be dropping us very
soon, like the withdrawal of the hand that gives
you the last shake. There was a fleet of smacks
ratching to the eastwards on our port bow, jumping
the green hollows heavily and crowding a space of
the cloudy sky and the jagged olive-green of the
hazy horizon with their chocolate-coloured sails; a
few gulls hung in our wake peering with arched
necks into the boiling eddies and balancing themselves like shapes of marble against the streaming
wind, now and again uttering hoarse cries as they
stooped to the foam which flew scattering from
the rolling coils of the waves like feathers from
their own beautiful breasts; right ahead of us
was a deal galley flashing through the seas under
her fragment of reefed canvas, with a couple of
men in yellow oilskins sitting to windward and a
fellow crouching aft; the wind was keen and damp

with spray as it blew in moans over the bulwarks and rushed with a shriek through the rigging into the staysails, and there was a hard look in the sky to the southward and eastward, away past the tiny red dancing blotch of the North Sands Head lightship, which made me suspect that a teaser lay lurking there in readiness for us presently.

We were heading to pass the Goodwins to the eastward, which would keep the land a shadow wherever it was. About three quarters of an hour after Florence had left the deck the tug dropped us. Lunch was on the table; I had slipped below to get something to eat, and I would have stopped there had Florence been visible, but not seeing her, and preferring the busy cheerful scene on deck to Captain Jackson's views on the decadence of the Royal Navy and Mrs. O'Brien's loud abuse of her native country, I was soon on the poop again, watching the tug pitching and flinging the green water in shining showers of emeralds over her forward deck as she swept in a long curve away from us, a fellow on the bridge waving his hat, and the thick smoke of the funnel blowing like flying scud straight into the land. Hands were aloft on our ship, canvas was rattling its folds, chain sheets were grinding and tearing upon the sheaves, and the crew were springing about in all directions, raising those hoarse peculiar cries which are to my ears as much a portion of ocean sounds as the seething of foam or the singing of the wind.

I remained on deck, constantly hoping that Florence would arrive. Though her aunt was apparently prostrate there was evidently no fear of sea-sickness attacking my sweetheart, for whilst we had walked and talked I took notice that she seemed to feel the ship under her as a horsewoman would a frolicsome mare, and to enjoy the vessel's jumping as though the dance were a hurdle-race. I stumped about, sniffing up the keen salt wind and tasting the spray on my lips and relishing the sweetness of it, my thoughts full of my darling, though some little attention I could give to the ship and the foaming and rushing sea through which the *Strathmore* was squeezing and rolling. Such were the fancies my talk with Florence had put into my head, that it seemed to me, if her father had wanted to play into my hands, he could not have done better than send his daughter to Australia along with Morecombe. Particularly had I noticed the resentment in her when she spoke of her aunt. The more she thought over the ruse, the more pained and disgusted was she bound to feel. It was not for her health, for her amusement, that her father had sent her away; no, but that Morecombe and she might be locked up in a place where no Jack Seymour could intrude upon her to whine out his love. Mr. Hawke's young friend would have her all to himself; and, backed by Aunt Damaris, would end in getting her to accept him; that was the idea, and to obtain that man as a son-in-law, merely because some of these days he would be making his wife her ladyship, Mr. Hawke was willing to send his child to Australia, lose her companionship for he would scarcely know how long, subject her to the dangers of the sea, and inflict upon her the attentions of the creature she had already refused! Would not such considerations vex and disgust my high-spirited girl more and more as she looked into and understood them? It was all new to her yet; only yesterday had she discovered the meaning of the voyage; but already had it done a deal of work in her feelings, as I could tell; and, faith, I should not have been much of a lover if I did not quietly rejoice over the possibility of her rebelling against her father's wishes in a manner sweeter to myself and more emphatic to *him* than was signified in the mere refusal of Mr. Morecombe's empty heart and itching palm.

We had left the North Sands Head lightvessel dancing fast and furious a long way astern, and the deep ship, pressed down pretty nearly to her covering-board by the weight of her whole topsails into which the wind was rushing with a shout as though it must presently burst through the strained, distended spaces, was heavily breaking her way through the quick fierce head sea of the

Channel, her forecastle dark and wet, her running gear blowing out in semicircles, the foretack groaning like a wounded giant with every weather roll of the hull, the crew in oilskins, the older salts among them casting their eyes to windward at the stormy look of the driving sky that way, and then aloft in evident readiness for an order to reef down; and the decks forward wholly cleared of the passengers by the flying wet. It was a winter-piece, for the wind was as raw as if frost were in it, the sea was a hard dark green out on the horizon, the clouds as they flew out of the south and east and swept like smoke over our mast-heads seemed to be full of snow, with their slate-coloured bellies fining into a whitish grey at the skirts, and though the distance was thick, yet there was the sharpness of outline you see in things on a clear frosty January morning in all objects this side the haze, such as the buoy that slided past us, rising and falling amid a showering of spray and leaning with the tide, in the white water that flashed and quivered upon the submerged Goodwins, in the two or three black-hulled smacks which were heading for the North Sea, burying their bowsprits with every chopping fall, and in the paddle-steamer that was passing us on our port quarter, her sides shining like oil as she lifted away from us, with her red wheel twinkling over the foam in which the next roll would bury it.

I was about to go below to be out of the wind for a spell, when the order to clew up the maintopgallant sail was given; and a minute afterwards another order was delivered, the chief mate echoed it, and the boatswain's pipe took it up with a long piercing silvery whistling, instantly followed by his hurricane roar of "All hands reef topsails!" I lingered to watch an old familiar scene. The topgallant halliards were let go, the sail clewed up, and the rigging jumped to the sprawling of the fellows who slapped the ratlines as they mounted the shrouds and swarmed over the top like revolving porpoises. Down came the three topsail yards with a tearing sound of whirling sheaves and rattling of chains, and then followed a thumping and thundering of canvas as the reef-tackles were manned, whilst the seamen heartily chorused, and the ship, with her way slackened and the pressure aloft nearly gone, bowed and curtsied with almost erect spars upon the head sea that poured in sharp concussions against her weather bow. When I saw the third mate jump aloft for the weather mizzen topsail earring, followed by the brass-bounders and an ordinary seaman or two, my fingers languished for the feel of a ratline and a reefpoint; but it did not answer my purpose to let the cuddy passengers—a few of whom had come on deck on hearing the noise—see me on the topsail yard, and guess from the spectacle that I knew the difference betwixt a backstay and a brass rail; so I kept where I was.

Reefing topsails is a lively thing to watch, boys, as you know, when there are hands enough for all three sails at once, and the men are nimble; for at such a time there will be plenty of wind—unless you're providing against a low glass in what Jack Spaniard calls a furious calm—and the screeching of it as it sweeps off the combing ridges with a slanting bound right up along the canvas, making it boom like a thousand drummer-boys at work up there, is the sort of accompaniment that is wanted to make music of the deep sea-notes of the men lighting over to windward and hauling out to leeward; the surges run along the bends with a wild washing noise: the wheel leaps in the hands of the man grasping the spokes as the sea smites the rudder and swings up full and gurgling under the counter; and there is a kind of strangeness in the recovery of the ship from the slope she has been rushing along with, and in the tumbling, rolling, straining, creaking pause as if something was wrong. Well, I stopped until the men were off the yards, and had mastheaded them with a rattling chantey at each halliard, and then taking notice as the ship leaned down again under her single-reefed canvas and snapped and worried the seas as she gained way, how a number of wind-bound craft in the Downs over our lee bow were shaping themselves out of the haze in rocking outlines, and how the coast there, which should be as white as milk in the sunshine, hung like a smoky louring of vapour betwixt heaven and water, I walked to the companion and trotted down the steps, feeling all the enjoyment of a special privilege now that my darling and I had been properly introduced, and we could meet without risk of a betraying exclamation or an equally traitor-like blush, such as Daniel had described.

On entering my cabin I found a man seated on a box close to Morecombe, who lay in his bunk moaning in the most dismal manner. The stranger stood up as I shut the door, and suspecting from his appearance that he was the ship's surgeon, whom I had not before seen, no doubt from the circumstance of his cabin and apothecary's shop being in the steerage under the cuddy, I asked him straight if he was the doctor, and he answered "Yes: I have been called to this gentleman by the steward. He is certainly very bad, I don't like his symptoms at all. Indeed I don't believe he ought to continue the voyage."

I peered into the bunk, and my eyes getting used to the gloom—for, you see, the sky was made up of whirling vapour, and the scuttle which the lee heel of the ship pointed at the sea let in but very little of what light there was—I made out Mr. Morecombe lying like a corpse, his eyes closed, his face of the colour of a turnip, with gouts of sweat all over it, with a kind of saliva draining from the lips, whilst the posture of his arms and half-closed hands indicated an exhaustive degree of prostration. I did not need the surgeon, whose name was Griffith—a young red-headed chap fresh from the hospitals, I suppose, and who had shipped like most sea-doctors do, to get experience by experimenting on poor Jack—I did not want him, I say, to tell me that Morecombe was in a very bad way. I really could not help pitying the fellow, as he lay with moaning noises breaking from his mouth and looking like a dying man, and, said I, forgetting that we should have to land the pilot, "If you think he should not pursue the voyage, what's to be done? We're bound right away out; there's to be no more stopping, I think."

"Well," replied the medico, "he can't go on like this. He must be got ashore, somehow, if he don't show signs of recovery. You should have been here twenty minutes since. Sick! 1 never saw more furious and dreadful retching," lowering his voice: "the veins on his head stood out like that," said he, holding up his finger, "and I expected every minute to see the blood come up out of him like a fountain."

"He seemed all right this morning in the river," said I.

"The water was smooth—but this is cwuel—it is

killing me ! " groaned the sufferer, to my surprise ; for by the looks of him I should have thought that if he was not past hearing he was certainly past speaking.

"Don't you think your nausea will subside ? " said I.   "Most people are ill at the first start, you know, but they recover when they feel the long deep sea-heave of blue water under them."

He made no answer to this, for a reason that was only too fully explained by a sudden explosion that I thought would have torn him in halves.   I dropped on one knee and supported him, whilst the doctor assisted him in other ways ; his throes and convulsions were truly formidable ; indeed I had never seen anything of the kind to approach his, and when I let him sink back I thought he had fainted ; he scarcely seemed to breathe, and his face presented a most ghastly appearance from the puffy discoloration under the eyes caused by his violent straining.

"I can't let this go on," said the doctor : " he must be set ashore somehow or other.   I'll not be responsible for his life if we carry him much farther."

"Well, sir," said I, " suppose you go and speak to the captain, and ask him to come and look for himself.   I'll keep watch here."

He assented, and left the cabin.

"Do you feel a little easier ? " I asked the poor

moaning creature, fancying that the last burst-up might have relieved him.

He replied in the faintest imaginable voice, "No, I am vewy ill—I am dying—the captain must land me."

"But," said I, "you told me you had done some yachting in your time. Won't you give yourself a chance? This is bound to pass if you'll hold on."

"I've done vewy little yachting—always in smooth water—never weally liked it," he gasped out: "this is killing—I shall never wecover—the captain must land me."

The doctor and he knew more about it, of course, than I did, for at that time I never reckoned sea-sickness a dangerous thing; perhaps because, never suffering from it, I had no sympathy with people affected by it. But since then I have heard of people dying of it, and only the other day read of a steamer that called at a port some miles out of her course to land a woman who was so ill from the effects of nausea, that she expired as she was being conveyed ashore. Yet, though I could not guess that there was any uncommon danger in Morecombe's sickness, it was easy to see that the man was suffering horribly, and that if there was no chance of his recovering shortly, he must be got out of the ship; for even the length of the Channel from the Downs to the Scillies would be leagues too much of a voyage for a stomach that promised to kill its owner by rupturing a bloodvessel or two if its agony was not ended ; I say I could see that ; and small as would be the notice I should have taken on my own account of the staggering rolling deck, yet the sight of Morecombe made me clearly understand what the rude and giddy motion must seem to him, with its accompaniments of creaking and straining timbers, the washing and thundering of water alongside and the deep hollow gurgle of the seas as they swelled up over the scuttle and veiled the immensely thick glass of it with the glimmering green darkness of their folds.

Presently the doctor returned with my friend Daniel, who stood awhile trying to catch sight of Morecombe, who lay in the dusk of the bunk, and then making out how fearfully ill he looked, he said with a deal of pity and good feeling in his voice, "I am sorry to find you so bad, sir. If you feel unable to continue the voyage, there need be no difficulty in setting you ashore—perhaps not yet a bit," said he, with a cock of his eye at the scuttle, "for there'll be too much wind and sea to enable us to do anything in that way this side of to-morrow, I fear ; but if you can manage to hold on until we fetch the Isle of Wight, the pilot'll be leaving us there, and you can go with him."

"I'm fwightfully bad," answered Morecombe, in so faint and choking a voice that the skipper had to put his ear to his mouth to hear him above the grinding and complaining noises in the cabin. Here the doctor spoke to Thompson, talking in a low tone that Morecombe might not hear him, so that I did not catch what was said; but there was great gravity in the medico's face, and by the glances Thompson directed at the sufferer, I could judge he was a good deal concerned by what he was hearing. Well, you know, sea-sickness is a thing for which no cure has been discovered yet; the doctor could do nothing, and it was plain that the only remedy for Morecombe was to put him on solid ground; and looking at him and thinking of Florence, I began to consider that nothing better could happen for us all than that he should leave the ship. Whether something to that effect was in Daniel's mind I can't say; but I fancied there was a kind of wink in the droop of the eye he turned on me as he slewed round on his heel to leave the cabin, saying to the doctor as he went that he was afraid there was no chance of landing Mr. Morecombe before next day, but he'd speak to the pilot to see what could be done. It went against my grain to leave the poor chap alone, so I told the doctor I would stop with him until dinner-time; and this I did, putting a wet towel to his forehead to keep the swooning feeling down, and supporting him when the deadly fit of retching seized him: but the job was one, let me tell you, I had not much relish for, as some of the attacks were so bad that I was thoroughly frightened by them, and expected when I let his head sink on the pillow to find him lifeless.

How on earth he could have come to sea with such a stomach as his I could not imagine. He must have travelled in his time, been upon the water if only for a short run, such as from Dover to Calais, or Holyhead to Kingstown; and would therefore know what sort of seafaring qualities he possessed. He was too ill to answer questions, was unable to speak indeed, and so I could only go on ministering to him and puzzling my head. And what a thing was this to come about! Here were we rivals for the same girl, capable on dry land of shooting at each other for her—following her to the other side of the globe: here were we, I say, in one cabin, one of us in the most horrible condition of sea-sickness, and the other nursing him! Just dwell upon this if you're fond of the unexpected.

CHAPTER VIII.

MEANWHILE, as I kept watch by Mr. Morecombe's side, doing what I could to soothe his sufferings, I heard the sound of running rigging thrown down on deck, the voices of sailors singing out at the ropes, and the muffled flapping of canvas. More reefs were being taken in, and the increasing violence of the wind was to be felt in the weight of the seas that lifted the vessel. We were booked for a regular Channel dusting: a black night was drawing up, and I pretty well knew that there would be too much anxiety felt on deck by pilot, skipper, and mates to allow room for thoughts of Mr. Morecombe. The first dinner-bell rang at half-past five; it was then quite dark, the cuddy lamps alight, the glass of the scuttle in my cabin like ebony, and the wind roaring in thunder outside. I stepped out and found the doctor talking to Captain Jackson in the cuddy.

" Well, Mr. Egerton," said he (I suppose he had

read this name on my box), "how's your sick friend ? "

" Much too bad to be left alone, that's my opinion," said I. " Go and look at him, doctor, will you ? And if you think proper, get one of the stewards to tend him, for he'll expire if he's not lifted in one of his fits." And there being ten minutes to spare before the second bell announced that dinner was served, I trotted up the companion-ladder to have a look around.

The wind seemed to be coming with the hardness of a gale as I put my head into it clear of the companion. The evening had come down in a shadow as black as a storm, and the darkness was made the thicker for the clouds of spray which were swept off the breaking crests of the sea and whirled like wreaths of mist through the rigging. The ship was under double-reefed topsails and reefed foresail. The wind was abeam, and under this small canvas the ship was pressing forwards, rolling most uneasily over the ugly, quick, short surges. There was not a star to be seen, not a ship's lantern nor shore-light. The water was as black as ink among the froth; there was never a gleam in it that I could see. A bright look-out would be needed on such a night as this in these narrow waters ; and in the haze of light that came up through the glass of the foremost skylight, I could see the figures of the pilot and the mate walking athwartships to and fro, pausing to windward to take a squint at the sea on that side, and then to leeward for a look at the ponderous shadow that lay on the water betwixt the main and the fore shrouds. Foreward the ship was in darkness; for the side lights were invisible aft, and no sheen was in the air from them; you could just make out the bands of topsails glimmering like the pinions of monstrous birds as they swayed overhead; but nothing above them was to be seen, so that the screaming and wailing that came down out of the hidden rigging was a kind of wonder. Every now and again a rush of damp swept up in a burst of wind, but the showers dried as fast as they fell, and the deck of the poop was a stretch of grey from the break of it to the wheel, where a yellow haze overhung the binnacle, and gave an outline to the figure that was grinding at the spokes behind it.

Well, we were holding our course and swarming down Channel at about five knots, as I might guess by fixing my eyes on any leaping surface of white to leeward and watching it slide away on the quarter. There was satisfaction in this, and so long as the wind enabled us to keep our jibboom pointed towards the Atlantic—why, it might blow half a gale for all I cared; so I went below, and in a minute or two the second dinner-bell rang, and those of the cuddy passengers who were not sea-sick came out of their cabins and seated themselves. Amongst them was Florence, and she was alone. I went round the table to her, and she pretended not to see me coming; but I knew better. There must be some kind of reflection of me in her shining beautiful eyes, or what did the little smile mean?

You will remember that I described the tables as forming this shape, **T**, the top cross running athwart. Well, in the centre of this thwartship table was the captain's place, and when he looked forward he commanded the length of the fore and aft table. There were two seats on either hand of him. He was waiting for the passengers to take their places, when I went up to Florence and asked her which was her seat.

"Here," answered Daniel for her, giving me a knowing grin; "Miss Hawke sits next to me—her aunt on my right. I like to divide the ladies. you had better secure that corner, Mr.—Edgboro', is it?" said he, pointing to the seat on Florence's left; and these being the skipper's orders, you see, I sat down, Florence being 'twixt Daniel and me. There were five besides ourselves. Everybody was sick, it seemed, but Captain Jackson and his wife, Mrs. O'Brien, Mr. Thompson Tucker, and Mr. Joyce. The cuddy fare was very good in those days—excellent soup, poultry, joints, decent wines, dried fruits, and such things; and dinner was not

only a long business, but it gave one plenty to do.
I see the picture at this moment of that dinner-
table on this first black Channel night I am telling
you about; the white table-cloth all agleam with
glass and plate, the burnished swinging trays tossing convulsively in the bright light of the large
pendulous lamps, ripples of radiance running about
the polished bulkheads as the heaving of the ship
brought the rays to bear on different points, the
passengers eating with very little avidity, pausing
often whilst in the act of lifting a spoon or fork to
their mouths when the ship gave an extra heavy
lurch, and frequently directing their eyes at the
skylight, the panes of which resembled squares of
ebony against the blackness, and reflecting the
shining table under them like looking-glasses.
Thompson, with his jolly red face, sat eating and
enjoying his dinner, and answering questions about
the weather and such things, and the stewards trotted
with solicitude past the people. But these matters
received but little attention from me. My darling was
close alongside ; I had her all to myself, and I talked
to her and nobody else, though I took great pains
so to manage my face that the passengers should
not guess too much of what was passing in me.

Aunt Damaris, she said, was not actually ill but
felt queer, and was in bed and not likely to get up
for a day or two, as it took her about that time to
conquer her nausea.

"Have you heard," said I, "how fearfully ill Mr. Morecombe is?"

"No, I have not heard about him, nor am I interested," she replied, with a curl of her red underlip.

When, however, I told her how dangerously sick he was, and what the doctor had said about him, and how there was a risk of his rupturing a blood-vessel and dying in one of his attacks, she looked up at me in amazement. "What will he do?" she asked. "Will he continue the voyage?"

"I think not," I answered. "He has begged to be put ashore; but that was not to be done in the face of such weather as this and with a black night drawing up. If he lives until we fetch the Isle of Wight, he will probably land with the pilot."

She fancied I was joking by saying "If he lives," but Thompson overhearing us, assured her that I was speaking the truth, and to confirm my words called out to the doctor, who was at the bottom of the table, "What's the latest report of Mr. Morecombe?"

"He's as bad as bad can be, captain. I looked in before dinner, and don't think he could be worse. You'll have to put him ashore, sir. If he's carried out to sea it'll be odds if he don't answer for it with his life."

Here the passengers took the subject up, and all sorts of questions and exclamations were let fly.

" You see how it is," I said to Florence ; " were he not so cruelly ill I should say he was being well paid out for following you. But his pursuit is not a long one. He is sure to go ashore with the pilot."

She was very grave and thoughtful, and said, " What an unexpected termination! What will Aunt Damaris say ? "

" I hope you'll let her find out for herself that he's gone," said I.

" I certainly shall," she exclaimed. " His coming was no business of mine, and neither is his going. It is perfectly indifferent to me whether he stays or leaves."

Well, we had much to say about the man and his dreadful sea-sickness, and the subject furnished me with more than one opportunity for quietly dropping a hand-lead into her heart, and finding what depth of water there was for me there, and what sort of ground the " arming " showed. And I was so greatly encouraged by my discoveries that, growing more courageous as the dinner progressed and my spirits mounting to the music of her voice's gentleness, ay, and *tenderness*, boys—a melody distinguishable above the muffled roaring without and the straining and creaking within—I asked her to tell me if she would like me to go away from the ship with sea-sick Mr. Morecombe. She peeped at me under her eyelashes, and said, " If you thought I would like you to go, you would not stop ? "

"You'd have a good right to distrust my love if I refused to do anything you desired," said I.

"Well," said she, "since you are here I don't want you to go."

I found her hand under the table and took it. She let me hold it a moment, with a trifle of pink in her cheeks, and then drew it away in a manner to signify, "I don't object; but you must not make love to me too fast." But this small stroke of eloquence was of no use. The feel of her soft little hand, crisp with the ring or two she wore, was too much for me; I was but a young man, I loved her so truly that never was a girl more loved by her sweetheart; and so whilst Captain Jackson talked at the top of his voice with the chief mate, who had come below to dinner, and Mrs. O'Brien was blathering about the pedigree of the O'Briens and the O'Shandrydans to Mrs. Joyce, and Daniel and Mr. Thompson Tucker and Mrs. Jackson and the doctor rattled away in brisk conversation, I poured into Florence's ears the hundred feelings and hopes which the touch of her hand had cast adrift from my heart; I told her of the misery caused me by her removal to Scotland, the fears which haunted me that her father would carry her away somewhere out of my reach, the despair that had possessed me when I heard that she was going to Australia, and that had determined me as my only chance to sail in the same ship with her and to risk her anger for daring to love her too well to suffer the ocean to separate her from me. If she thought me presumptuous for talking in this fashion she did not say so nor look so; indeed, my lads, the idea she gave me by her manner of listening was that she would rather have had me talkative than shy. Now and again she would take a side-long peep at me, and when I told her how utterly I had been crushed by her letter to Sophie in which she said that she was going to Australia, until the idea of joining her in the voyage pieced my heart together again, she said, " I knew that would grieve you terribly," letting the words slip out and then averting her face with a little blush as their significance struck her. But, you see, this was not the first time we had met—not the first time she had discovered I loved her; there was the memory of many words, of many thoughts between us, and her locket was on my heart, and she was being sent away partly because of my love for her, and I was proving my love by being with her and following her unto the very ends of the world; could our eyes meet without a world of meaning springing from the encounter of our glances? If her love for me was not yet full-grown, it was born—it had an existence, it was coming forward. And though a few hours before, when I lay hiding away from her, I could not have dared to believe that she had any other feeling for me than a simple kindness, I had not sat half an hour by her side at that dinner-table without feeling as sure as that her eyes were beautiful, her smile the most winning in life, her voice a melody sweetly played in tune, that many more days would not pass without her finding the young sailor by her side sovereign of her heart, as she was already the delight and glory of his life.

These thoughts ran through my talk with her like the central line of hemp over which the strands of a rope are laid, and made me so joyous that I would sometimes fancy she peeped at me for the pride which the happiness in my face gave her as the cause of it. When we quitted poor Morecombe as a topic we were not in a hurry to return to him. Indeed it was plain to me that her former indifference to the man had developed into real disgust through his chasing her on to the water where she could not escape his attentions; and any reference to him humiliated her, as you might suppose of a high-spirited girl who would be ashamed that I or anybody else should know that her father and aunt had lent themselves to a cheap poor conspiracy to entangle her with a creature mean enough to play the unmanly part allotted to him.

Thompson and the chief mate left the table to go on deck, and presently the pilot made his appearance in a shaggy coat glittering with moisture and a red nose at the end of which

sparkled a large drop of salt water hanging there
like a jewel.   Captain Jackson tackled him on the
subject of the weather. Mr. Thompson Tucker and
Mr. Joyce withdrew to their cabins, but Mrs.
O'Brien and Mrs. Jackson kept their seats and so
did Florence, who seemed perfectly happy at my
side and in no hurry to see if she could be of any
use to her aunt. I congratulated her upon her
fine sailorly qualities, which were not a little
remarkable, let me tell you, in her as well as in the
other ladies who had mustered at the dinner table ;
for the *Strathmore* was pitching and lurching in the
abominable fashion that is only possible to a big
ship in Channel seas where the confined surges
run fast with a short savage play as unlike to
the rhythmical long-drawn heave of ocean billows
with the wide gleaming valley between, into which
a vessel swings with a cradle-like floating plunge, as
the motions of an unballasted kite are to the stately
sweeping of a balloon upon the waves of the wind.

"Have you decided yet upon returning to your
real name?" she asked.

"I will do whatever you wish," I answered;
"but will it be wise to let your aunt know who
I am?"

"What could she do if she should know?"
she asked, with a gleam of mutiny in her eyes.

"She may make a fuss," said I, "and surely
there has been too much fuss already."

"If I may not call you Seymour I cannot call you Mr. Egerton," she exclaimed.

"You can speak of me to her as Mr. Egerton," I replied, "and think of me as Jack, can't you, darling?"

"Oh, don't call me darling," she said, "it is not right. I don't mind Florence *now and then,* but darling is—is almost wicked."

"If it is not wicked to think of you as darling, it cannot be wicked to call you so," said I.

"Do you prefer," said she, not looking so very shocked after all, "to keep the name you have taken?"

"Yes, I do; it would set the passengers talking if they found I had shipped under an assumed name. And what need is there that your aunt should know who I am till after a bit?"

Well, presently she consented, manifestly against her will; but she would see the force of my objection respecting the passengers, and then again she was too angry with her aunt for the snare she had laid for her to mind what she would think if my identity came to be revealed, whilst on the other hand any uncomfortable opinions the other passengers could form of me were sure to embarrass her, foreseeing as she must have done that my love for her would soon be noticed by them. This little matter being settled to my satisfaction, we got talking about my relations at Bristol, and then she told me how unhappy she had been made by her papa's wish that she should marry Mr. Morecombe, and hinted at some painful quarrels that had occurred at Dunkeld, which she said had made her glad to accept her aunt's offer to return with her to Sydney.

"Both Aunt Damaris and papa said my health would be improved by a sea voyage, and that was the ostensible motive for the journey," said she; "and I pretended to believe that that was the only reason, though," added she, with a lovely tinge of red in her cheeks and looking down as she spoke, "I never doubted that you were the cause. But to think," she exclaimed, warming up and fixing her eyes on me, "that the voyage was planned wholly and simply to bring Mr. Morecombe and me together! Oh, I cannot bear to think of it, indeed I cannot! How *could* papa be induced to take such a step?"

"Don't let that thought trouble you, my darling," I exclaimed, overjoyed by her candour, and groping for her hand which she let me retain: "if you only loved me one little bit as much as I adore you, Florence, you would not find anything to be angry with in a scheme that has ended in making me the very happiest man in the whole wide world."

Well, I dare say you're wondering how the dickens we could be talking in this fashion with-

out the people who were sitting . at the midship
table hearing us.   But there was not an ear in
that cuddy that could have caught a syllable of
our speech unless it had been brought as close to
us as we were together, so full of noise was the
hollow interior with the roaring of the wind, the
straining of bulkheads and creaking of timbers, .
the half-stifled thunder of seas striking the ship
and falling forwards in storms of spray which
sounded like a discharge of musketry heard at a
distance, and with the gabble which the pilot and
Jackson kept up.

Presently Mrs. O'Brien and Mrs. Jackson withdrew, and Florence went to her cabin.   I asked
the pilot if we were lying our course.

"Why, yes," says he.   "Lyin' our course? to
be sure we are! how else should we be lyin'?"
and he looked at me under his thatched brows
with a pair of eyes which might have passed for
glowworms in a thrush's nest, as if he would say,
"Don't try to come it over me·with any nautical
terms.   I'm not to be gammoned."

"Well, Mr. Pilot," said I, "you see if we were
heading south, you know, we shouldn't be lying
our course, should we? for I recollect learning at
school that the Atlantic bears west by magnetic
compass from the English Channel, and we must
get into the Bay of Biscay before we can double
the Cape of Good Hope."

"What's all that got to do with it?" asked the pilot, who was one of those surly sea-dogs I delighted in worrying. "You asked if we was lyin' our course, and I said yes. How else should we be lyin', with the wind three points free and nothin' to stop us as I knows on?"

"You're wrong, sir," exclaimed Captain Jackson, "in talking about doubling the Cape of Good Hope. You don't double it in going to Australia. Doubling means coming down one side of a headland, rounding it, and sailing up the other side."

"Thank you, sir, for your information: it is very interesting," said I. "Nautical terms are exceedingly difficult to understand. Mr. Pilot, will you tell me what a scuttle-butt is?"

"A thing they drowns rats in, ain't it, sir?" answered the pilot, hoarsely, looking with a grin at Captain Jackson.

"And what part of a ship is the main jibboom in?" I inquired.

"Well," says the pilot, "in my young day it used to be bolted to the first strake under the wales, but custom's waried since then, and I'll allow if ye seek it ye'll find it mostly atop of the long-boat."

"There is no main jibboom, sir," exclaimed Captain Jackson, taking pity on my ignorance. "But I'll tell you what there *is;* there are ships which are allowed to leave port a sight too deep in the water, sir, and we're on board one of them at this moment. D'ye feel her straining, pilot? It's enough to tear out her bottom."

"Well," said the pilot, "I didn't stow the vessel, and whether she's deep or light's nothin' to do with me. My business is to give her a clear 'rizon, and that I'm doing, though this young gentleman here doesn't seem to believe as that we're lying our course."

"Oh yes, I do," I replied, "now that you tell me we are. How dreadfully high the wind is! Do you think if I go on deck there is any danger of my being blown into the water?"

"Ay, werry great danger," he replied; "if I was you I'd go to bed."

"I'm not sleepy yet, but when I do go to bed, Mr. Pilot," said I, "I hope if you should steer us on to the rocks or anything like that, you will instantly call me, so that I may have a chance of saving my life."

He mumbled a blessing on my eyes as I left the table and entered my cabin to procure a pipe of tobacco. A small bracket lamp swinging against a stanchion shed a faint uncomfortable light upon the little interior, in which I spied Mr. Griffith holding Morecombe's wrist in his hand. The unhappy sufferer had been undressed and got properly to bed. There was a smell of physic about, a sort of chloroform flavour mixed with brandy which made the atmosphere anything but pleasant. The clothes suspended on pegs against the bulkhead swung wildly, the heeling of the ship brought the sea alongside close, and rendered the wash and thunder of it a very distinct near sound; and the cabin deck was a surface that seemed to slant in half a dozen different directions all at once. I asked Mr. Griffith how his patient did, and he replied, "Bad enough. His prostration is very great. Feel his hand." I took it, and found it as cold as a piece of iron and slimy with moisture like the dew on a dying body. I could not see his face, for it was in deep shadow, and partly turned towards the ship's side; if he was awake he did not speak; no sound came from him, and I was glad that the constant moaning he had kept up when I sat with him had ceased. I was so concerned for him that it was a positive comfort to feel that we were making good headway and would, if the wind held, be off the Isle of Wight in the morning. However, I could be of no use, so I took my pipe and stepped out on to the quarter-deck for a smoke, sheltering myself by standing under the break of the poop to windward against the chief mate's cabin.

There was plenty of wind on that black night, and the whistling of it in the rigging was as shrill as though congregations of wild fowl were being swept along and screaming as they drove; but it seemed to me there was less weight in the pouring blast than there had been an hour or two before, though another little creep of it to the eastward had put a true wintry touch into the rawness of its cold. Small wonder that the decks were deserted. The gleam of water came out of the darkness in the lee scuppers and every roll to windward brought the inky fluid up the weather deck like the run of a tide on a shore, creeping up and down with a regular pendulum swing. It was a wild feeling you got when you looked at the mainmast standing plain for a height of fifteen feet or so in the cuddy light, with lines of gear coming down, and belayed to the circle of pins that girdled it, and then found the vast spar vanishing at that elevation in the howling blackness as though it had been sawn off. The dim space of topsail glimmering on high scarcely seemed to belong to the ship. The water washed past with a whiteness in the foam of it like the unsparkling surface of frosted silver, and when the ship rolled over to leeward on the send of a sea, with a kind of lull up aloft where the wind found less to split upon in the slanting fabric, the froth looked to roll up to the horizon and the sea standing above the topgallant bulwark was like the slope of a hill buried in snow. Once when the ship came over to starboard on the side of a surge that left her spars erect, I caught sight of a kind of phantom thing, a vague pallid shadow a short distance off, and coming and going in the darkness just before the main rigging. I got on to the lee poop ladder to look, and made the object out to be a three-masted schooner that we had overhauled and were slowly dropping astern. Upon my word she was the one thing, I somehow felt, that was wanted to complete the mystery of the dark scene; for she gave you something for your eyes to rest on, though all the while she was as vague and illusive as a spectre, with her port light like a bloodshot eye fitfully showing over the surface of white under her bow, then vanishing as a black coil of water rose up between her and us, whilst the reefed canvas faded if you watched it steadily as though it had dissolved into the whirling ebony that was shrieking over her, and you had to look a little away from her to catch a fresh sight of the faint wan surfaces.

Well, having smoked my pipe, I went into the cuddy, where I found the chief mate, a man named Thornton, a square-faced burnt-up fellow, with a glittering blue eye that tumbled about like a monkey's. I suppose he had found out by the look of us at dinner that the skipper and I were old chums, and he asked me to accept his apology for his manner last night, "for," says he, "I had not seen you before, Mr. Egerton, and I couldn't quite make out your object in standing at the skylight and looking down into the cuddy for ten minutes at a time with scarce a move," and then there rolled over his face a grin which gave me to know that he for one had smelt out something of my business in that ship. However, for my part he was welcome to find out all he could; I minded nobody but Aunt Damaris, and to tell you the truth I was beginning to think that even if *she* were to discover that I was Jack Seymour, nothing very serious could result in the face of the lovely malicious gleam that had shot into my sweet one's eyes when she had said at the dinner table, "what can she do if she *should* know?"

CHAPTER IX.

I BREAKFAST WITH FLORENCE.

IT was a queer ordering of fate, as any man will allow, that I should have had to nurse Morecombe in the English Channel, when in Bristol nothing could have pleased me more than the privilege of twisting his neck. It was strange enough that he and I should have come together in one cabin; but think of my ministering to this sea-sick rival, hoisting up his head when a tremendous fit of nausea convulsed him, putting brandy to his lips, chafing his hands, and doing my dead best to hearten up the unfortunate creature by begging him to remember that in a few hours he would be out of the ship, ashore and himself again! I did not undress myself that night. The temperature was desperately cold, and I foresaw that it would be no joke to tumble out of my bunk unclothed in response to the gurglings and chokings and strugglings which from time to time went on in the bed under me. You would suppose that

what Morecombe had gone through would have
been enough to kill a horse : but some men take
a deal of destroying.　Bad he was as bad can be ;
the doctor had said it ; but never will I believe
that he could not have got over his sickness had he
stuck to the ship and given himself time.　In spite
of his terrible prostration—and terrible it was—he
could find a voice, now and again, faint indeed, but
still a voice, to curse the sea in those fashionable
oaths in the nice conduct of which he was a perfect
master—and I'll do him the justice to say he never
showed himself the least obliged to me for the
trouble I took to attend him, but on the contrary
accepted my services as if I was a steward, and in
that ship simply to give him brandy when he asked
for it and to put my arm under his head when he
yawed at the coverlet.　It was wonderful to me
that the chap didn't get drunk : for he had nothing
in his stomach but brandy, of which he drank very
plentifully, I can tell you : quite enough to have
shifted *my* ballast.　But perhaps he was used to
strong drinks, or, what was more likely, his condition enabled him to stand up under a press of
sail that would have capsized him under ordinary
circumstances.

It was not my policy, however, to encourage
him to continue the voyage, as you may suppose.
Indeed I lost no opportunity to heighten his fears
by telling him that the doctor had said he could

not possibly live to reach the mouth of the Channel unless a change for the better in his nausea was immediately visible, and that the only chance he had to preserve his life was to go ashore with the pilot. I also assured him that this Channel was little more than a pond compared to what we must stand by to expect in the Bay of Biscay; "where," said I, "the waves roll mountains high, and even old sailors are prostrated by the dreadful motion."

"Yas," he murmured, in the faintest, most sea-sick tones you could imagine, "I have heard of the Bay of Biscay. It is not likely I shall twy it. Curse and confound, etc., etc., this beastly wolling. I thought it would have knocked you up. You were ill this morning."

"It's the smooth water that affects me, strangely enough," said I. "The moment the ship begins to heave, I recover."

"Doocid odd," he gurgled. "Nevar heard of anything more extwaordinawy. When will this beastly ship stop? What time to-mowow will the pilot leave? Why the dooce must I go on suffering all through to-night? Can't the captain find a harbour somewhere to dwop anchor in?" And then he cried out for more bwandy, and asked me to wipe his face, whilst the bedclothes heaved upon his chest in horrid sympathy with the rolling and pitching of the vessel.

But it was very seldom that he spoke at length
as above. Sometimes he would lie for an hour
perfectly mute and motionless, as I would know
by peeping at him over the edge of my bunk, and
then an attack would seize him and he would
groan and moan and sing out for me with a sort
of selfish terrified shriek in his voice which never
failed to plump me alongside of him in a breath.
I got very little sleep that night, though he gave
me some peace in the small hours. I turned out
at seven in the morning, having slept since four,
and had a look at my friend who lay with his eyes
closed. There was sunshine on the water and the
scuttle was brilliant with the flash and tremor of
it, and light fell in a stream from the bull's-eye in
the deck, so I could see him very distinctly. I
was perfectly staggered by his appearance. His
face was hollow and dark, and the lids of his
closed eyes had a greenish waxy look as they
seemed to float rather than to lie in the livid cups
under his brows. I put my head into his bunk to
listen, for when I saw him I could no more have
told you whether he was dead or alive without hearing him breathe or seeing him move, than I could
have cured his nausea. Well, he was breathing all
right, and a good deal relieved by this, and thankful
to heaven for the sunshine that was promise of a
fine morning outside, I freshened myself up with a
wash, making no noise, and went on deck.

The foul night had blown itself out; a bright blue sky was overhead with a dash of woolly cloud here and there sailing down it, and the sea was a light luminous green that darkened away up at the horizon and stood like a streak of olive-coloured paint against the silver azure beyond. The ship was under all plain sail, braced sharp up on the starboard tack, but making good way under the brisk morning breeze that seemed to come with a flavour of land in it. There was just enough sea to keep the noble ship curtseying as she drove along full of the sparkling of brasswork and glass and the wet glitter of the decks newly washed down, and her sails of a star-like whiteness in the glorious morning sunshine. Smoke was blowing away from the galley chimney, cocks were crowing in the hencoops, there was a coming and going of 'tween-deck passengers, and a sound of the crying of children rising up from below through the booby hatch. I got on to the poop, drinking in the pouring of the fresh north wind as a man will who comes on deck on a fine morning after eight or nine hours of a small cabin, and heartily thankful, for the sake of Morecombe, that the weather was bright.

I said good morning to the pilot, who was standing with one hand on the weather main backstay, and he responded with a surly nod, singing out to me as I passed on to join Thompson, " Better not look at the compass, sir, or ye'll be swearing we're not lying our course." But in spite of his request the first thing I did after shaking hands with Thompson was to take a peep into the binnacle, and found that we were heading a course that was to bring us in sight of the Isle of Wight and make visible there the signal we should be hoisting for a boat. Daniel at once inquired after Morecombe, and I gave him a short account of the night I had passed with that gentleman.

"Upon my word," said he, drawing me out of the hearing of the helmsman and obliging me to walk the deck with him, "this adventure of yours should make a yarn to please the girls. What goodness! what humanity! Instead of smothering your rival, there you have been sitting up all night with him, your arm round his neck, swabbing his face, and pouring brandy into him. Will he go ashore with the pilot, do you think?"

"I hope so," I answered. "He looks deadly ill; I've done my best to scare him, but he may change his mind if he sees the sunshine."

"You mustn't let him do that," said he, with his face like the rising moon in a November fog; "you don't want him to stop, of course?"

"Not I; I'd be glad to heave him overboard, if I thought he could swim ashore."

"Then," said he, "take care to tell Griffith that the fellow was several times in the act of dying last night, and that you only recovered him by a miracle. The doctor will believe you. *He* won't want to have a sick man after Mr. Morecombe's pattern on his hands, and it shouldn't need much of a hint to make him *order* the youth ashore with the pilot, on the ground that his case is beyond him whilst he keeps afloat."

"I don't think any strategy will be needed," I replied; "Mr. Morecombe is not likely to proceed. Why, in less than twenty-four hours he has been reduced to the sickliest object that you ever saw in your life."

"Serve him right," said Thompson. "What business has a man to thrust himself upon a girl who doesn't want him? I noticed your young lady yesterday morning at breakfast, when Mr. Morecombe got alongside of her and fell a-squinting at her through his eye-glass. Jack, she wouldn't look at him! What manner of creature can this young swell be to put himself in the way of being snubbed and spurned in a fashion to make a chap with any kind of sensitiveness pitch himself over the side."

"He's been punished enough," said I, "and nothing remains but to get him out of the ship. At what hour do you hope to land the pilot?"

"Some time this forenoon, I reckon. The old girl walks through it, eh, Jack? Watch the water passing—it's like looking out of a railway carriage window;" and he pointed over the rail where the little surges were pouring towards us in emerald green lines which melted into snow as they ran, the yeasty seething flashing up dazzling white in the sunshine, with here and there a scattering of smoke-like spray upon which the fragment of a rainbow would stand an instant. There was no land in sight, and the course we were steering showed that we were a trifle to the southward of the fair-way track owing to the wind having drawn ahead for a couple of hours during the night, and sent us ratching that way. Against the thin pearlish blue over the horizon, you could catch in places a glimpse of a vessel's canvas with a vague kind of shine in it, like what a first quarter moon has when the sun is up; and in the west and south, a shadow of smoke lingered in a serpentine posture upon the wind, indicating the existence of steamers whose funnels had drawn down behind the sea. As I stood leaning over the rail, watching the greenish copper of the ship shooting through the coiling white and emerald with a sound like the hissing of red-hot iron, and noticing how the radiance of the water was reflected in the glossy bends which the crests of the surges combed down into the brilliance of a mirror, my friend Daniel talked to me of Florence, with a fine sentimental twang in his voice, congratulating me on her beauty—as if I had had a hand in *that*—on her evident affection for me, on the pleasing nature of the romantic adventure I had embarked on. He told me that though he was not what is vulgarly called a lady's man, he had a tolerably comprehensive knowledge of the sex, and flattered himself that on the whole he understood them pretty well; and therefore, when he assured me that Miss Florence Hawke liked me, I was to allow no more misgivings to trouble me on that head, for he was not a person given to talking without knowing what he meant.

"I'm not cocksure of the law," said he, "and we've unfortunately got no parson on board; but if you should bring matters to a point when we're on the ocean, I should be perfectly willing to read the service over you, if you don't mind taking your chance of the matter being illegal in my hands. I've got an idea that the skipper *can* join folks together in holy wedlock, and that a splice of that kind is not to be drawn asunder; but I won't swear to it, for it is a question I've never taken the trouble to look into. Any way, you and the lady can talk the thing over, and if you and she are agreeable and don't mind a trifle of risk in such a matter, why, then, all you'll have to do, Jack, will be to put a mark in the prayer-book where the service lies, so that I may find it without groping, and I'm at your command."

I thanked him heartily for this fresh instance of

his kindness, and told him I would not fail to call upon him in that way should Miss Hawke express her wish to be married at sea.   Soon after this we went to breakfast, and I was a bit nervous as I stood in the cuddy door watching the passengers assemble at the table, for I thought the bright sunshine and the mild curtseying of the ship would have put Aunt Damaris on her pins again. But there was no sign of her ; Florence came forth alone, and immediately I walked up the cuddy, saluted her, and took my place alongside her. How beautiful she looked ! how clear, and pure, and luminous her eyes, as if the spirit of the deep had passed into them !   The morning radiance streaming down the skylight sprinkled a light like gold-dust over her hair, and I saw Daniel squinting at it out of the corners of his eyes, as if he couldn't understand how that kind of sheen came to lie on her head.   Well, mates, I could not meet her glance now, without feeling and understanding that we were sweethearts at last.   Hitherto it had been on my side mostly, but I had fondled her hand last evening, I had told her more than ever I said before, and when I sat down in the seat next hers, and spoke to her, and she turned her eyes to mine, I knew as though she had spoken it that the night had worked a mighty change in her for me, that her heart, which had been no more than a bud when the evening gathered, had become a

flower for the morning sun to shine on. How is it
a fellow can tell that a girl loves him when she
does not speak, when, not to save his soul, could
he recall a syllable from her to justify his knowledge? This would make a good question for a
debating club; and if any community of young
Pitts and Foxes will go to work and deliver their
views on the subject, they may count on Jack
Seymour reading every word of what they say.
For my part, I am no fist at handling problems of
that kind. You know sailors can smell ice when
they can't see it, amid a blinding snowfall that is
colder than ice. That's wonderful, thinks the
landsman; but it's true. And sailors, by squinting to leeward, will sometimes see a gale of wind
in a sky as blue as an Irish girl's eyes, and barely
have time to reef down before it is upon them.
That is wonderful too, thinks the landsman. But
Lord preserve us, what are such wonders to your
discovery of a girl's love of *you* by the feel of your
instincts? I was in the thick of the miracle the
moment Florence and I came together that morning, and the beating of her heart upon mine was
as plain to my adoration of her as if the darling
were in my arms and her lips at my ears, telling
me all about it.

However, even if we had been alone, her love
was too much of a bairn to quit the warmth of her
eyes, and there only was it to be sought at present.

But we were by no means alone; for though Aunt Damaris was missing and Morecombe was on his back, other passengers, who had been sick yesterday, came out and took their places this morning—Mr. and Mrs. Marmaduke Mortimer, the newly-married couple, who sat so close together that the meal was a perfect jostle between them: and Mr. Thompson Tucker, a thin, rather blear-eyed young man, who was going to seek his fortune in Australia; and Mrs. Grant and her daughter; and the Joyce family, six in all, counting the nurse; not to mention Mrs. O'Brien, and Captain Jackson, R.N., the doctor, and Jack Seymour and his sweetheart, and jolly-faced Daniel and the chief mate. The only other lady (excepting Aunt Damaris) wanting was Mrs. Jackson, about whom her gallant husband shouted out to Daniel as follows: "Thank you, captain, she is not ill, but she is uncomfortable. A better sailor never wore petticoats, as you might have noticed yesterday. But, sir, there is a sluggishness, a heaviness, a topsy-turvy nauseatingness in the movements of an overloaded ship, which are enough to capsize the stomach of a female figure-head, sir, and Mrs. Jackson has temporarily succumbed, not to the motion of the billows, but to the rapacity of owners;" and he glared around him with a quarter-deck scowl, as much as to say "I'm in a quarrelsome mood—better not contradict me, anybody."

Of course, my first question to Florence was after her aunt. She was better, my darling answered; "she is breakfasting in her cabin, but she talked of coming on deck to-day if the weather remains fine."

"I hope she won't make her appearance," said I, "until Morecombe is gone. She may dissuade him."

"How is he?" she asked, smiling as if it would need very little to cause her to break into a hearty laugh. I told her that he was no better, if he was not worse, described his haggard appearance, the wonderful change that had come over him since we had left the river, and said there could be no question that he would go ashore with the pilot. As I spoke, Mrs. O'Brien called out to the doctor to know how the poor "say-sick gintleman was, him that manes to go ashore, Mr. Griffit." The doctor answered, "I have just seen him. He is very low, ma'am. Captain, he says he could not bear the sight of food, and the mere smell of the breakfast violently affects him. It's a bad sign."

"Why, sir?" demanded Captain Jackson.

"Because, sir," responded the doctor, "it means that the nausea is still strong in him, for the only symptom of recovery that I know of in sea-sickness is the return of the appetite. Nothing but brandy has passed the gentleman's lips since this hour yesterday, and how is he to support life, sir, without food, and to contend with the exhaustion that follows his sufferings?"

"I merely asked for information, sir," said Captain Jackson. "I am satisfied. His sufferings would be less if we had more freeboard. Another inch more of depth would have killed him, as another foot more of side would have made a sailor of him, at once. Stew-ard, more tea hee-ar!"

"He must be sent ashore, doctor," said Thompson, taking no notice of the navy man's talk. "I presume that is his wish?"

"I can answer for that," said I, addressing the passengers generally, "as his berth-mate."

"There is no alternative," exclaimed the doctor. "He is utterly unfit for the sea; and it would be sheer madness on his part to pursue the voyage, as it would be sheer cruelty on my part to recommend him to do so."

Nothing could be more decisive, and Daniel, giving Florence a half-look that followed on to me, sung out to the steward to turn to after breakfast to get Mr. Morecombe's traps packed ready for getting over the side.

"What do you think of this, Florence darling?" I whispered. "Is it not immense?"

She returned no answer, not trusting herself to speak at the moment, as I might reckon by the merriment of her eyes, which betokened laughter (that would sound unseemly) dangerously near. Meanwhile, all the passengers were calling questions to the doctor about the danger of sea-sickness, Morecombe's symptoms, why one should suffer more than another, and the like, and the cuddy was busy with chatter.

"What will your aunt say when she finds him gone?" I continued, watching the laughter fade out of her face like a light slowly withdrawn from alabaster.

"I don't know, Mr. Seymour, and I don't care," she replied.

"Do call me Jack, Florence—give me the name you think of me by. If you don't, you'll be calling me Mr. Seymour as you have just done, and what will become of me?"

She nibbled at a piece of white roll, looking coyly down.

"Say Jack, darling!"

"Well, to please you I will call you Jack," she answered, saying nothing about the "darlings" I was bestowing on her.

"It's a very easy name to pronounce," said I. "Sophie and Amelia gave it me at once, on the very first evening we had ever seen one another— as *you* can remember, for you were present."

"Why do you go on entreating?" she exclaimed, laughing. "Haven't I said I will call you Jack?"

I fancy Daniel overheard this, for I spied him

grin, though he was listening to Mr. Thompson Tucker questioning Mr. Joyce as to the chances the Colonies offered a young man who couldn't dig and who declined to beg. In truth, Daniel sat a good deal too near us; but there was no help for it, and on the whole the arrangement was to my taste, providing Aunt Damaris kept t'other side the skipper when she should come to the table.

"How surprised," said I, "your father will be to hear that Mr. Morecombe has abandoned the voyage."

"Is your uncle likely to talk of your having sailed in this ship?" she asked.

"You know him," I answered, laughing; "he cannot hold his tongue, I am afraid."

"Then the news is sure to reach papa's ears!" she exclaimed, pursing up her sweet little mouth with a scared look in her eyes.

"But he will know," said I, "that you were ignorant of my intention to join you."

"He is not likely to believe it," she replied. "Oh, what a bad character you will have earned for me! But is it not proper retribution—Jack?" said she, bringing out my name with a little hesitation, for the first time, and pronouncing it with a kind of softness that thrilled me, quite apart from the delight of hearing the sound of it on her lips. "I never should have desired you to take this voyage with me against papa's wishes;

but neither should I have been here had I guessed that Mr. Morecombe was to accompany us; and since no liberty of choosing a companion was allowed me, could papa be angry at finding me glad that things have happened as I could have wished?"

There was a droop in her voice, for she was confessing. And oh, the magic of her meaning, that gave a new glory to the sunshine, a lovely rhythm to the steady heave of the ship, that put a perfect melody into the hoarse chorus of seamen handling the braces on deck, that made a heaven of that vessel's cuddy, and angels of Captain Jackson, and Mrs. O'Brien, and Daniel, and all the rest of them. But we were at breakfast: her hands were busy with plate and cup and knife and fork, and I could not grasp them; there were people near us, and I could not seize the moment to ask her to tell me she loved me. Indeed, as it was, I discovered that we were being noticed, especially by the newly-married pair; and so I had to haul off and put on an abstracted face, and talk to Daniel about last night's change of wind, as if I would not have given all I owned in the world for ten minutes' use of a quiet corner where there was just room for two of us.

Well, when breakfast was over, I went into my cabin and found one of the under-stewards at work lashing or "cording up" Mr. Morecombe's box, and collecting his odds and ends of sticks, guns, etc. I had no mind to linger, for I had had quite enough of the sick man, and so was loading a pipe, meaning to clear out in a moment, when Thompson and the doctor came in.

"Sorry to find you still so bad, Mr. Morecombe," said Daniel, evidently struck by the fellow's hollow looks: "however, you'll recover like magic the moment you're ashore, where I shall hope to set you in another two hours or so."

"It's a cursed hardship that I couldn't be landed sooner," replied Morecombe from his pillow, speaking in such weakly notes that it was a job to hear him. "There ought to be some pwovision made to land people who suffer as I do, instead of dwagging them on and on till they're nearly dead. I'll kick up a wow about this when I get home, curse me if I don't. What wight have people to dwag fellahs about when they're dying?"

Thompson mildly explained that it would have been · impossible to put him ashore during the night owing to the weather.

"How much longer, then, am I to be kept here?" moaned the sufferer. "Do you mean to dwag me about until I'm dead?"

"Is it your wish to be put ashore?" inquired Thompson.

"Why the dooce d'ye ask me?" answered Morecombe, staring wildly at the skipper. "You know it's my wish. You ought to have landed me yesterday, when the doctor told you how I was sufferwing; see if there won't be a jolly wow over this when I get back. I'll expose the Company as a swindle, confound me if I don't. What wight have you to take my money and put me into a wotten old cwadle that's never stopped wolling since we left Gwavesend, and go on lugging me about in it when I'm dying? I'll wite to every paper in the country, curse me if I don't. When do you mean to land me, eh?"

"I'll leave you to talk to this gentleman. doctor," says Thompson, without the least temper in his manner. "You had better get him dressed ready to go ashore when a boat arrives;" and. so saying, he stepped out of the cabin, followed by me. "I thought you said your friend was dying. Jack?" said he, as we mounted the companion steps. "Why, there's life enough in his temper alone to furnish out a ship's company. What an ass the man is, to be sure! I've met a few swells in my day, but never the like of that chap."

"Well," said I, "I can assure you I had no idea the fellow had so much jaw left in him. Had you been with me last night you would again and again have thought him at his last gasp, as I did. Did you notice his face?"

"I did," he answered. "Oh, he's been bad, and *is* bad: and I shall be glad to get him ashore."

He walked up to the pilot, who in a few moments went below to breakfast, and I stood near the wheel to have a look around me. The wind had freshened into a magnificent sailing breeze, and had gone away into the north-east. With every sail pulling and all sail on her, every yard-arm looking aft as the spars ascended, the jibs swelling out upon the slightly bowed jibbooms, the *Strathmore* was walking through it like the clipper that she was, a belt of foam racing past to leeward, and a sharp playing and flashing of glass-like water to windward where the surge that rolled away from her weather bow met the oncoming run of the waves, and broke them, and was itself shattered into a tumble of glittering green, full of bubbles and feather-shaped patches of foam. Away on the starboard-bow was the dim bluish shadow of land, whilst astern the seething wake of the ship ran away in a line of snow in which the sunshine kindled a thousand glories of green and yellow and blue and diamond-white, as though some hand under the counter were emptying bagsfull of gems upon the water. Presently one of the apprentices came aft, took the ensign out of the flag-locker, and stopped the fly of it with a rope yarn. This converted it into what is called a "whiff" or "wave" or "waft" or "wift," or in plain English a signal for a boat, and bending it on to the peak signal halliards, the youth ran the flag aloft where it shook its straight-jacketed length against the blue sky.

CHAPTER X.

IT was half-past eleven before any notice was taken of the signal, and then you might have seen a white sail shining upon the sea to the right of the land that had broadened ahead, and was now on either bow, and taking the unmistakable configuration of the Isle of Wight coast between Dunnose and St. Catherine's Point. All this while Florence had remained below, but suddenly on removing my eyes from the pilot vessel that was coming down to us, with a sharp heel of her mainsail, like the weather pinion of a gull rounding into the eye of a strong gale of wind, I glanced behind me and saw Florence and her aunt. They both stood near the mizzenmast, and Miss Damaris was holding on to one of the belaying pins that circled the spar. I was very completely taken aback by the sight of her, but had mind enough left in me to note her attire, which consisted of a small brown straw bonnet, over which was drawn the hood of a long thick cloak, so that, with her sharp hard bony face peering out of the cavernous head-gear, she might very well have passed for a lean Roman Catholic priest, rendered cadaverous by a large number of midnight vigils and mortifications. She did not look the sweeter for the spell of sea-sickness she had suffered from, and her keen greenish eyes travelled swiftly about, as she ran them over the sea, and the ship and the passengers. When Florence met my glance, a slight smile curled about her mouth, and she looked up at the stopped ensign with a sort of inquisitiveness, as if she partly suspected what it meant, but would like to make sure. I hardly knew what to do for a moment, whether to address her or "make tracks." I was in a manner fascinated by the old woman, and my stare attracted her notice presently, for she gave it me back with a bit of a scowl that, so to say, forced me to act; so stepping up to her with a pluck at the brim of my hat, I said in my politest way that I was sorry to have learnt from her niece that she had been ill; would she allow me to get her a chair?

"No, thank you," she answered, with a touch of old Hawke's pomp in her manner, coupled with a large dash of acidity, and a brisk look of surprise at Florence, as if she wondered how her niece and I could have become intimate enough to talk about her in so short a time.

" Will you tell me the meaning of that flag ? " said Florence, with a world of amusement in her face, and looking lovely beyond expression in her hat, that was looped up on one side with a feather that rattled along the scuppers of it, and a warm tight-fitting jacket, with fur upon the sleeves and neck and bottom.

" It is a signal for a boat," said I, " to take the pilot ashore. Yonder she comes—that white sail there."

Just then Thompson passed us, and seeing his friend Damaris on deck he lurched up to her with a deep-sea bow. " Glad to see you up, Miss Hawke," says he ; " but then you know you're an old sailor, and I couldn't dream of allowing you more than one day to suffer from sea-sickness."

" I should want a month," she answered in her sharp manner, with a kind of peck forward of her scythe-like nose, much as a pigeon moves its head when it walks, " if I were not an old sailor, for of all rolling ships the *Strathmore* is the worst. Don't contradict me ; I'm sure of what I say. What have you been doing with the vessel all this time, captain ? I hope there'll be no more pitching this voyage. It was shocking last night—I wonder I have a whole bone left. Never again will I take a stern cabin. Where are we, sir ? What land is that ? "

" The Isle of Wight, ma'am," answered Daniel.

"Well, I'm sure you've taken time enough to reach it," she exclaimed.

"We shall be heaving-to in a moment for that boat," said Daniel; "and then, Miss Hawke, when the pilot has dropped over the side," giving me a look that made me tremble, for I wanted no freemasonry of that kind under the shadow of Damaris' hatchet countenance, "we will brace the yards around again and fairly start for beautiful Australia. And a fine run we shall make, no doubt. What do you think, Mr. Edgemore? By the way, Miss Hawke, will you allow me to introduce an old schoolfellow of mine to you—Mr. —— "

"Egerton," I exclaimed, covering up the interpolation by a profuse bow, whilst Daniel left us to give some directions to the chief mate. Aunt Damaris inclined her angular body, and Florence pretended to be engrossed by the spectacle of the approaching pilot cutter. I could not help thinking that the sound of Egerton put a pleasanter look into the old lady's face. She ran her eyes over me in a sharp quick inspection of my clothes, paying close attention to my boots, and dwelling upon the silk handkerchief round my neck; and then said she, "Are you going to settle in Australia, Mr. Egerton?"

"N—no, I think not," I answered. "I'm just going to have a look round."

"I hope you're not going out with the idea of

making your fortune," said she. "You'll be disappointed˙ if that's your dream. Money is just as hard to get in Australia as in England. I mean gentlemen find it so. Mechanics and labourers manage, but there's no room for gentlemen." And she cast her eyes upon the Isle of Wight, as though she would suggest that I had better get ashore whilst the chance remained, if I was going to Australia with the notion that I could make my fortune there as a gentleman.

"I am not going to Australia for the sake of money," I replied blandly. "I am fond of travelling by water, and I am particularly anxious to see the lovely Bay of Sydney."

Florence looked round as though wishful to check any approach to equivocation. But what was I to say? and wasn't my whole existence on shipboard what is called in Dublin a "loy" and in Newcastle a "lee"?

"Have you been sea-sick, Mr. Egerton?" asked Damaris, rounding off the name as if she liked pronouncing it.

"I did not breakfast in the cuddy yesterday morning," said I, rendered resolute by the lovely exhortation in my darling's eyes to be as accurate as I possibly could; "but I am sorry to hear that there has been a good deal of suffering among some of the passengers."

"Yes, one gentleman," said she, with a glance

at Florence that instantly turned her face into marble as it stood between me and the sweep of soft blue sky over the quarter, "has, my niece tells me, been very ill. He must expect to suffer at first: but there is very little movement in the ship now, and he ought to feel better. Do you know, Florence, I have a great mind to send the steward to him with my compliments and ask him to make an effort to come on deck. The sunshine and the air are sure to do him good."

"You had better not interfere with him, aunt," said Florence quietly; "he will come on deck in due course. If the man is sick, it will be cruel to send him your compliments."

"Don't call him the *man*, Florence," exclaimed Aunt Damaris, with a kind of saw-like sound in her throat, and her old nose gave another peck out of the hood.

It was very certain from all this that she had no idea how exceedingly ill Morecombe had been or was. Florence had merely told her that he was sea-sick, and having been confined to her cabin the old lady had had no chance of learning the truth. It was no part of my policy to enlighten her. All this while the pilot boat was bearing down fast upon us, sweeping along with a run of snow past her glistening sides and the sunshine pouring past her full on to the towering coast, that stood like a vast fortress upon the sea.

Land was in sight now all the way along our starboard beam, melting into mere faint blue blobs as the Sussex shore trended towards Worthing and Brighton, whilst right ahead you might just catch a glimmer of the coast about Durlston Point, with here and there a coaster or a smack creeping along. And now while Aunt Damaris seemed to be considering within herself whether she should send her compliments to Mr. Morecombe, an order was shouted from the poop, the crew came tumbling aft, the lee main braces were let go and the great yards laid aback amid a deal of singing and stamping and yells of "belay!" The ship still leaning under the tower of canvas upon her came to a stand, and you could hear the water washing with a sloppy sound all along her weather side, and, just under the lee where the shelter of the hull was, the oil-like surface was darkened by the skurrying of the draught down over the rail and shooting away in a hundred swift lines like the track of the long-legged insects you see on the surface of a stream on a hot summer day.

Now it all at once flashed upon me that I should not be doing my duty either to Florence or my cousin Sophie if I missed the chance of the pilot going ashore to send a letter to my cousin to tell her that Morecombe's presence aboard was the fruit of a conspiracy, and that my darling had no more idea than I that he was to make the voyage with her, and I also felt it due to my uncle's fine sense of the ridiculous to relate why and where Morecombe's voyage had come to an end. So I said to Aunt Damaris, "Will you allow me to suggest, madam, that if you would like to write a last line to your friends ashore, now is your opportunity, as the pilot will be landing presently and will take your letter."

She turned to Florence and said, "I wrote at Gravesend—there is nothing to add. Would you like to write?" I caught Florence's decisive resentful "No" as I walked away, thinking to myself, "Nothing to add, eh, old girl! You'll see presently."

When I entered my cabin I found Morecombe, fully dressed, sitting in an American chair. His luggage I had noticed piled under the break of the poop, ready to hand over the side. The poor wretch looked so miserably ill, so wan, haggard, death-like, that for the life of me I couldn't help heartily pitying him, and it was human nature perhaps that my sympathy should even stand higher than it would have done under other circumstances, for my triumph over him was enormous in all ways, too remarkable altogether not to render me very generous. I went to my trunk, saying whilst I looked for the writing-case, "Your sufferings will soon be over, Mr. Morecombe; the pilot cutter'll be alongside in twenty minutes or so."

"Wha's that you say?" he mumbled in a thick voice, smiling meanwhile like an idiot. The strong smell of brandy in the cabin, coupled with his manner, caused me to look at him attentively, and I then perceived that he was intoxicated. I could not be surprised, for if ever a man's stomach was empty, his was; and when a fellow is in that state you know it does not take much to capsize him. He had swallowed brandy plentifully in the night without appearing the worse for it, owing maybe to his sufferings; but here he was now with several caulkers too many in him, and when his glazed eyes rolled in the hollows under his brows and he grinned his imbecile grin as he said "Wha's that you say?" I thought to myself, "Oh, if Alphonso could only see his beauty now!"

"I say, ole man," he cried in a kind of moaning guttural, "come ashore too, will yah? going t' Austwalia's wot. Come along! Where's th' boat?" He tried to rise, but his legs buckled up under him and he fell back again, looking at his shanks with drunken gravity. "Can't stand," he muttered. "What cursed wolling—nothing's steady here—it's woll, woll, woll. I'll wite to the papers. Captain's a wascally impudent cweature— doctor's a duffer—dunno his business. I say, ole man, call steward, will yer?"

I sent the steward to him, and sat down at the cuddy table to write a few lines to Sophie, giving her all the news I could find time to put into my letter, and particularly dwelling upon Morecombe's drunken condition at the moment of his departure from the ship. "Here, steward," said I to Hay, who had come out of Morecombe's cabin, "put that in the bag for the pilot, will you? And," lowering my voice," try to hide the gentleman as you get him over the side. I mean don't let the passengers see more of his condition than you can help—that is if you assist him to the gangway. Who's made him drunk?"

"Oh, himself, sir," answered Hay. "He's been calling for brandy all the morning. The doctor told me to let him have as much as he wanted. 'Anything,' Mr. Griffith said, 'to stop his sickness till he's out of my hands.'"

I returned to the poop and found the pilot boat within a quarter of a mile from us, coming along nobly, and our decks full of people watching her. All the cuddy passengers, including Mrs. Jackson, lined the rail, and Florence and her aunt stood at the break of the poop, close to the starboard ladder, where they commanded the quarter-deck and gangway. I perceived a bit of feminine malice in this on the part of Florence, and when she turned and spied me standing a fathom or two behind her, a gleam shot into her eyes that would have made me laugh outright had not her Aunt Damaris been within earshot. "Stand by ready with a line one of you ! " sung out the chief mate ; and in a few minutes the large powerful craft hauled down her foresail, shifted her helm, and swept alongside. The pilot without ado shook hands with Thompson and the chief mate, touched his cap in a sort of all-round manner to the passengers, wished us all, he was sure, a prosperous voyage, and dropped into the cutter.

I drew nearer by a couple of paces to Aunt Damaris. The second mate on the main deck was giving orders about Morecombe's luggage, and his boxes and sword-stick and umbrella and macintosh were handed along and passed over the side. Presently Morecombe himself emerged from the cuddy front, propped up by Hay and a couple of under-stewards. You never could have guessed how his spell of sea-sickness had changed him by seeing him in his cabin. The brilliant sunshine on the quarter-deck was the light to view him in. He turned his inebriated tallow-white face up at the people who looked down at him from the poop, and I saw Florence take a step back with the recoil of a person utterly dismayed.

" Why," cried Aunt Damaris, in a shrill tone, " it's Mr. Morecombe ! Where is he going ? What's the matter with him ? " And the whole of her face, with a foreground of brown bonnet, forked out of the hood, as she stretched her neck with her hands up and her mouth open.

"How d'ye do, Miss Hawke?" exclaimed the wretched creature, forcing the stewards to come to a stand while he wrestled to free his arm that he might pull off his hat. "I'm going home. Too much wolling for me. Been half killed by following your advice. Take your love to 'Phonso? Tell him no more wotten sailing ships for me. Good-bye, capt'n—look out—I'll expose you for dwagging me about when I'm dying."

By this time the condition of the man was plain to everybody, and the seamen and 'tween-deck passengers were all on the broad grin, some laughing out. Even among us aft, where there would be more delicacy if not more sympathy, you might have heard an occasional titter.

"Now then, how long is the gent going to keep us waiting here?" roared the hoarse voice of the pilot over the side.

"Why, Florence," I heard Aunt Damaris exclaim, seizing her niece's arm, " has he gone *mad?* Is he actually *leaving* the ship?"

"Ay," said the chief mate, who stood near us, and who would not suspect that Mr. Morecombe was a friend of hers; "and don't you think it's time that he left? Why, he looks a corpse, ma'am—and a drunken corpse too!" he added with a half-laugh.

Meanwhile the stewards were shoving Morecombe towards the gangway; and being as I reckoned

almost as much delirious as intoxicated, he was
jabbering nonsense all the time, sometimes shouting it, cursing and swearing in such a way that
Mrs. O'Brien, and Mrs. Jackson, and Mrs. Grant
and her daughter walked aft out of hearing, and
Florence would have gone too, I believe, only that
her aunt, who stood petrified, had a tight hold of
her arm. It was like a row in a street to see the
squalid crowd of emigrants pressing round Morecombe as he was bundled into the gangway. A
pitiable sight truly, and very distressing to me;
for after all the fellow was a gentleman, although
a puppy and a fool; he had suffered fearfully, and
if ever a drop too much was excusable in a man
it was so in him at that time; and I say it went
desperately against my grain to see that chap as
white as if he had been confined to his bedroom for
six months, with his moustache bedraggled, his hat
jammed upon his head, his neckcloth awry, and his
hollow face the merest phantom of the handsome
countenance he had brought aboard with him,
drunkenly swearing at the captain and the ship,
trying to address Florence and her aunt, and all the
'tween-deck passengers and sailors pressing round
him and laughing at him and passing jokes.

Never shall I forget the look of disgust in my
darling's face. All her old dislike of the man was
worked up into a sort of horror, and I give you my
word she watched him as if he were some offensive

kind of animal. Her aunt stood like a woman who beholds a ghost. I could see her gaping at him as her lean face shot out of her hood. She never spoke after her exclamation of amazement to Florence. Once I thought she meant to go down to him, but it was at the moment when his pleasant language drove the other ladies away, and she never shifted her feet again until the sailors had handed Mr. Morecombe over the side. There was a rush of passengers to see the cutter leave, and I supposed from the laughter which rang along that Alphonso's friend was making a sad fool of himself: but I had no chance of looking, for when he was being bundled through the gangway Florence had turned to me and said, "What a horrid scene! is he not intoxicated?"

"Very much so," I answered: "were he sober he would have less life in him."

"I am astonished! I cannot believe my senses!" cried Aunt Damaris. "Surely he cannot be drunk! he must be mad."

"I say, captain," bawled Captain Jackson from the rail where he stood looking at the cutter, and addressing Thompson, who was waiting for the boat to get away to haul the main yards around, "can't you order the fellows down here to shove off and leave us? That drunken vagabond is swearing in a manner not fit for the women folk on the main deck there to listen to!"

"Is this Mr. Morecombe a friend of yours, madam?" said I to Aunt Damaris.

"A friend? Why do you ask, sir?" she answered, with her sharp face full of bewilderment, shame, and indignation.

"He shared my cabin," said I, "and I can tell you about his sickness if you are sufficiently interested to listen."

"Oh, pray come away, pray come away!" cried she. "I cannot hear you for the disgraceful noise those people are making;" and she led the way aft, going indeed to the extreme end of the poop.

"Did you say you could tell me something about him, sir?" she exclaimed, with a sharp peck of her face at me as she tackled me afresh.

"I know him only as a person who shared my cabin," I answered. "He was excessively sea-sick, and in my opinion is well advised to leave the vessel, as I believe another day or two of what he called 'wolling' would have killed him. I was up pretty nearly all through the night with him. Is he a gentleman? I was disposed to consider him respectable until I heard his very wicked language."

"Don't ask me any questions about him!" cried the old lady. "Florence, could you have believed this of him? Could you have imagined him capable of such conduct?"

My darling pursed up her mouth and looked at

her aunt steadily, then dropped her eyes without speaking.

"What could be taking him to Australia?" said I. "He could not be going there for the love of the people of that country, surely, for he spoke in great contempt of them. I hope, madam," said I, in the mildest tone I could assume, "that I shall not be giving offence if I declare him, on my honour, to be one of the greatest asses that was ever let loose by nature upon the world. If Captain Thompson were not busy I would call upon him to give you his opinion of Mr. Morecombe. Was he going to seek his fortune? You should have been boxed up with him, as I was, and listened to the imbecilities he delivered himself of in the intervals of his sickness. What could have induced him, do you conceive, to attempt a voyage of which the first twenty-four hours have very nearly killed him?"

"I have requested you not to ask me any questions about him, sir!" exclaimed Aunt Damaris, shrilly. "Florence, come with me downstairs. I am quite unnerved. Could anything be more extraordinary? Fancy leaving the ship *drunk*; never giving anybody the least idea of his intentions—and think of the whole of his passage-money being wasted!" And making a kind of snap at Florence's arm, she walked hurriedly to the companion, giving me a stiff bow just before she disappeared down the steps.

CHAPTER XI.

WELL, by this time the mainyards had been swung, and the *Strathmore* was heading on her road down Channel, fairly under way, on her own hook, for the other side of the world. The swell of the sea had gone down, there was no weight in the brisk small surges which the merry wind had set a-rolling, and the fine ship, with all plain sail on her, from the flying-jib to the mizzen-royal, swept steadily along with a heel of the hull that sloped her canvas against the blue sky and the white sunlight in the south, that was making a blaze of silver of the water over the port bow. It was a day fit to keep a mute grinning for the fulness of the life and the light of it. You saw the high clouds blowing like bits of mother-o' pearl out of the distant green land, which shelved in and out with a space of lustrous white right abeam, where Durlston Point yawned into the Solent, and the wake astern, spreading into a fan of foam, seemed to be full of leaping mackerel, with the sparking up of glittering lumps of water where the windward line of the track collided with the little seas and shivered them. Of all that numerous company of human souls which the ship was bearing to a distant land, there was surely none happier at heart than I. It was not only that Morecombe was out of the road, it was not only that his manner of going was the completest victory over her father and aunt that Florence could have won, it was not only that my darling was in the ship with me and that I knew I had her love; the magic of the sea was in me too, mates; all the freedom and delight that comes blowing to a man upon the salt, sunlit wind, all the gladness of health and imagination that is swept up like spray out of the heave of the coiling billows and that passes into the heart as the spirit of a pure and generous cordial works its way into the brain. I stood lost in thought, but with straining eyes, as I may warrant, gazing at the flickering gleam of the pilot cutter's canvas as it hovered upon the bright green waters before melting into the film of dim land beyond.

It was now lunch-time, the passengers were in the cuddy, and I joined them; there seemed to be no more sea-sickness, though I questioned if the Bay of Biscay would not revive a qualm here and there. But there was no excuse for nausea now, for though there was a sort of breathing in the water, a respiration rolling up as it might be out of the ocean towards which we were heading, with a kind of yearning response to it in the floating hurl of the ship, it was too long-drawn to take notice of, and the deep *Strathmore* seemed to be sailing as steadily over the foam which her shearing cutwater flung under and along her bends as a sleigh over a level plain of snow. Aunt Damaris and Florence were already seated when I sculled round the side of the table, and took the place I had heretofore occupied; the old lady had decked herself out in a cap and mittens, and there was a hard wooden look on her face. When she noticed where I had seated myself, she lay back so as to peer at me from behind Thompson's broad shoulders, on which I said, "Did you speak, Miss Hawke?"

"No, sir, I did not," she replied, whipping herself erect as a length of bent whalebone recovers itself.

"I saved your old post for you, you see," said Thompson to her.

"But why do you separate me from my niece?" she inquired, inspecting him severely from the level of his eyes, for she and Daniel were of the same stature, sitting and standing.

"Why," he answered, "if I put you both on my right or left, there would be one of you that couldn't by any possibility be next to me. Now I couldn't forego *you*, and at the same time I didn't want to lose the happiness of having your niece by my side; so how should a plain sailor work such a traverse as this except by placing himself between you?"

Well, she couldn't help herself, for to have made Florence change her place would have been rather too marked a proceeding, with all the passengers there looking on; and then, again, do you see, she might not perhaps have been sure that Florence would obey her. Meanwhile during this brief skirmish my darling sat quiet, glancing at the people, and not appearing to hear what her aunt was talking about. I said to her, speaking low— and unless her aunt dodged Thompson's square figure she never could tell, if we sank our tones, whether Florence and I conversed or not—"After the very humiliating defeat of Morecombe's plot, your aunt, I suppose, will give up playing duenna."

"Do not mention that man's name to me," she replied softly. "I am so disgusted that I do not even like to think of him. I am sure the motion of the ship has driven him crazy. What language for a *gentleman* to use!"

"He was drunk," said I; "the poor wretch did not know what he said. Before we shelve him, tell me, my pet, what your aunt thinks of him?"

"What would she think of *you*, could she hear you call me your pet?" said my love, hiding her face by looking close into her plate.

" Are you not my pet ? " I whispered.

" You say I am, and I suppose therefore I must be," she replied.

" My pet for life, darling ! my pet to—— "

" Florence," rasped out Aunt Damaris, with her sharp nose projecting beyond Daniel's cravat ; " don't you hear me speak to you ? "

" No, aunt," she replied, colouring up. " What is it you say ? "

" Do you want me to borrow Captain Thompson's speaking-trumpet ? " cried the old lady. " I'm asking you if you have my smelling bottle in your pocket ? "

Florence found the bottle and passed it.

" I'm afraid," whispered I, " that your aunt is a little quick-tempered. I don't like to hear my darling addressed so sharply."

" Oh, she is terribly mortified by what has happened," she replied. " And you must know that she is in the utmost fright lest the passengers should suspect Mr. Morecombe and we were previously acquainted. She is very sensitive as to other people's opinions of her." *That* I might have suspected of Alphonso Hawke's sister. " She nearly went into hysterics when we left the deck. She advocated the man so warmly after they were introduced in London, and took papa's side so strongly ! She feels thoroughly humiliated, and is the more angry because she cannot quarrel with *me* about him, and has nobody else that she can open her mind to."

"You must have had a great deal of courage to accept her as a companion for a long voyage, Florence."

"Yes," she answered quickly, and with the tiniest show of warmth, "but then I did not know the meaning of the voyage. It is explained now, but I do not regret being here;" and she looked at me.

The impassioned answer I was about to make was baulked by the navy man calling out, "Captain, Mrs. O'Brien is under the impression that the young gentleman who has left us is the son of a baronet of old family. Is the lady right?"

"Ye'll find I am," exclaimed Mrs. O'Brien.

"We shipmasters are never supposed to know anything about our passengers," replied Thompson blandly. "Our duty is to convey them safely from port to port, and endeavour to make them happy and comfortable whilst they are with us."

"And quite enough too," said Mr. Thompson Tucker. "A man's business is nobody's but his own."

"Quite so," observed Mr. Marmaduke Mortimer, who, along with his newly-married wife, was exceedingly polite and amiable to everybody when not engaged in being affectionate.

"There's Miss Hawke perhaps will tell us about

the gentleman," cried Mrs. O'Brien, coming out very easily with Aunt Damaris' name. " I believe, mam, you had met before ? "

" I am really unable to give you any information about him," replied the old lady very grimly, and with an expression of face I was left to imagine, not being able to see her. Daniel glanced at me, and I at Florence. If the passengers had supposed that Aunt Damaris was previously acquainted with Morecombe, this answer of hers put their doubts at rest. Apparently nothing had restrained them from speaking their minds about the youth but the idea that the Hawkes were friends of his, which they would have got perhaps from seeing him sitting and talking with them in the cuddy—as I did—when we were in the river.

" Does anybody know," observed Mrs. Jackson, " what object Mr. Morecombe had in coming into this ship ? Surely he couldn't have embarked *only* for the purpose of being sea-sick, and then drinking himself intoxicated and using profane words."

" I suppose he forfeits his passage-money, captain ? " said Mr. Marmaduke Mortimer.

" Oh yes," answered Daniel; " that's gone as completely as he has."

" What could be taking him to Australia ? " persisted Mrs. Jackson. " If he had any motive in going there at all, it is so very odd that he should abandon the voyage within a few hours of his commencing it."

"He's a lunatic, Maria," said her husband, "and as bad a specimen of the kind as ever I encountered."

I felt for Florence's hand and gave it a squeeze; there was a disconcerted look, with a touch of pain and shame in it, in the darling's face, but the pressure brought out a little smile.

"He was driven out of the ship by sea-sickness, Captain Jackson," said I. "He was no lunatic. He shared my cabin and I witnessed his sufferings. The doctor there will tell you that the steward had orders not to stint him in brandy, the only specific that would give him life enough to put on his clothes and leave the ship."

"I did not conceive that he would make himself drunk, Mr. Egerton," said the doctor.

"I've been a temperate man all my life," said Daniel: "but had I suffered as Mr. Morecombe did, I'd have been willing to swallow the English Channel had it been brandy or whisky. Captain Jackson, you could have seen in the young gentleman's face what he had gone through."

"Ay, but his language!" cried Mrs. O'Brien. "Sure it was horrible, captain. He drove me away, and the dreadful words still ring in me ears."

"Oh, come, it wasn't so bad as all that," exclaimed Mr. Thompson Tucker. "A few strong words, you know, Mrs. O'Brien, but really nothing more than an enraged lord would bestow upon a clumsy valet."

"Besides," said I, "the man didn't know what he was saying."

"But the words would be in him when he was sober," cried Mrs. O'Brien, "so that makes him a bad person any way."

"That's just it," remarked Mrs. Grant. "If there's wickedness in the heart, it does not matter whether the tongue speaketh it or not."

"Well, I don't know about that," said Mr. Thompson Tucker. "It mayn't matter to the man, perhaps, but it's not all the same to the company he's in."

"If Mr. Morecombe is really a baronet's son," exclaimed Captain Jackson, with immense emphasis and in a sort of summing up way, "all that I can say is, I am very sorry to hear it, for such a creature as he would be a disgrace to White-chapel."

Aunt Damaris left the table, and in a few moments Florence followed her.

The others sat a while speaking their minds very freely about Mr. Morecombe; but as the subject was tiresome, and it was no part of my business to defend the absent man's character, I went on deck to meditate upon the numerous things which had in the most unexpected way turned out to my advantage, one of the first in importance, in my opinion, being Aunt Damaris' answer to Mrs. O'Brien. Think of Alphonso's sister pretending not to know anything about Morecombe! What shame that piece of shamming expressed—what disgust! Sir Reginald Morecombe's son positively disowned by the sister of the man who was plotting like the very spirit of mischief to get his daughter to accept him! Why, had Morecombe left the ship in the most dignified manner, taking a respectful and reluctant farewell of Aunt Damaris and Florence, and followed by the sympathy and admiration of the passengers, I should have accepted his departure as a marvellous stroke of good fortune for me. But going as he had—drunk and swearing—amid the gibes and laughter of the 'tweendeck people, causing by his behaviour all the passengers aft to wonder who he could be and rendering Aunt Damaris too heartily ashamed and disgusted to admit that he was a friend of hers and Florence, made the whole business a sort of miracle of good luck. It was entirely beyond any plot that I could have contrived for my own advancement; my cleverest wishes never could have reached up to the perfectly simple but exquisite ingenuity of accident.

The ship was sailing fast; the wind blew with a

cheerful humming into the gray hollows of the swelling canvas whose face glared like cotton at the sun over the lee topsail yardarms ; and there was a deeper green in the curve of the long and scarcely perceptible swell that under-swept a flashing hurry of surges which ran at the deep and steady ship abeam with a feathering and flaking of their crests, and went away to leeward in oil-smooth billows. The decks made a picture to fill the eye ; children running about in the sun-shine 'twixt the galley and the bulwarks where the cable-range lay thick and massive, whilst the foot of the swollen foresail arched over transversely with the shrouds and backstays ruled black against the gray of the shadowed cloths ; groups of people on the forecastle hanging over the rail and watching the passing water, or walking to and fro with their hair blowing to the strong down-draught of blue sunlit wind pouring under the foretack or out from the hollow of the topmast stay-sail, and a shifting of shadows all along, and a gushing of white light between the sails, and an eager sparkling of glass and brass in fresh places as a gust would blow with a moan over the bulwarks and heel the ship by a quarter of a strake, or as the long swell rose full at her forefoot and slowly lifted the flying jibboom-end with a tender sinking of the counter towards the snow of the wake that whirled out from under the quarters.

After a little Aunt Damaris and Florence arrived on deck. I was standing forward of the port quarter-boat leaning against the rail, and thought it best to appear not to see them. So I looked to be absorbed in watching the foam rushing past under the channels, and when I took another peep over my shoulder I spied them in conversation with Daniel and Mr. Thompson Tucker. I was deep in thought when I heard somebody say, "Mr. Egerton," and turning I found Aunt Damaris at my elbow. She was alone, and Florence on the other side patrolling the deck with her arm in Daniel's. "Mr. Egerton," said she, in a much milder tone than I should have thought possible in the possessor of so lean and acidulated a face, "did not you tell me that you shared Mr. Morecombe's cabin?"

"Yes," I replied, breathing a little quickly, "that is so."

"You know," she continued, very polite and still very mild, "that that gentleman's extraordinary manner of leaving the ship has excited much observation among the passengers. Mrs. O'Brien, as you probably heard, quite conveyed the idea that she supposed Mr. Morecombe and I were acquainted previous to our meeting here. Can you tell me, Mr. Egerton, if you ever heard him say anything likely to produce such an impression?"

"Well," said I, "if you will have the truth, Miss Hawke, my answer is 'Yes.'"

" Oh, indeed ! ' she exclaimed, starting.   " What was it he said ?"

" The notion he gave me was," said I, speaking slowly, with a cautious reference to my conscience, and at the same time much enjoying this unexpected privilege of plain speaking, " that he and you, and a gentleman whom he vulgarly ridiculed as an old Australian cock, had plotted this voyage in the hope that he would sicken your niece, who had already rejected him, into accepting him. I gathered that he was in want of money, although the son of a baronet and apparently very highly connected. I inferred that he had embarked on this voyage as a commercial speculation. There seemed to be no love, no liking even in the matter. He was wanted, I understood, because of the title that would come to him at his father's death. That's all I know about him," said I coolly.

Aunt Damaris' face was a curious picture. Pale and gaping, eyes goggling, brows arched with horror and amazement, and indignation writhing in her lean features, it formed as it stared forth upon me out of her bonnet one of the most striking and impressive recollections of a life not wholly undiversified.

" I hope, Mr. Egerton," she gasped, " that you didn't believe him. Pray was he *drunk* when he talked in this manner ?"

" He was very sea-sick, but not drunk," I replied.

She bit her lip, she looked round at Florence, and seemed in real distress of mind. "How very dreadful," she exclaimed, "that he should talk to a perfect stranger in that way." Then, cocking her eye at my face with a very earnest look at it, she appeared, as the Scotch say, to take a thought, and said, "Walk with me up and down, will you, Mr. Egerton?"

"With pleasure; let me give you the support of my arm; there is a slight heaving in the ship." And, hooked on to each other, off we stumped the whole length of the deck in the tail of the Joyce procession, whilst Florence stared as if she distrusted her eyesight, and Daniel seemed to be one immense grin from his boots to his cap.

"Mr. Egerton," said Aunt Damaris, after a short pause, and with a sort of tremulous sucking in of her breath before she spoke, "I am sure you are a gentleman."

"You are very good, Miss Hawke," said I. "I hope I am—I try to behave as one."

"Your name speaks for itself," she continued. "But I like your manners. You'll excuse my plain speaking—I'm old enough to deserve forgiveness for being candid. I was much pleased by the way in which you defended Mr. Morecombe at lunch against the sneers of Captain Jackson."

"Well," said I, "I have no opinion of Mr. Morecombe; but the man had suffered, I had witnessed what he went through, and it was right that I should give my evidence."

"His behaviour at the last was most odious," she exclaimed, holding on tight to my arm in her agitation. "It seems incredible that a person of breeding should get drunk and use such language."

"Why, yes," said I, "but as he was a perfect stranger to us all, his conduct need not signify."

Her grip of my arm tightened, and she said, " It would ease my mind to speak out. As a gentleman, Mr. Egerton, you are, I am sure, to be trusted."

" Implicitly," I exclaimed.

" Well, then," said she, "what Mr. Morecombe told you was not wholly false, but dreadfully exaggerated, in consequence, as I do not doubt, of drink. His statement to you places me in a most awkward position—that is, if you should think proper to repeat it, which I trust and pray you may not, for if the passengers were to hear the story it would make the voyage exceedingly uncomfortable to me."

" You need not fear, Miss Hawke," said I tenderly, and with a small squeeze of her bony arm against my ribs; " not a hint of Mr. Morecombe's exaggerated, if not drunken, statement, shall ever escape me."

" Thank you, Mr. Egerton. You know what the passengers think of him," she continued, her manner so mild that you might fairly call it soft.

"Had he joined this ship merely as an acquaintance, I should not object to owning him as such; but there were other reasons. He exaggerated horribly, I assure you, but his story to you was not wholly false."

"I suppose," said I, in an off-hand way, "that your niece will be rich, and that he was pursuing her in compliance with her papa's wishes, but against her own."

"Ye—yes," said she, with great reluctance in her manner, "that to a large extent is it. I was deceived. When I was introduced to him by my niece's papa—my brother, sir—I took him to be a very gentlemanly young man, and was most favourably impressed by him. This, too, was my brother's opinion, and we certainly thought him a desirable match for my niece. Who could have imagined that he would have acted so disgracefully in this ship! so vilely as to force me to imply that he was an utter stranger to me, and to oblige me to be begging you to conceal his story from the passengers, that we may escape their impertinent chatter during the time we are in the vessel!"

"You have my warmest sympathy, Miss Hawke, I am sure; and as to my secrecy you may count upon me as if I were a priest. I shall dismiss his story from my mind—more especially all that part about this voyage being a plot, and the ship a rat-trap in which he was to catch your niece."

"What a horrid creature!" she exclaimed. "Fancy anybody calling himself a gentleman talking like that of a young lady! A rat-trap! I wish I could catch him in one! I should like to punish the odious fellow!"

"Then I am to assume, Miss Hawke," said I, "that he did not join this ship at the wish of your brother?"

"No, I won't say that," she answered. "You may assume that he did—my brother believing, as *I* did, that he was a gentleman in feeling as well as by birth, and a not undesirable acquisition to our family. But the very moment I arrive in Sydney I will write a letter to Clifton that shall undeceive my brother in that respect. A desirable match! Why, after his misconduct, his manner of leaving the ship, his dreadful language, I would no more dream of sanctioning his alliance with my niece than of allowing her to wed one of the sailors at the end of the ship there."

The old rasp was in her throat as she delivered herself of these words, but it clearly did her good to ease her mind. It was what the old creature wanted; the chance had come, and you may reckon I didn't baulk her. On a sudden she let go my arm, stepping out nevertheless very briskly alongside of me, and accommodating her old legs with much dexterity to the inclined deck and the occasional floating heave of it, and looked at me attentively with a preliminary anxious peck towards me of her chopper-like face. "I really don't know," said she, "what you can think of me for talking to you so candidly and, indeed, I hardly know what to think of myself. You see how it has come about, don't you? Shame forced me to tell Mrs. O'Brien I could give her no information concerning Mr. Morecombe; and then I discover that among those who heard that answer were you, Mr. Egerton, to whom that wretched young man had related a most exaggerated story, equal to a lie, sir, indeed. A rat-trap? the horrid creature! Why did I ever place myself in such a position? I simply desired to oblige my brother and to promote the interests of my niece, as I believed. I trust you will not speak to your friend the captain? Pray consider how intensely mortified my feelings would be if I conceived that Mr. Morecombe's aggravating falsehoods were to pass about, and get from us here to those low passengers who actually made a sort of rag-fair of the ship when that miserable person left the vessel. I could never show my nose on deck; I never could. I am dreadfully sensitive."

I assured her again in the most emphatic language I could employ, that no syllable of what either she or Mr. Morecombe had related should escape me. On this she took my arm again, and became wonderfully gracious. Regularly as we came abreast in our walk of Daniel and Florence on the weather side of the deck I would note my darling peeping at me with laughing eyes, whilst the natural red of the skipper's face would occasionally take a sort of apoplectic duskiness from the severity of his pent-up merriment. My keen anxiety to be exceedingly polite to Aunt Damaris, my perfect willingness to do anything she required, no doubt rendered my behaviour and society very pleasing. Indeed, to speak the truth, I had always made shift, ever since I was a little boy, to " get on," as it is called, with old ladies. I can't tell you what there was in me to please them, but they always took to me. What Florence had implied of her aunt—that Morecombe's conduct had established a heavy grievance in her mind, and she was crazy through not having anybody to open herself to— was proved now that she had hold of my arm and found me sympathetic. I never knew an old tongue to rattle on as her's did. Had I been her lawyer or her oldest friend she could not have been more garrulous and communicative. She told me in what part of Sydney she was born, how her father had made a great deal of money by buying a piece of land which was now crowded with fine houses ; how her brother Alphonso had acquired a fortune by breeding sheep, and so on ; and then she would talk of Morecombe and abuse him, declaring that she should never cease to wonder at her blindness in not perceiving that his manners when they were introduced were the cheapest kind of social veneer, hiding a very despicable nature. But, said she, her brother's praise of him had greatly prejudiced her in his favour, and then you see he was a baronet's son, and very highly connected; "and what made me more willing," she exclaimed, "to help the project my brother had in sending my niece with me to Australia in company with Mr. Morecombe was the annoyance that had been caused him by a Mr. Jack Seymour, who had met his daughter at Clifton, and had fallen in love with her."

"Oh, indeed," said I, feeling my throat turn very dry: "there has evidently been no lack of complication in all this business, Miss Hawke."

"Too much for me, I can assure you, Mr. Egerton," she answered; "indeed it is enough to make me thankful that I am a single woman and spared all the anxiety of children. However, indignant as my brother will feel when he hears about Mr. Morecombe, and reflects that he has spent his money in vain—for I must tell you that the pitiful creature actually *allowed* Mr. Hawke to pay his passage to Sydney—it will console him to know that the voyage effectually puts a stop to the pursuit of the underbred person who was paying attention to my niece through the medium of his cousins."

"Yes, that ought to console him," said I; "the voyage is not hopelessly aimless."

" Quite the reverse," she cried. " What I shall tell my brother is that nothing more fortunate could have happened: for it enabled us to discover the real character of that worthless creature Mr. Morecombe before it was too late—I mean, before my niece had become his wife: besides putting an end to the mischievous attentions of the person I have named, who, my brother told me, had been a sailor, and was a very common insulting youth."

Lucky, thought I, that this is not said in my darling's presence! If it did not force her to betray me by look or by speech, might I be hanged! As for my own feelings, why, all the effect the words had was to set me laughing, to cover which I exclaimed, " Thanks to the interest you take in your niece, Miss Hawke, both the common sailor youth and Mr. Morecombe are effectually cleared away out of her road."

" Yes," she answered, smiling grimly, in sympathy with my laugh or out of politeness; " the voyage was well planned after all, though the consequences to me might have been exceedingly disagreeable had Mr. Morecombe talked as freely to the other passengers as he did to you."

And then, after a bit of a pause, she said, " I think you told me that you are not going to Australia to settle ? "

" No, I shall probably return in this ship."

" Do your family reside in England, Mr.

Egerton?" she asked. It was the most fortunate thing in the world that Florence quitted Daniel at that moment and joined us. There was a long family catechism in each of the greenish eyes Aunt Damaris turned upon me, and I was trembling on the verge of a bottomless pit of equivocation when my sweetheart unconsciously came to my rescue.

"You know my niece, so there is no need to introduce you," said the old lady most graciously. "Florence, my dear, I have been taking I don't know how many turns, and it is astonishing how much better I feel for the exercise."

"You certainly look the better for it, aunt," exclaimed Florence, with a rich note of laughter in her voice, and glancing at me with her eyes rendered brilliant by the contrast of the soft warm colour on her cheeks.

"I hope," said I, "that this is only the first of many walks of the same kind, for nothing could be more agreeable to me," and with a slight bow and a lift of my hat I sheered off, noting with intense satisfaction the gratified look in Aunt Damaris' face.

Well, soon afterwards they went below, and I saw no more of them for the rest of the afternoon. Thompson came up and began to joke me about my conquest over the old lady, but finding me full of thought, he had the good sense to leave me alone after awhile. The manner in which the old lady had opened her mind to me set my thoughts flowing in a new channel altogether, and I stood for I don't know how long a while leaning over the rail, with my eyes upon the water and my brain whirring like the machinery in a locomotive factory, until I believe the people forward imagined I was sea-sick. We were sailing a good ten knots an hour, and before I left the deck the darkness had closed around and away over the starboard bow; distant maybe seventeen miles was Portland High Light, a mere spark, but the sight of it made me reckon that if this wind held we should be on with the Start before midnight, and that the Scillies would be on our quarter by noon next day. It was fine sailing, and when the dusk came along, with a scattering of sharp bright stars among the high clouds, the ship became a phantom; and I lingered for five minutes after I had turned to go below, with my hand on the companion, to watch the spectral glimmering shadows piled one atop of the other as they rose, until coming to the royals you spied nothing but what might pass for a streak of mist hanging over the topgallant sails and blowing along with the ship. There was noble music in the chanting of the bow-wave as it rolled away from the cutwater, and you would have fancied that some of the children belonging to the 'tween-decks had clambered aloft, and had broken out into singing for joy of the wonder of the sight of the stars that looked to lie close to the towering mastheads, had you heard the strains that poured down from the shadowy fabric on high and the flute-like whistling of the wind as it swept through the hundred ropes of all sizes which ran taut from the ship into the gloom over her.

CHAPTER XII.

When I left the deck and entered the lighted cuddy, I forgot all about the wonderful evening picture, and thought only of Florence and the score of matters I had in my mind to say to her; and mighty pleased was I when, on everybody being seated, I peered past the captain and found Aunt Damaris' place vacant.

" She complains of a headache," said Florence ; " I think you made her walk too much."

" I am sorry that her head aches, but I'm glad she's not at table," said I. " Her absence enables me to be fluent, and I want to tell you what our talk was about."

" Oh, she has told me everything," exclaimed Florence, laughing. " Don't you think her a rather strange person ? "

" Well, rather," I replied. " But, for all that, I fancy I could like her if she would let me. She called Jack Seymonr, it is true, a vulgar insulting person : but that, my darling, is because she doesn't know what a charming creature he is."

"Are you sure of that?" said Florence, giving me the chance of a peep into her eyes, the depth of whose pure sweet beauty I was always on the look out to sound. "Let me tell you she considers Mr. Egerton a most gentlemanly young man, refreshingly unaffected, yet with something very thorough-bred about him too, and a real treat to talk to after Mr. Morecombe. I am using her own words, Jack."

"You must be joking!" cried I, on the broad grin.

"Indeed I am not," she answered. "You appear to have won her heart. But dear me! what will she say when she discovers who you are?" and a delightful air of puzzlement came over her face as she mechanically glanced along the table at the people who were talking and laughing as they gobbled over the plates the stewards put before them.

"I have been turning that point over in my mind," said I, "and the conclusion I have arrived at is that your aunt ought not to know who I am. If there is a chance of her liking me as Mr. Egerton, then what is to stop me from making her affectionate by paying her all the attention she will allow me to bestow on her? *Then* when the mask is dropped at last she will be too fond of me as *a man* to bother over the name I go by. Do you see that, my pet? She shall think me in love with her for the sweetness of her disposition. I'll overwhelm her. Those old ladies are wonderfully credulous. Nothing to do but to eye them pensively, and forthwith they go and buy new caps."

"What's the joke, Miss Hawke?" asked Thompson, hearing my sweetheart's laughter. "Jack making fun of somebody, I'll wager. He's too much of a monopolist to suit my book. He engrosses all your attention and gives me no chance to edge in a word. Talk of concealing his feelings! of misleading all these ladies and gentlemen and Miss Damaris Hawke! Why, the workings of his heart might be watched from the flying jibboom end."

Though he spoke low, it was nevertheless terribly alarming to hear him joke in this fashion, for his voice was by no means melodious, and even his whispers had something of the sound of a straining timber in them; so I gave him an imploring look along with a glance at Florence (who was smiling with a little confusion in her expression) as if to entreat him to spare me for *her* sake. But if I had felt the necessity of behaving with caution before the passengers, I should certainly not have stood in need of a hint from him. The truth is I had made up my mind not to let the suspicions or curiosity of the cuddy folk hinder my courtship.

I had no intention of suppressing my love for
Florence when others were by, and it was a
question very shortly to be settled whether indeed
I should think it worth while to conceal my passion even when Aunt Damaris was looking on.
However, Thompson was not to be put off; he
insisted upon conversing with Florence; whereupon
I talked to Mrs. Grant, who sat at the after-end
of the length-wise table nearest ours, but I was
soon deep in whispers with Florence again. She
told me that after I left them her aunt had indulged
in a number of surmises respecting my birth, connections, and social position, and that when she had
done extolling me she fell again upon Mr. Morecombe, denounced him as an impostor, said that
there never could have been an atom of affection
in him for Florence, seeing how glad he appeared
amid his drunkenness to leave the ship, and re-
ferred again in a great passion to the young fellow's
comparison of the *Strathmore* to a rat-trap. She
was mortified and disgusted in all ways, Florence
said; by the idea that he had given me the whole
story of his relations with the Hawkes, by his
withdrawal from the ship and the ignominious
failure of Mr. Hawke's scheme, by his going away
drunk amid the scorn and laughter of the passengers; and her dislike and indignation were
increased by the conviction that, had he remained
in the vessel, he would in due course have told all

hands, from the cuddy to the forecastle, why he was in the ship, and why he was making the voyage to Australia. "And best, or worst of all, Jack," said Florence, "is my aunt's fear that the passengers will guess that we knew Mr. Morecombe before he joined the vessel, so horrified was she by his being intoxicated and everybody jeering him."

"Does she not commend your good sense in having refused him now that she professes to have found out what a poor creature he is?"

"I don't want her commendations. She is heartily welcome to go on abusing Mr. Morecombe as long as she pleases, but the moment she couples my name with his or connects me in any way with his wretched attempt to make a voyage to Australia, I beg her to cease, and she does, Jack."

"Would you be angry if she coupled your name with mine?"

"No," she answered: "why do you ask? In the hope that I should reply yes?"

"Oh, my darling, never wonder at any questions I ask you! Nothing ought to surprise you in me— no, not even if you should catch me dancing on my head. Are *you* not enough to turn my brains? Every look you give me with your beautiful eyes robs me of something of my wits. Only the other day I met you for the first time in my uncle's house at Clifton, old Flora at your feet. I fell in love with you plump; ay, Florence, it was the completest header mortal man ever took. Well, sweet and amiable as you always were, I hardly dared think of you, so immeasurably remote did your father's behaviour cause you to seem to me. And now, after weeks of horrible fears, here we are together; here am I calling you my darling, and although you have never yet told me that you love me, yet don't I *know* that you do; don't I *know* that your darling heart is mine—ay, as we stand now on the very threshold of our long voyage, though I never dared dream that I should have wholly won your heart until the Australian coast was some thousands of miles nearer than it is at present."

Well, she coquetted a little: she whispered that I was a very conceited person to conclude that she was in love with me; certainly she liked me very much, indeed she had liked me from the hour of our first meeting, and she was glad I was in the ship, and that her aunt had praised me; but was I quite sure that she had given me her heart?—and as she asked this she looked up at me with eyes so fond that the temptation to kiss the beautiful loving face that shone within an easy stretch of my lips was just one of those things which a man must set his teeth hard together to resist. From time to time I would catch Mr. and Mrs. Marmaduke Mortimer eyeing us with smiling approval, whilst some of the others, particularly Mr. Thompson Tucker, would direct surprised glances at us, as if they were very much astonished by the rapid progress I was making. Hitherto, partly on account of the motion of the ship, the nausea, the general sense of bewilderment induced by the novelty of the surroundings, we had not attracted attention; but, as the dinner on this day advanced, it was impossible not to see that we were detected, that the passengers were beginning to indulge in silent surmises, and that the general conclusion would be (if the truth was concealed) that either Florence and I were lovers before ever we boarded the *Strathmore*, or else she was a most impressionable young lady to be won in an hour, and I a most wonderfully smart hand at love-making.

My darling saw all this as plainly as I, but it did not seem to give her the least trouble. Never lose sight of one thing, lads: the whole job was a romance that any girl would enjoy. Florence was the heroine of the performance; all that was happening was a tribute to her; two young men had pursued her to sea, and she would know very well that, if the full story were to be related to the passengers, the only effect it could produce would be to make her an object of great sentimental interest on board the ship. It was altogether different with Aunt Damaris. If the part *she* had played were to become known, why, all hands would be triumphing and laughing over the failure of the plot; and claiming to be a sensitive woman, and being in a ship full of people whom she could not quit her cabin without encountering, why, you see, she would be just as eager for secrecy as my darling was indifferent to discovery. So that is how matters stood on that evening of September 30th, Portland High Light being visible on the starboard beam, and the ship sailing a bold ten knots an hour with her jibboom pointing west by north for the Atlantic Ocean.

The weather was fine when I turned in at eleven o'clock, after having stumped the poop for near upon an hour, in company with Daniel and Captain Jackson, who had seen some service in his youth and had a memory well stocked with yarns of the navy as we know it in Marryat's books, and who proved to be a very decent companion when he was not grumbling. The fore and mizzen royals and flying jib had been taken in, but all else was held on with, and the wind coming with a rush across the black water drove full into the immense squares of canvas that soared up in the gloom, and heeled the ship channels under. She was going through it like a steamer;—indeed there were few steamers afloat at that time which could have held their own with her in that strong, steady breeze and smooth water. You could hear the stem ripping through it forward in a kind of crunching sound that came along aft with the noise of the wash of the surge thrown up; and, now and again, when an extra puff gave a sharper inclination to the pallid spaces overhead, you would see the white water shoot inboard through the scupper-holes; while looking down at it from the poop, the rail of the maindeck bulwarks seemed to be flush with the yeasty smother, so that, let me tell you, it needed genuine nautical toes to keep a grip of the deck at such times, for, to leeward, the ebony water, with here and there a gleam of froth on it, appeared to start from the top of the line of hencoops and run right up among the windy stars which flickered wan and small among the driving clouds vanishing in the south.

Amid the humming and trembling of the rushing ship, every hanging thing at an angle of 33° with the deck, as I allowed, I turned in and lay for perhaps half an hour thinking of Florence and Aunt Damaris and how this voyage was to end; wondering whether Florence would marry me in Sydney, or force me to wait until she had her father's consent, and if he ever would consent, and if not what Florence would do, until I fell asleep to the lullaby of the hissing and streaming of water alongside, and the jar and croak and groan and complaint of timber and panel strained in their strong fastenings by the enormous leverage aloft. Soundly I must have slept, as I afterwards came to know, for when I awoke there was half a gale of wind blowing, and all hands had been on deck clean throughout the middle watch—that is, from midnight until four—shortening sail. Yet I had heard nothing! Coils of rope had been flung down, reef-tackles, clewlines, and buntlines manned, halliards let go amid hoarse songs and a tramping of feet and orders bawled out with hurricane lungs—in vain ! The gale was news to me when I awoke at eight o'clock next morning, though it had been blowing since midnight.

It was a job to dress, for the jumping of the ship made me sprawl about horribly, and, though I flatter myself that my sea-legs were as good as any man's aboard the *Strathmore*, yet thrice did I plump down upon my nose before I succeeded in shipping all that I required to render me fit to be seen on deck. The first thing I did was to look aloft and note how the yards were braced, and found them pretty nearly square. That was the main point; anything but a head wind in the Chops: and here were we swarming along under close-reefed topsails and reefed foresail with the staysail swagging in the calm beyond with a hard blow of the sheet against the forestay, and then a rounding out of the cloths to the yaw and swing of the driving ship, a small hurricane of brilliant wind pouring into us betwixt the starboard after quarter-boat and the mainbrace bumpkin, and a heavy sea coming after us like cliffs ; walls of water almost, up and down, green-ridged and sparkling with spray, swept along, and half-obscuring them as a bride's veil conceals the beauty it covers.

This will do, thought I, if it only holds as it is. So long as we could run before it there was nothing to complain of. I had a bit of a job to scramble out of the companion, for the wind came hard enough to leave you well content to hold on for a minute or two, without striving to make head against it. There were two men at the wheel in yellow oilskins, and the set faces that looked out of their sou'westers gleamed with sweat. Hard work I knew it must be to steer that flying ship, with a heavy sea on the quarter that kept her head as wild as a swing, and the helm was grinding up and down, just as you may notice a coachman whirling a carriage wheel when washing it. The pitching of the ship was a real sensation. You'd see her bows swooping down to the base of the glittering green arch that was rolling away ahead of her until her forecastle deck looked as flat as a floating saucer upon the water, whilst the foam was flying like wool out through the headboards, and the sea beyond stood up like the side of a hill; and then down would go the stern of the vessel as the surge that ran roaring under and past her, swelling nearly as high as the bulwark rail and giving her the while a mighty lurch, left its hollow for the ship's counter to sink in; and up with a noble majestic motion would soar the bows, until the crest of the sea slipped away from under the forefoot, and left the gale to blow the huge fabric with a long floating roaring sweep down the weltering slant of the dark and thunderous trough.

We were making noble progress, and our wake danced away into the bluish haze miles astern like the white dust of a road passing over hills. The sea was fuller of life than ever I can remember seeing it, for there was a constant flash of sunshine among the clouds to give a splendour as of shining emerald to the billows in places and a startling glory of prismatic white to the foam ; so that what with these irradiations, and the whirling olive-coloured shadows of the clouds, and the varying tint of the surges which changed from dark to light green as they swept along and shifted their forms, the ocean to the very confines where the horizon resembled a line of mountains seemed to be one vast surface of leaping and rolling colours. You must be in a sailing ship to enjoy a gale of wind. She lets you feel the genius, the spirit of the wild disturbance. In a steamer you have the alliance of a power that neutralizes the thrilling inspirations of the conflict. The champing of the engines vibrates through the shriek of the blast, and the sense of *mechanism* makes the battle inglorious to the feelings. But in a sailing ship you ride the whirlwind, if you do not direct the storm. The life of the vessel is due to the mighty power she grapples with and influences to her own existence. She strips like a pugilist to the encounter, and whatever delight is born of such defiance of enormous force as is illustrated by a vessel lying-to with her head to the mountainous billows and looking up into the eye of the hurricane, or of such audacious appropriation of the titanic power of the elements as a ship's arrow-like speeding before the gale conveys, comes from the sailing vessel alone.

If ever this thought was strong in me, it was so that morning when I stood against [the weather mizzen-rigging watching the action of the plunging ship and the dazzling masses of foam thrown from her bows and her grand domination of the ridged and hissing brows of the huge seas which rolled transversely under her, and listening to the whistling and screaming of the wind aloft where the close-reefed canvas was pulling at its sheets as if it would crack in halves the solid yards which stretched them, whilst the very tautest lines of the running gear were blown out into semi-circles, and the foot of the reefed foresail stood up under the forestay in an arch that one moment framed nothing but the huge green undulations over the rail, and the next nothing but the sky of the lee horizon where the driven clouds lay thick before the howling wind.

Well, my lads, for three blessed days and nights did this strong wind blow, with a bit of a lull now and again that never gave the officer of the watch time to shake out a reef, and a shifting of four points only, coming back to its place before it blew itself out. The sailors liked it, you may take my word, for it gave them a fair watch below and little enough to do when on deck: and if ever a sea-blessing rumbled forward, you may safely bet it was to be heard in the galley where the rolling and the pitching set the cook and his mate scalding their dainty hands, and made every successful cuddy meal a notable feat. I pitied the 'tween-deck passengers, for the tarpaulins were over the main-hatch gratings and there was no ventilation for them save by the booby-hatch, through which no daylight was visible until you stood chock under it and looked up at the break of the poop; and my old experiences of what would be doing down there were lively enough to save me the need of a peep to realize the sense of sliding chests and clattering tin dishes and pannikins, and crying children and bewildered women, pell-mell in the twilight of the dim oil lamp that swung heavily from a beam.

I am not going to tell you that this was a whole gale of wind, though maybe I am making it seem so: had it been *that*, the deep ship could never have run before it; we should have hove-to and lay tossing about with a drift to the southward instead of bowling out our fair twelve geographical miles and making a run in every twenty-four hours of those three days equal to hard upon five parallels. But nevertheless it was violent weather; talking was difficult at table or anywhere else, and for that reason nothing of moment unless it were a look or two passed between Florence and me. On the third day, however, of this noisy blowing, I was passing through the cuddy in the afternoon when I saw Aunt Damaris and my darling seated on a cushioned locker near the piano. I clawed my way over to them, and asked the old lady if she would like to see the ocean. "It's a fine sight," I shouted; "I'll engage to hand you safely through the companion."

"Very much obliged, Mr. Egerton," she answered, the saw-like notes in her voice making her speech clear enough: "I have no wish to lose the little hair that time has spared me."

"You ought not to let this gale blow itself away without taking a look at it," said I.

"I have no doubt it is very fine," she replied, "but I prefer to remain under shelter. Pray don't suppose that I have no conception of the height of the sea. You should go and sit in our cabin! I was never whirled about like this when coming to England, not even off Cape Horn."

"Stern cabins are a mistake, madam," cried I. "Whatever movement there is in the ship you get the most of there; not to speak of the grinding of the wheel-chains over your head and the jar of the rudder."

"Quite true, Mr. Egerton; you appear to know all about it. Positively one would suppose that you had been a sailor," she bawled, with her eyes, that were close set in her face, fixed upon me.

"Oh," shouted I, noticing the smile that came and went over Florence's face like a touch of the sunlight on the rolling snow outside, "every landsman knows that the wheel is over the stern cabins and that the rudder is in the water under it."

"You are used to the sea as a yachtsman, perhaps?" she exclaimed. "No person unaccustomed to the motion of a ship could move about as you do. Only half an hour ago Mr. Thompson Tucker was dashed down on the deck when leaving his cabin, and was very glad to regain it, I assure you."

I had no objection to her thinking that I knew the sea as a yachtsman, for it would probably be the only form of sailoring she would think genteel, so I blandly smiled in her face, and turning to Florence sang out, "Since your aunt will not trust herself on deck, may I have the pleasure of taking you there?"

"I am afraid I shall be blown overboard," she answered, piping out the clear music of her notes nobly.

"Have no fear," said I. "You will enjoy the

scene, and the wind will refresh you after your confinement in the cabin."

Aunt Damaris made no objection, which surprised me exceedingly. My darling raised her beautiful eyes to the skylight, and after a moment's hesitation consented to accompany me. She had to go to her cabin first for her jacket and head-gear, and I handed her to the door of it, squeezing her little fingers tenderly during our progress as you may reckon, and whilst she equipped herself I took her place at Aunt Damaris' side. "I am exceedingly sorry," I called out in her ear, putting all the amiability and sympathy I could pack into the strong voice I was forced to exert, " that the motion of the ship should inconvenience you in your cabin. Mine is very much at your service, if you would like to use it. It has two bed-places; Mr. Morecombe had one of them."

"Oh, you are very obliging; but no, thanks, we will stop where we are," she answered. "Pray don't mention Mr. Morecombe's name; he has quite gone out of my head, I assure you, and I don't want to be reminded that he has an existence."

I bowed to signify obedience, or at least I made the best job I could of a bow under those tossing and rolling conditions, and then congratulated her upon her appearance, telling her that I had been afraid her health would suffer from her imprisonment below. "But I am glad to see," said I, viewing her earnestly, "that that has not been the case; doctors say that the sea air makes people live long, but my notion is that it makes people look young. There is nothing like it for brightening the eyes and purifying the complexion."

She would have been more than human, indeed she would have had to be an angel instead of an old maid, not to have been sensible of this piece of flattery, which I reckon on the whole was pretty neatly administered, considering what a green hand I was at such work. You would have perceived the Eve in her old lean bony composition stirring under the compliment and warming into a smile, faint indeed, because, you see, she was an elderly lady, and would suck a lollipop of this kind cautiously, making pretend that she had nothing in her mouth. Just then Florence came out of her cabin, and I sprang forward to give her my hand, for superbly as she would poise her lovely figure to the motion of the sea, here was a deck quite impracticable to any woman's feet, even though they should have twinkled under the gauze of *la première danseuse de la monde*, whatever her name might be.

"Be very careful," squealed Aunt Damaris.

"Have no fear, madam!" I shouted: and leaving the old lady to think what she pleased of my behaviour, I passed my arm under my sweetheart's, linking the darling firmly to me thus, and helped her up the companion steps. The moment her dear little nose was above the companion, she put her hand to it as if she thought it had been blown off her face. She struggled for breath, dragged at me as if to descend the steps again; but I was not going to lose her. The privilege of having my darling alone with me was so great that I looked about to see how we might obtain shelter for a half-hour's quiet talk. The wind blew screaming betwixt the rail and the keel of the quarter-boat griped at the davits, and was unbearable. The gale was on the quarter, and blew right along the poop, and there was no shelter to be got this side the maindeck, where the sight the sea offered would be an imperfect show. This was a confounded nuisance, but could not be helped. Had the wind been right abeam, why, a square of canvas in the mizzen-rigging would have made a summer-house, with the hencoop for a seat, and the fowls talking to themselves at our heels; but a wind blowing over a quarter gallery might as well be sweeping through the spokes of the wheel for all the shelter a poop will yield you; so there was nothing to do but carry my pet to the mizzen-mast, and station her against it and myself alongside of her. There was some little protection here; but the wind raved as it cut itself in halves against the great spar and united t'other side with a screeching whistle, and our ears were so full of the infernal piping that love-making would have been an easier job in the forecastle, with the watch below snoring at the top of their throats, and every timber and every plank in the bows groaning as they parted the swelling tons of water.

Shipmate, did you ever stand on the deck of a vessel sweeping over a foaming rolling sea, with your heart's delight alongside of you? No? Well, if so be you are a single man, and your sweetheart is agreeable, make the experiment and think of Jack Seymour. There will be a perfume in the gale, richer to the taste than the most aromatic of languid hothouse sweets, a glory in the flying sunbeam such as never yet dazzled in the most tropical of the luminary's flashings, a nobleness and grandeur in the swelling and creaming liquid acclivities the like of which was never before sensible to you even in the mightiest of old ocean's conflicts with the storm-fiend, and such a boundless, intoxicating, thrilling sense of liberty and happiness, that upon my word, on second thoughts, I don't know whether you ought to risk the emotion unless you are cocksure that your soul is too strongly built to be blown up by the immense number of square feet of moral and spiritual ether which an experience of the kind I am talking about will sweep into it. Oh, my lads, to look into my darling's brilliant eyes, all ashine with wonder and awe and delight, and turn from them to the wild picture of hurling waters and flying ship and rushing sky, was to behold such a meaning and spirit in the splendid stirring scene that the ocean seemed a new thing to me, the great commotion of the gale a revelation.

CHAPTER XIII.

I SAVE A CHILD'S LIFE.

IT is not always blowing at sea, whatever ladies may think, though to be sure I have known a ship leave Adelaide and carry a storm with her from abreast of Cape Horn to Ushant, when, after a hundred and forty days of grinding and tossing, there fell a calm with light baffling breezes from the eastward which kept her groping about the Chops until passengers and crew made up their minds that the tormented hooker they were aboard of was just the *Flying Dutchman* that was doomed never to reach her destination. Nevertheless, it is not always blowing at sea, a mercy sailor men are grateful for; and with us it happened that the gale, which had swept us south a distance of eight hundred miles in seventy-two hours, expired when the last of those hours had come round, and left us rolling in a dead calm on the verge of the Horse latitudes. We were in warmer weather now, and the sun climbed up over the calm, very hot indeed, with a sea like heaving quicksilver shot with scores of colours, as a daguerreotype plate is when you slant it about to the light. I remember that particular forenoon well, though we had many others like it. The awning was spread over the poop, and the blue sky between it and the rail made a frame whose tender azure was here and there piebald with lumps of white cloud, one peering over another like a lot of bald-headed giants forking up over the sea-line. The ship had spread every stitch of plain sail belonging to her to catch the flutterings of air that crept along the water, blurring the polished folds with streaks that had a look of ice in the distance; and she was managing to sneak along fast enough to leave a few holes in the sea under her counter, and to keep her course steady at the lubber's point, allowing for the swing of the swell. Everybody, save the watch below, was on deck; and it was enough to make a man thoughtful to stand at the break of the poop, and to turn his eyes forward and then aft and observe what a mob of people were being kept alive by nothing more than a few caulked planks. The steerage and 'tween-deck passengers filled the quarter and main decks and forecastle; they walked about in pairs or conversed in groups, or sat sunning themselves in the ardent beams to the enjoyment of which they would bring a particular relish after their long confinement to the gloom and noise and

bewildering motion below; the children played in
the scuppers, thoughtful faces looked into the
wonderful ocean distance as if seeking to create
upon the remote and polished line some image of
the Pacific shores, whither they were bound in
search of bread if not of fortune, whilst sailors
were at work aloft on jobs it would be idle to
describe, and a spun-yarn winch was rattling on
the forecastle, and the sailmaker and his mates
flourished their shining needles and tarry twine
over some stretch of fore and aft canvas.

The cuddy passengers were scattered over the
poop, Captain Jackson and his wife in American
arm-chairs with books in their hands, Thompson
Tucker on his back on a hen-coop, a cigar in
his mouth, and his head in a coil of rope,
Mrs. Grant and her daughter knitting or doing
some work of that kind, and the Joyce children—
pretty little infants, one a boy, with long fair curls
down their backs, and blue eyes, all as like one
another as peas are or eggs—playing bopeep round
the compass stand before the foremost skylight.
Aunt Damaris and Florence were on chairs near the
mizzenmast, the former looking at the sea with her
mittened hands locked upon her lap, and my
darling reading some book from which every now
and again she would lift her eyes and steal a
peep at me, who walked quietly too and fro past
her with the chief officer, Mr. Thornton. Presently

Captain Jackson yawned loudly, got out of his chair, and joined us.

"What's the weather going to be like, can you guess, Mr. Thornton?" said he. "Is there any sign to be found in this westerly swell?"

"I don't think it means anything, sir," replied the chief mate.

"It was just hereabouts," said the navy man, in his loud voice, and taking all hands within reach of his notes into his confidence, as his way was, "that a thunderstorm demagnetized the compass of his Britannic Majesty's ship *Wren*, in which I was then a midshipman. It came on as black as my hat, though the daylight was abroad, being four o'clock of the afternoon, and there whizzed out of the mud overhead such a flash of lightning as never saw I the like of since. It put the whole sea on fire, sir; it was as if all creation had been plunged into the infernal regions. Well, when the thunder was gone, and it must have taken a long five minutes for the echo of that crashing boom to roll away out of hearing over the slippery smoothness—not a breath, mind you—we saw the binnacle card spinning round like a teetotum. Its sensibility was killed, sir. It was never afterwards worth a dump. Fortunately, we had a spare compass on board, or we should have had to steer by the stars, of which, by the way, we never obtained a glimpse, for it came on thick that night and remained so a whole fortnight." And our friend looked triumphantly around him as he usually did when he spun a marine yarn, just as though no experience that ever befell him was to be matched by what anybody else had seen or suffered. It was never my policy at that time to appear to have any knowledge of the nautical calling, otherwise I should have liked to tell Captain Jackson that the effect of his thunderstorm was not so extraordinarily uncommon as he supposed, I myself having been in a ship during a magnetic outburst which reversed the poles of the compass, so that when the officer of the watch went to see how the vessel was heading he could not believe his eyes; the compass pointed north by east, and our course was south by west. There was a regular outcry; the man at the wheel was abused, and he swore he had never shifted the helm; the sailors thought the ship bewitched, for did any one hear of a ship suddenly slewing around sixteen points without anybody taking notice of the change, the vessel having steerage way at the time? The cause was discovered after a bit, but the general consternation was very fine whilst it lasted.

"Strange things happen at sea," said Mr. Thornton; "I was once in a ship that sprung a leak, and how do you think it was caused? Why, by the sounding-rod, sir. We had tried the pump-well so often that, hang me, Captain Jackson, if at last the rod had not passed slick through the ship's bottom."

"That's nothing," said Captain Jackson. "If you're fond of wonders, listen to this. I was in a ten-gun brig, and left Hong Kong for Foochoo. Off the Bashee Islands we had to heave-to in a gale of wind, and in the middle of the storm we struck something with such force that all hands thought we were ashore and must go to pieces. We sounded without finding bottom, and the land was invisible. What could it be? Well, sir, the brig began to make water, and gangs were sent to the pumps. We managed to reach Foochoo, and when the vessel was surveyed, what do you think was discovered? Why, sir, that a sword-fish had pierced the solid oak and sheathing with its sword, that was three inches in diameter, and had broken short off, leaving a space of an inch wide on either side through which the water flowed." And with that he cast another triumphant look round.

A little of such nautical talk went a long way with me when Florence was in sight; and our walk to and fro regularly bringing me abreast of her and her aunt, I dropped Captain Jackson and Mr. Thornton, to address myself to the ladies.

"Well, Miss Hawke," said I to the aunt, "here is fine weather at last, almost perhaps more than we want. Don't you prefer the last three days gale to this?" and I seated myself on the edge of

the skylight close beside her.   Florence closed
her book and looked up at me with a smile.

"I like the wind to blow us along," replied
Miss Damaris, "but not great waves which
throw one off one's balance and make existence
quite horrible.   Pray, Mr. Egerton," sinking her
voice, "what was the chief mate talking to you
about just know, before Captain Jackson joined
you ? "

"About his profession,—about ships."

"Oh, I thought as you passed that I overheard
one of you mention the name of the person who,
as I told you, so far as I am concerned, has no
further existence."

"You mean Mr. Morecombe.   I solemnly assure
you that his name was never mentioned ;" and
struggling to think for a moment what could have
made her imagine that the chief mate and I had
been talking about that man, the recollection of a
phrase Thornton had used flashed upon me, and I
burst into a laugh.   "I'll tell you what you heard,"
I exclaimed; " the chief officer was contrasting this
ship with another he has sailed in, and said that
her floor had *more camber* than this—meaning, as
he explained, that it was higher in the middle than
at the stem and stern ; that's the phrase you must
have caught and mistaken."

She peered into my face as if she would read me
through, and said, with a deal of acidity in her

voice, " Well, you see I have ears. I don't mind—indeed I can't help others talking, but *you* have given me your word——"

" And I am keeping it," I exclaimed, flushing up a bit, for I did not at all relish her utterly unfounded suspicion.

" Aunt, you are unnecessarily sensitive; I am surprised that you should question Mr. Egerton's plain assurance," said Florence, bringing out Egerton with a little struggle, but speaking with warmth for all that.

" Florence, how dare you! I am not questioning Mr. Egerton's plain assurance. I believe what he says. Mr. Egerton," turning to me and giving me a very gracious bow of her head, " I fully believe you, sir, and I beg your pardon if—— "

" Oh, pray, Miss Hawke," I began.

" Unnecessarily sensitive, Florence!" she whipped out, interrupting me, and rounding again upon her niece; " how is it possible that you can consider me so? Didn't I tell you that that horrid young man had told Mr. Egerton some odious stories about us when he was intoxicated—I don't mean you, Mr. Egerton—dear me! I am quite fluttered. And do you think I am unnecessarily sensitive because I desire that his wicked exaggerations should not be known to the passengers ; least of all," said she, lowering yet the rather hoarse whisper in which she was speaking, and eyeing Captain Jackson grimly as he passed by with Thornton, "that dreadful naval person there, who roars like a bull when he talks. Do *you* think me unnecessarily sensitive, Mr. Egerton?"

"I do not, madam," I replied, with great emphasis and just one peep at my darling's eyes which were upon me; "and I sincerely trust you will never deem me capable of betraying the trust you have honoured me with."

"No, indeed I have the highest confidence in your honour as a gentleman," said she, unbending her manner into the suggestion of a complete apology. "I hope you will forgive me."

"Oh," said I, "you embarrass me—forgive a lady!" And I flourished my hand and bowed, and she bowed, and Florence, who could not conceal her merriment, dropped her book as an excuse to hide her face. I saw Mr. Thompson Tucker staring at us out of his coil of rope. No doubt he wondered what was making this old lady and me so deucedly polite to each other.

"You talked, Mr. Egerton," said Aunt Damaris, soothingly and very graciously, "of returning in this ship. I presume, therefore, you will stay about three months in Sydney?"

"About that time, I believe," I replied, beginning to breathe short, for even when she and I were alone this sort of questions always bothered me terribly; but they were scarcely endurable when

Florence was near, for I did not dare venture upon a fib in my sweetheart's presence.

"It will give me much pleasure to see you at my house when you are in Sydney," said the old lady.

"You are extremely good," I answered. "Nothing will give me more happiness."

"That's a very long invitation, aunt," said Florence, laughing.

"Mr. Egerton has been exceedingly polite to me," responded Aunt Damaris, "and if there should be anything *colonial* in what you call the length of this invitation, my dear, I hope he will pardon my Australian manners."

There was something in the manner in which she said this that caused my darling to give me one of those intensely meaning glances which sweethearts, whether they have beautiful eyes or not, have a knack of casting at one another. I had not up to that moment addressed her, nor could Aunt Damaris have guessed the true state of our hearts from any single sign between us when she was present on previous occasions; but it happened when Florence lifted her eyes to my face in the manner I have mentioned that her aunt was looking at her full; and the effect of it upon her was shown by the speed with which she whipped round her sharp old face to stare at me. I gazed mildly into her greenish eyes until she removed them to Florence again. Well, thought

I, she'll be stumbling on the truth sooner or later, and then she'll be finding out who I am, and then—and I was musing in this fashion, whilst in the pause that fell upon us I watched the operation of Florence's intercepted look in the old maid's mind, noticed it stiffening her as the ideas it bred increased in number until her face took the hardness of a ship's figure-head, the thin under lip tightening into a mere line, and her sharp nose standing out with a heaving nostril past the lank sausage curl that embellished her starboard cheek, when I heard a sudden small plash over the port side, followed by a woman's long ear-piercing shriek that penetrated from one end of the ship to the other and came down in a sharp clear echo out of the sails.

I was too old a hand not to know what the soft peculiar sound of that plash signified, even though no yell should have followed to make a horror of the thing; I sprang in three bounds on to the hen-coop abaft the mizzen rigging, and looking over saw a child floating with its hands raised upon the glass-blue surface within a couple of feet of the ship's side. The vessel, as I have said, had steerage way upon her, and was moving through the water at the rate of about a mile and a half or so an hour. I threw down my hat, and singing out to Thompson, "Pitch me a life-buoy," I jumped into the mizzen chains and dropped into the sea. I was a fairly

good swimmer, though from want of practice no
hand at a long bout.   Slowly as the ship was
moving, and rapid as my movements had been, I
was surprised when I came to the surface to observe
the distance the two little lifted arms—for that was
all I could see—had already dropped astern.   I
knew that children drown quickly, and I struck
out with all my strength, taking the exact bearings of the child's hands by a group of heavy
white clouds on the horizon: and fortunate it was
that I had presence of mind enough to do that
same, for before I reached the spot the child's
arms had disappeared, but I could see the little
body just below the surface quivering in the
refraction of the wonderful translucent azure of
the water, and with a bit of a dive and a quick
grasp I had the bairn's head out of it, and looked
about me for the life-buoy.

There was the circular white thing within a few
kicks of my feet, hove, as I might guess, by a
sailor man, and in a few moments I had it under
my armpits, and the child atop—not dead, heaven
be praised! but nearly choked with the salt water
in it.   It was Mrs. Joyce's little girl—one of the
three children that had been playing about the poop
at hide-and-seek.   I held her on high, she was but
a feather in my hands, with a slant of the head to
let the water drain from her throat, and I could hear
cheers and cries rolling in a sort of broadside from

the ship's starboard bulwarks, which were black with the swarming of sailors and passengers, whilst aft stood a crowd motioning and shrieking. I tell you it was strange to hear those sounds coming along the smooth surface—every note clear as a bell, through a confusion of hurrahs and hysterical screaming, and the loud orders of the mate directing the hands, who were franctically at work in clearing away the quarter boat ready for lowering, mixed with the flapping of the canvas beating the masts as the vessel lifted with the swell and the straining of spars and the chafe of the running gear.

The ship came round very slowly to the faint draught that was stirring aloft, and if this had been my first experience overboard I should have found something like a new sensation in the sight of the stretch of water between me and her gleaming hull, leaning her shapely checkered side out of the yearning gurgle of the swell until you could see the water sparkling as it drained down the bends past the sheathing into the sea. But a man who has tumbled off a yard-arm into a smother of yeast and a hollow full of roaring can't be expected to make much of an adventure overboard in a calm, with a life-buoy around him and plenty of sunlight for him to be seen by.

The boat came down into the water with a rattle and a splash, the oars broke into a silver shining as they were raised after the first dip, and in a trice the little girl and I were lifted into her and rowed alongside the ship. The child was handed up to twenty pairs of arms extended to receive her, and I, dripping wet and feeling more like a water-rat than a man, scrambled into the mainchains and so got aboard. From the mainmast to the cuddy-front the deck was just a block of people, and there being plenty of mothers among them, they would have made some kind of fuss over this very cheap, mild exploit had I not hurriedly shoved through them on my way to my cabin, saying in reply to their "Well done, sir!" "A mother's blessing on you, young man!" "There's the right kind of stuff in you, sir!" and the like of such exclamations, "Oh, it's all right. It's no more than a ducking for either of us."

And yet, small as the incident was, it was of the right kind to cause a sensation : it was a break in the monotony of the sea-life; then again, no kind of excitement caused by accident upon the ocean surpasses the thrill sent through the heart by the fall of a person overboard, and all the women, and maybe all the fathers in that ship, would find a child tumbling into the water much more moving than had a man taken an involuntary header; and so combining these points with the electrical effect of the piercing shriek that followed the accident, the rush to the side, the shouts and screams of men and women, I could not be surprised to find the crowd of 'tween-deck and other passengers very much stirred and somewhat enthusiastically demonstrative as I passed through them.

I stripped and dried myself, and was soon completely dressed, and lighting a cigar stepped through the cuddy, up the companion ladder, to the poop. The moment I showed my nose Daniel pounced upon me: "Jack," cried he, "it was smartly done. The child owes its life to you. The least delay would have been fatal, for the child was under when you reached her." And as he said this up bustled the passengers, Mrs. O'Brien, full of Irish impulse, using her elbows that she might force her way to shake hands with me, Mrs. Jackson jostling Mrs. Grant, Captain Jackson jamming Thompson Tucker against Aunt Damaris, Mrs. Marmaduke Mortimer sobbing as an emotional young wife knows how on such occasions, and her husband hovering on the skirts of the others, waiting to catch my eye. It was what an actor would call an ovation, whatever *that* may mean, if it don't signify the pelting a fellow-creature with rotten eggs, and I was so exceedingly disconcerted that I was heartily sorry I hadn't turned in when I stripped myself instead of coming on deck.

"Mr. Egerton," cried Mrs. O'Brien, "ye're a hero; there's the makings of a thrue mother in you, and my blessin' upon you as a widow who has been a mother herself."

"It was a very smart thing, Mr. Egerton, let me tell you, sir," shouted Captain Jackson. "Had you been a sailor, you couldn't have shown more presence of mind."

"Mr. Egerton," cried Aunt Damaris, "I must shake your hand. Your conduct is truly impressive."

I am sure I cannot remember what I mumbled in reply to these and a dozen other courtesies and compliments. The smallness of the exploit made me feel that there is a deal of unconscious irony in the most generous of human impulses, and I was sensible of blushing like a girl as I bowed and wagged my head and begged them to say no more. But I was not to be let off yet; for on a sudden I heard a voice crying out, "Where is he? where is he?" and up rushed Mr. Joyce, the others making way for him, and seizing my hands he endeavoured to speak, but his voice failed him, and he looked at me only with the eyes of a man whose heart is full of tears.

"How is she?" I asked.

"Oh!" he answered in broken tones, "she will take no harm the doctor thinks. Nothing is to be feared but the shock to the nervous system. She is talking to her mother—' and breaking down, he called God's blessing on my head in barely articulate words.

His gratitude was so affecting that for the life of me I couldn't help a mist creeping over my eyes.

To God bless a man is but a conventional phrase : but when a father says the solemn words, when the blessing of the Almighty is asked for you by a man whose child's life you have saved, and who speaks with sobs in his voice and his face made infinitely affecting by gratitude, the sentence takes a wonderful significance, you feel there is more in it than sound, and the memory it gives is something to linger like a shining light in the mind for many a long year.

He explained how the accident had befallen. The forward end of the hen-coops which ran down either side the poop stopped short within half a dozen feet or so of the termination of the raised deck, leaving the rail open : the child had gone behind the square end of the coop to hide, and the nurse catching sight of the wee body at the instant it toppled backwards and overboard, sent up the wonderful shriek I have mentioned. I should have imagined that nobody but the mother could have delivered such a note, but be that as it may, when Mr. Joyce had explained how the thing had happened he again grasped my hands as if he would embrace me, and then hurried below to see after the little girl.

After a bit the other passengers drew off. Of all those who lived aft the only one who had not approached me was Florence. She had kept her seat, though I knew that her eyes were upon me all the while I stood surrounded by the others. Aunt Damaris had rejoined her, and seeing this I stepped up and seated myself on the edge of the skylight, just where I was before I went overboard, and addressing the old lady I said, " You were good enough, Miss Hawke, before our conversation was interrupted, to give me leave to call upon you at Sydney—— "

"Oh, how can you talk so coolly? " exclaimed Florence. "Do not you know that you have just saved a little child's life? It was nobly done." And she put out her hand. I took it and pressed it, lifting my cap as I did so.

" Don't speak of such a thing as that as *noble*," said I. " There was no risk. The sea is calm— the ship is scarcely moving. I had a life-buoy to support me. I should be a poor creature if I could take credit for such a twopenny job as that."

"You are a very enigmatical person, Mr. Egerton," said the old lady, eyeing me as if I had grown three or four feet since my bath. "You seem to treat the saving of life very lightly, sir. *I* think your conduct wonderful. How you can come back here and resume the conversation after an incident that made my very brain reel I cannot imagine."

"Why, Miss Hawke, I so value your kind invitation that I did not want this little upset to turn it wholly out of your mind, which might have happened if I did not take care to recall it."

"This little upset! How can you give the very near drowning of an infant such a term?" she exclaimed. "But perhaps you are used to danger, sir," eyeing me attentively, and then she said, doubtfully, "and yet you are too young to have seen enough to harden your nerves. I need not ask if you are in the army?"

"No," said I, feeling confused, "you need not ask that, Miss Hawke."

"Indeed," she went on, scanning me, "you have much more the look of a sailor than of any other profession I can imagine. The way in which you sprang from your seat there as if you knew exactly what had happened and where the child had fallen was quite nautical." And she fixed on me a keen scrutinizing gaze that was barely saved from grimness by the reverence my behaviour had excited in her mind.

"Well, you are not a sailor, are you?" said Florence, smiling and coming to my relief, the need of which she would perceive in the flush in my cheeks and my bothered air.

"No, I am not," I replied, which was true enough, for a man is a sailor only so long as he is in the calling.

"If you were you would not disown it," she continued, with a light coming into her eyes and a proud eager look into her face, as if she wished me to see her heart and the thoughts of me in it. " It is a noble calling, and no higher compliment could be paid you after what I *will* call your noble act, than to say you deserve to be a sailor."

Aunt Damaris twisted her lean face from her to me and from me to her with the old pecking of the nose that was like groping for information. At this moment Mrs. Joyce came up the companion hatch, and immediately catching sight of me ran up to me with her arms outstretched, and literally locked her hands round the back of my neck.

" Oh, Mr. Egerton," she cried, sobbing and crying and looking wildly into my eyes with her face close to mine, " how am I to thank you for saving my darling's life ? What am I to say to you ?" And almost incoherent in her language, as people violently affected often are, she called me noble and generous and brave, blessed me again and again, let go my neck to grasp my hand and kiss it, and then turned to Aunt Damaris and my darling—maybe because they happened to be near —and asked them to tell her if I was not the most courageous—— But avast! there is too much self-praise in all this to make its repetition agreeable to me, though having a yarn to relate I must tell you what happened in it.

Moving as the father's thanks were, the mother's went much deeper into my heart. I heard a sound of sobbing behind me, and afterwards learned that it proceeded from Mrs. Marmaduke Mortimer, whilst the tears stood in Florence's eyes and Aunt Damaris hung her head.

"He thinks nothing of the action," said the old lady, when Mrs. Joyce had ceased. "We were conversing before he jumped into the water, and no sooner has he changed his clothes than he comes back and goes on talking as if saving a child's life were no more than catching a fly."

"Nevertheless, Mrs. Joyce," said I, "I thank God for the privilege of preserving you from a great grief. Tell me now how the little darling does."

"Oh, very much better than we had dared hope," she answered. "I do not think there is anything to fear from the shock to the system, as she is almost too young to suffer in that way. She has asked to see you and give you a kiss? Will you come down to her?"

"Assuredly," I replied, and I followed her to the cabin occupied by the nurse and the three bairns. The father and Mr. Griffith were there—the other children and the nurse being in the parents' cabin —and the child lay in the top bunk under the scuttle, snug in the sheets and her fair hair covering the pillow. Mates, did any of you ever save the life of a fellow-being? If so you'll know what sort of feeling comes into one when one stands and looks at the living face and the grateful eyes, and hears the low notes of thanks, half-checked by overwhelming emotion, which but for one's action, be it great or little, would be white and dead and still. The name of this little girl was Lily—and a flower of that kind she looked, a bud rather, with the sunshine of her hair upon her.

"My darling," said I, bending over her, "I know the doctor does not want you to speak. I have come to give you a kiss, and to tell you that to-morrow you will be able to get up—at least I hope so—and run about the deck again : only you and your brothers must mind never to go near the edge of the ship, for it is not good for little boys and girls to tumble into the sea."

And so saying I kissed her tiny mouth and passed my hand over her hair and drew away. The father and mother were crying—and to speak the truth, my lads, so was I : at least there were tears in my eyes. But I whisked them off, and after exchanging a few words with the doctor and receiving another outpouring of fervent thanks from Mr. and Mrs. Joyce, I withdrew to my own cabin to stretch my back in my bunk until lunch-time, thinking that I had best not put myself too much in Florence's company when Aunt Damaris was alongside until my pet and I had settled upon some definite line of policy.

CHAPTER XIV.

FLORENCE CONFESSES.

IT does not take much to make a hero of a man (for a few hours) on board a ship, where there's nothing to talk about except the rate of speed, and what's for dinner to-day; and so at lunch I found myself a conspicuous figure, the ladies smiling at me, the gentlemen begging the honour of taking wine with me (the custom was not yet dead) whilst the stewards favoured me with their best attention. Florence as usual sat betwixt me and the captain, Aunt Damaris having up to this time made no objection; but the meal was very nearly over before I could manage to tackle her in one of our quiet, half-whispered talks, for now that Griffith had said that the child was doing very well (Mr. and Mrs. Joyce being absent from the table) the passengers felt at liberty to talk freely about the accident and to ask me questions, such as how I had managed not to hurt myself by jumping into the water (this was Mrs. O'Brien's), and how I managed to keep myself afloat in my clothes, whilst Captain Jackson exclaimed that if he hadn't known me to be a landsman by the questions I had asked the pilot, he should have supposed I was a sailor: "by one circumstance I took notice of, sir, and that was your having taken the bearings of the infant; for she had vanished before you reached the spot, and if you hadn't fixed her locality by some object—a cloud I take it, sir, for there was nothing else—why, then, all I can say is, little Missy Joyce would have been at the bottom of the ocean by this time."

The ladies shuddered, and Daniel pointed to the Joyces' cabin, with a grimace at the navy man. But the subject was too fascinating to be dropped. Mrs. O'Brien remembered the narrow escape of her little brother from drowning in the Liffey; Mr. Thompson Tucker knew a man who was a cousin of a fellow who had saved a bargee's life by heaving an open umbrella to him; and Captain Jackson had some remarkable stories to relate of Navigating Lieutenant Jones who jumped overboard in a heavy gale of wind and saved a marine who had tumbled over the side in a drunken fit, and of Master's Assistant Smith who had drowned a purser's mate in a squall by heroically jumping right on top of him when he was in the water, in the manly effort to save his life: to all of which I was bound in courtesy to listen.

However, when at last the conversation

slackened, Florence said to me, " You don't seem to care what I think of your conduct, Jack."

" You may be sure of that, my darling," said I with fine irony ; " you know that your opinion is of no consequence to me at all."

" Well," she continued, smiling, " whether you care about my opinion or not, I will tell you this, you ought to be proud of what you have done. It is a glorious thing to save a life."

" So it is, Florence, but we'll say no more about it, my pet. The child is rescued, is well, and there's an end. I have something more serious to talk to you about. Only, confound it, with your aunt making a fender of the skipper's elbow t'other side there, talking seriously is almost impossible. If Mrs. O'Brien looks, Miss Damaris will look, and if *she* looks she'll see."

" First, what is a fender, Jack ? " asked Florence, giving me my name now very easily, and with a distinct relish in the utterance.

" Why," said I, " something that you put over a ship's side to prevent it from being chafed."

" I am no wiser," she exclaimed. " But never mind. What is it that you want to talk to me seriously about ? " and she peered at me with one of those coquettish glances which in most girls never fail to set a man's heart galloping.

" How can you ask ? " whispered I. " I have told you I love you—have I not, Florence ? "

She pretended to look for something between her and Daniel.

"Answer me, my sweetest girl," said I, whispering always.

"Yes, you have," she replied, giving me a view of her left cheek that was full of colour.

"And do you know," said I, "that you have never yet told me that you love me?"

"Oh, don't talk to me in that way—here," she exclaimed, with her eyes on the tablecloth. "I am sure Captain Thompson hears you, and Mrs. Marmaduke Mortimer is staring so hard."

I peered at Daniel, but he had his shoulder towards us and was chattering briskly with Aunt Damaris. "Am I never to be alone with you, Florence?" I whispered. "It is fearfully hard to pretend not to care about you, and I have to do that when we're not alone. Can't you manage to come on deck this evening for a little walk with me: you gave me to hope you would not allow your aunt to have her own way altogether with you."

"If it is fine I will see," said she.

"It will be fine," said I. "Come up to breathe the fresh air; say at half-past eight. I have much to talk to you about."

She let me know she consented, though without speaking. Soon after this we left the table and I went on deck, where I found the ship sailing with

a wind blowing over the taffrail, topmast and
topgallant-stunsails aloft, the mainsail hauled up
and all the canvas from the royals down swinging
in and out as the vessel curtsied on the following
swell, beating the masts with a pendulum-like
movement and a sharp drumming of reef-points.
When you looked over the side it was like gazing
into the sky, so rich, limpid, profound was the
blue of the water, and there was a kittenish
playfulness in the tiny surges which ran along with
us for the space of a breath and then dissolved in
silver.　Northwards, whence the wind was blowing,
the ocean was an indigo blue, sloping and rounding
against the lighter heaven with the clear configuration of a swelling space of pasture land : but
this most beautiful colour grew paler as the sweep
of the sea-line took it east and west towards the
south, where the little clouds which passed over
our mastheads seemed to be waiting as if like a
flock of sheep they had found their pen down there:
whilst the hot white sun shining a little way on
the right of them, put the brilliance of snow
upon them for the sea beneath to reflect, so that
over either cathead the water ran away from the
cutwater in an azure that fined down into a kind
of satinish grey upon the horizon, making such a
contrast of the ocean blue deepening as it drew
upon our quarters that I have no words to express
the beauty of the sight.

Well, most uneventfully the afternoon passed: I lounged, smoked, conversed with first one and then another, inquired after little Lily Joyce, took a few turns with the father, and so killed the afternoon. Aunt Damaris and Florence came on deck for a while, but some of the other passengers gathered about them, there was no room for me, and no chance if there had been room to do more ·than carry on the humbugging masquerade of which, though we were not yet a week out, the obligation was beginning to eat into my soul; and so I stuck to the forward end of the poop, always thinking and plotting and scheming when I was alone, and wondering if ever I should have the luck to win the consent of that darling there to be my wife, and in what fashion our marriage was to be brought about. I happened to be delayed a few minutes after the second dinner-bell rang: and when I entered the cuddy everybody was seated, two of the usual lot only, Mrs. Joyce and her daughter, being absent. Mr. Joyce stood up as I passed him, as if I were the Prince of Wales, and grasped my hand afresh. This would not have confused me alone, but coming as it might be right athwart the discovery that I had already made, namely that Aunt Damaris was in the seat hitherto occupied by Florence whilst *she* was on Daniel's right, I was thrown right into the wind by it, coloured, stammered, asked after the child in a foolish way, and then pushed on, coming to a stand at the port end of the thwartship table.

There was a vacant place next to Florence, and I might have taken it, but besides that this deliberate mooring alongside my darling would have struck all hands as a very significant piece of behaviour, it would have been clearly an act of rudeness to decline what I was bound to regard as Aunt Damaris's offer of her own company. So after just pause enough to recover my confusion, whilst Thompson grinned at me and Florence fixed a Madonna-like gaze on the skylight above her, I took my customary place and fell to the plate of soup the steward put before me. After a brief silence between Aunt Damaris and myself, during which I had been expecting her to give me some reason for changing her seat, I was about to make some commonplace remark to her when she said, in her abrupt, pecking way, "I hope you are none the worst for your wetting."

I told her I was not: on the contrary, I thought I was the better for it.

"I believe I was a little short with you this morning," said she. "Pray did I express my sense of your heroic conduct in such a manner as to satisfy you? I *admired* your behaviour."

"Why," I answered, wondering at this talk, "you complimented me very much more hand-somely than I deserved, and so you may

suppose that I was a great deal more than satisfied."

"Then that assures me, Mr. Egerton," said she,
"that the impressions my friends like to make out
I produce on others are *not* what they represent.
My niece said I had as good as affronted you."

"Oh, indeed not," cried I; "very much the
reverse, believe me."

She screwed her head round to look past Daniel
as if she meant to repeat my remark to Florence,
but observing her and the skipper deep in conversation she returned to me. "I don't deny," she
continued, "that I am a little short tempered at
times. Who is not, pray? And really, Mr. Egerton,
you will bear me out when I say that the annoyance
I was subjected to at the beginning of this voyage
would have ruined the sweetness of an angel. It
is a perfect horror to me," said she, sinking her
voice with a sharp look along the table, "even
to *recall* the man in thought: and speak of him I
will not. You know what I mean. Had his
dreadful exaggerations been circulated, I should
have locked myself up in my cabin. Happily they
were restricted to you—they came into the keeping
of a gentleman—I am therefore safe. But oh, dear
me! how can my niece wonder that I should be
short tempered sometimes?"

"It was a terrible trial for a sensitive lady like
yourself," said I, "and a very narrow escape. And

a still narrower escape," continued I, turning my eyes on the keen bony old profile, "for your charming relative."

"Yes, no doubt. We'll say no more about it, sir," she exclaimed, not relishing this. And then, softening her manner, and speaking with a sort of forced indifference as if she talked merely for the sake of saying something, she asked, "Are you engaged in any business in England, Mr. Egerton?"

"No," I replied, "I am what is called a gentleman at large."

"Oh, indeed; that is a nice condition of life for a young man with brains, who is temperate and can devote himself to high pursuits such as going into Parliament and things of that kind. Have you any ambition in that way?" says she, with a bit of a smile that gave me the idea that my saying I was a gentleman at large had impressed her.

"I have sometimes thought of it," I replied, "but there's no use going into the House, you know, Miss Hawke, unless you can speak. I can *talk*—but I can't speak."

"Oh! but the social position is worth a good deal," said she, "whether you can speak or not. Probably you may have what, I believe, is called in England county interest?"

"Well—no! not exactly," said I, as if I was not sure.

" Is not Egerton a good name?" she inquired, still keeping her respectful bit of a smile. "I don't know. I ask for information. I believe there is a Lord Egerton. Is he any connection of yours?"

" One ought never to say no to a question of that kind," said I, beginning now to understand why the old woman had shifted her seat. "When people are of the same name, it is impossible to say whether they are relatives or not. Hawke, madam, is a very good name. Possibly you will be in some way connected with the famous admiral who beat De Conflans last century?"

"I don't think that can be," she replied, "for I cannot remember hearing that we ever had an admiral in our family, though my brother who lives at Clifton has taken the trouble to find out that we can go a long way back, and was talking of having a tree made. Have you a tree?"

" Not in my possession," I answered. "But my father had one"—in his garden, I might have gone on to say, but my answer went far enough.

" What is your father, Mr. Egerton?" she inquired carelessly, pretending to be more intent on the piece of fowl on her plate than on me.

" He was a solicitor," I answered.

" Ah, indeed; the law is a nice calling: so very respectable. There's a deal of money to be made at it too," says she, munching away at her dinner: and then she asked if my mother was alive, and

if I had any brothers or sisters, and where I lived
when in London, and so on. By this time it was
quite plain that she had exchanged places with
Florence for the purpose of pumping me: and as
she was not likely to attempt a job of that kind
without some reason, it dawned upon me that she
might have discovered that I was very much taken
with her niece, or that her niece was very much
taken with me, and that she had determined to find
out who I was and all about me, with the view of
putting herself between me and my darling, or of
allowing me to take Mr. Morecombe's place. You
will please understand that her questions had not
the character of rudeness they may appear to
possess as written. She tried—without much
success, I admit—to put a sort of maternal manner
into her inquiries, as though she would have me to
know that she made them not in the least degree
out of curiosity, but simply because she had taken
a fancy to me, and was interested in me, and
wanted for that reason to learn all she could about
me. But as I have said, my suspicion being
raised, I was very careful to give her truthful
answers to her questions, so that the only deception
she should be able hereafter to charge me with,
would be the sailing under false colours. To be
sure I constantly expected to find her turning her
green scrutinizing eyes upon me, suspecting who I
was by my replies; but it was quite evident she

had learnt nothing of Jack Seymour from her brother, outside the fact that he was a vulgarish sailor youth; and vulgarish mayhap I did not strike her as being, although she had talked as if she was willing to believe I knew something about the marine life.

Anyway, the mere circumstance of my supposing that she was pumping me in order to discover the extent of my eligibility as a marrying man, caused me to take extraordinary pains with my behaviour. I slipped several pretty compliments into her with considerable adroitness; and I give you my word, incredible as it may appear, in the tail of our conversation we actually grew sentimental—I don't mean as regards each other, but in our talk. It came about in this way. One of the stewards in passing the Mortimers capsized a small quantity of wine down the young wife's back. The sudden chill made her scream, whereupon Marmaduke fell into agonies of excitement and throes and convulsions of affection. Had the wine been a bucket of scalding water, and his wife half boiled by it, the disorder of the husband's mind could not have been more extravagant. He mopped her and swabbed her and caressed her, implored her by the name of Letitia to tell him if she was hurt, conjured her to be calm for his sake, and finished in his excitement in sweeping a decanter, a plate, and his knife and fork off the table.

Well, when this business was over, I said to Aunt Damaris, "What an affecting thing is the love of a newly-married couple!" meaning, you see, to be sarcastic, and never doubting that she would take me in that sense. Greatly to my surprise the grim, acidulated old lady heaved a sigh and said:

"It *is* affecting, Mr. Egerton. It is a dream—it soon passes—and that makes it affecting. But as a spectacle it moves us—some of us I should say—in another way; as reminding us of that which might have been, but never never came to pass."

Hallo! thought I, is it possible? Can *she* ever have been in love? And I gazed at the angular old countenance, showing hard and tense past the sausage curl, with a feeling approaching to awe. However, it was not my part to let her sigh for nothing, so I said, "I suppose, Miss Hawke, it is the doom of all of us to have what I may term blighted passages in our lives. But heaven is very merciful, madam, and teaches us how to forget that we have suffered."

"You are wrong, Mr. Egerton," she answered; "there are some natures that never *can* forget. There are scars which descend to the grave with one, but that is because the wounds were very deep and cruel."

"You speak feelingly, Miss Hawke," said I, thinking to myself, "And this is the sentimental

old lady who would have foisted that ass Morecombe upon her niece, and made the darling
miserable for life."

"You would think I had reason, were you to
know all," she answered, with a tremble in her
voice expressive of emotion that amazed me in her.
"It is too much the fashion to ridicule old maids.
I know nothing more objectionable and vulgar.
There are such things as marriages in heaven, Mr.
Egerton."

"I have heard of them," said I sentimentally,
"but never could quite grasp—— "

"Well, sir, *I* am married in heaven," she exclaimed, looking at me intently. "A beloved youth
died, the grave closed over him; he sleeps in
Sydney, and for thirteen years I never omit visiting
his resting-place once a month when at home.
In life we were betrothed, and his death married
us. No clergyman could have made us more one,
Mr. Egerton; and I know," continued she, casting
her eyes upon the skylight with a look of devotion,
"that when my time comes, the first to—— "

Plump at that instant came a small damp swab
through the open skylight on which Aunt Damaris's
eyes were fixed; it upset a number of things on
the table immediately in front of us, and caused
commotion enough to make the old lady squeal out.

"Who did that?" roared Daniel in a great rage,
hopping out of his seat. "Mr. Thornton, jump on

deck, sir, and find out who threw that swab here. Steward, pick the beastly thing off the table ! ''

All was bustle and noise. Mr. Thornton rushed out of the cuddy, and while one of the stewards removed the swab, others were baling up the sauce that had been upset, collecting the nuts, almonds and raisins, etc., which had been sent flying, and making the table presentable.

"It was that skylarking apprentice Murphy, sir," said Mr. Thornton, returning and resuming his seat. "The second officer had left the poop for a minute, and Murphy and another apprentice fell to chucking that swab at one another, and Murphy's last throw hove it through the skylight."

Daniel said nothing, but I thought I could detect the threat of a heavy " work up job " for Murphy in the inflamed profile of my old friend. The apparition of the swab—which the ladies should know is a sort of mop composed of old rope, used for drying the decks—put an end to Aunt Damaris's romantic references to the beloved youth who slept in Sydney. It was holy ground to the old lady, and not proper for me to intrude on unless she invited me to walk in again; and so the matter dropped. I was sorry, for not only was such a subject as that quite in my vein at that time, so that I could have listened to her with flattering sympathy and attention, but it was valuable as a revelation of her queer character. After the swab had been cleared away the conversation grew general, and then the ladies withdrew, leaving us gentlemen to sit alone over the wine, though no smoking was allowed in the cuddy. Daniel had smoothed his countenance, and it shone with his native good nature. I leaned towards him and said, "Skipper, I want my sweetheart on deck this evening for a half-hour's patrolling of your poop. If she offers to go on deck after dark, the aunt may think it her duty to follow. This will be objectionable. Will you manage to convey your compliments to Miss Florence after the second dog-watch, and ask her to take a few turns with *you?* Your invitation will make the thing shipshape in the old lady's opinion—always safe with the *dear* captain, you know, Daniel."

He grinned, and answered, "Yes, Jack, I'll oblige you; though, hang it! you seem to forget that I told you I should give up making love for you after the introductory business. I say, what did ye think of that swab coming down? How came such a thing as that knocking about the poop? Left in one of the quarter-boats, I suppose. It frightened somebody. Was it *you* that howled?"

I told him it was Aunt Damaris, and nothing having detained me at the table but the desire to get him to promise to ask Florence on deck that evening—thereby doubling my chance of having her to myself for half an hour—I left the cuddy.

The wind had shifted during dinner, and was blowing a very mild gentle breeze a little to the southward of west; the yards were braced to it, the stunsails in, and the ship sneaking through the smooth water on which the shadow of the evening hung dark. There was a streak of new moon overhead in the wake of the faint flush in the west where the fires of the sunken luminary were expiring. It was like a paring of pearl, without power to silver the dark wings of vapour which went slowly past it. The time was the second dogwatch, and all the crew would be forward on the forecastle, yarning and smoking, and taking sailor's pleasure; there was a fiddle going, and a hoarse, not powerful voice, was keeping it company. But nothing could be distinguished from the distance of the poop save the huddle of figures under the foresail, with outlines of them seated upon the rail, and rising and falling against the glimmering stars over the horizon. Upon the main deck the people moving about were distincter; you could see a haze of light in the great main hatchway, one grating of which was off; but the gloom along the bulwarks, melting into deep shadow about the galley and against the forecastle entrance, gave a kind of magnification to the deck appurtenances; the scuttle-butts, the winch, the foot of the mainmast, the coils of gear hung upon pins, and all such matters looked twice their size

in the graduated sweep of dusk, and the sails had
a soft large loom as they rose one above another
to the left of the streak of moon, every edge being
a clear white line of canvas against the darkness,
with stars glittering as it might be upon the bolt-
rope, whilst forward under the arched foot of the
foresail, past the shadowed groups of people there,
you could see a space of the great bowsprit and
jibbooms shooting into the dusky folds of the night
in the south. A sound of rippling water came up
from alongside, with a welling and gurgling under
the counter when the long delicate ocean swell
gently raised the noble ship, and went past her
with an ashen light in its broad brow which
stretched the star reflections it caught into lengths
of silver wire; and every heave seemed to set the
liquid shadows where they lay heaviest upon the
sea-line, flowing betwixt the stars and the water
like a thing that swarmed and thickened and
thinned to the motion of the wind.

You may talk of the loneliness of the deep being
felt most by the solitary watcher, by the castaway,
by the last of an abandoned boat's crew ; but to
me the sense of the ocean's tremendous solitude is
never more oppressive than on such an evening as
this I am describing, when the decks are full of life
made phantom-like by the dusk, and when the ear
goes away from the laugh and the murmur of
voices, and the eye from the swarm of moving

visionary shapes, to the distant starlit soundless space of sea, to those leagues of weltering waters along which the night-breeze passes moaning. Lads, it is the contrast of the life humming and stirring about you with the visible Eternity sweeping up to the ship from the height of the sky overhead, from the bottom of the fathomless ocean underneath, from the infinitude of the distances which girdle you, look where you will, that presses the feeling of loneliness with the weight of frost upon the intelligence of a man who makes one of the crowd in a ship and looks away over her bulwarks into the silence and darkness of the calm ocean-night.

But such thoughts as these would create but a very brief mood in me at that time. I hung about killing the evening as best I could; thinking a good deal of old Aunt Damaris and the queer stuff she had talked to me at dinner, and praying in my heart that she would not think it necessary to join Florence. The dew was heavy and glittered along the hencoops. One by one the people quitted the forecastle, eight bells were struck, the wheel was relieved, the watch on deck turned in, and only a few figures could be seen walking the forward decks. I peered through the skylight and saw Thompson Tucker playing at chess with Marmaduke Mortimer, Mrs. Mortimer sewing close beside her husband; Mrs. O'Brien nodded over a book, and Miss Grant was writing. Captain Jackson tramped the deck with the chief mate. Presently Captain Thompson and Florence came along the poop. It was too dark for me to be sure of them until they were close. Daniel said, "I have begged Miss Hawke to breathe this beautiful air and survey this calm ocean. But as you are more poetical than I, Jack, I will leave you to point out the wonders of nature, and I am sure you will forgive me, Miss Hawke, for taking advantage of the settled look of the weather to turn in." And without more ado off he went.

My darling laughed lightly and said, "What a strange man Captain Thompson is! But I like him very much."

"I have been waiting about for you," I exclaimed, "as if this deck were a country lane in Clifton. It was I who asked Thompson to invite you to take a walk," and I explained the reason.

"Aunt Damaris would certainly have accompanied me if the captain hadn't sent a very polite message by the steward," said Florence. "You are very clever, Jack. Almost too clever for my aunt, I believe."

"She is not likely to come on deck, is she?"

"No—there is too much dew. I am not to be more than twenty minutes," she said. "But this is delightful; I certainly shall not hurry;" and

dark as it was, I could see the gleam of starlight in her eyes, in the phantom-like glimmer of
her face, as she looked up at the stately, pallid,
shadowy heights of canvas silently doing their
work, and round upon the ebony of the sea.

"Will you take my arm? There is heave
enough to justify me in asking you."

She did so instantly, and we slowly patrolled the
deck. I talked a deal of impassioned nonsense to
her at the first going off: more than I have the
conscience to repeat. Loving her as I did, boys,
it was perfect happiness to have her sweet hand
nestled against my side, her dear face close to me,
and to enjoy her company amid a kind of ocean-
loneliness, so to speak—for the dark decks and the
black sea beyond inspired that feeling—which
seemed to bring us closer than ever the land
could have done in a commune of that kind. She
must have guessed, if she put herself in my company in this way, that I should make love to her,
and she let me do so as never had she suffered
before; and after awhile I won from her the ad-
mission I had made up my mind to get from her.
It came as we stood a minute or two looking at
the sea, just abaft the main rigging, where the
shadow of the mainsail threw a deep gloom upon
the deck; I had her hand in both mine, and, with
my lip to her ear, I asked her to tell me she loved
me—just to speak the words—that I might be surer

than ever her heart was mine, surer than I could be by looking into her eyes.

"Surer!" she whispered, with a little tremble in her hand and in her voice. "Have you such faith in *words?* But since you wish me to speak—oh, Jack! I am afraid I do love you. You are a wicked boy to have brought me to this confession, but I cannot help myself."

Well, whether she liked it or not, I had kissed her before the last syllable of her answer was fairly off her darling lips. I was just fit to jump clean overboard in the excess of my joy. Why, I had actually won her heart—won her fairly to love me and to confess it—ay, and to confess it in such a manner that, by the words, the tremor of the voice, the whole yielding of herself in the significance of the answer, the sweet and beautiful truth of it was as plain to me as the slice of silver moon that symbolized, as she looked down upon that silent ship and upon the two young lovers on her deck, the first passage of a sentiment that was to become like it full-orbed in time and as pure too. Won her to love me and to confess it! Think of that, said by Jack Seymour of this beautiful Australian girl, whom, but a few months before, he had hardly dared to lift his most secret dreams to!

It took me some time to collect my mind, to think reasonably, to talk, in short, as if I was not a stark, staring lunatic. We were then walking the deck, and my heart's delight, all her confusion gone, all her embarrassment vanished—thanks to the tender cover of the darkness—was talking to me with a glad light note in her voice, and a sort of freedom and ease as if something that had been between us was removed, as if she felt her heart fairly beating on mine at last.

"But what plans have you, Jack?" she was saying; "you told me you wanted to talk to me seriously, and so you have, you bad boy; and I also intended to talk to *you* seriously; for what have you done for my sake? You are following me to Australia; what are your plans? I have never liked to ask you this question before, but I do not mind doing so now," said she, with a little dying away of her rich voice.

"My plans, darling, are to marry you," said I.

"Oh!" she exclaimed, in a frightened way, "but you mustn't talk like that. You may say you love me, but you mustn't *dream* of marriage."

"Why, Florence—confound—ahem! not *dream!*" cried I. "Why, my own sweet darling, what do you think I love you for, but to be your humble, adoring husband till death parts us."

"Oh, yes! I know," she cried, still in a very frightened way; "but I couldn't *think* of marrying you without papa's consent."

"Well, my darling, we must get it," said I,

feeling somehow as if Murphy's damp swab had been flung at my head, and that it had penetrated to my soul.

"I would go on loving you for ever, Jack, but never could I become your wife without papa's permission," said she, in a voice of such plaintive melody that the yearning wash of the water alongside and the complaining of the light breeze as it sighed into the glooming folds overhead seemed the fittest accompaniment in the world for it.

"Then, Florence," said I, "you must write home to your father from Sydney, tell him I am with you, tell him we are *resolved* to marry, that you can only consent to return to England as my wife; and that letter, coming on top of your aunt's report of Mr. Morecombe, will bring us his consent."

"He would be more easily influenced by Aunt Damaris than by me," said Florence. "Oh, Jack, I wish she knew who you were! As Mr. Egerton, she thinks you a delightful person—she does indeed."

"But if you told her who I am, Florence," said I, "the good impression I have produced would be swallowed up in the earthquake the news would produce in her soul. Will it not be wise for me to go on steadily improving her liking, until I have brought her esteem to such a height that discovery won't affect her?"

"Do you think you'll ever be able to do that, you conceited boy?"

"I don't know, but I can try. What made her shift her seat to-day? She pumped me violently, asked if I was a connection of Lord Egerton, who my father was, and so forth. My darling, don't think me a puppy for the idea that she put into my head, but upon my word and honour, the anxiety she showed to find out all about me, my calling, my social position, my relations and so forth, was quite enough to cause me to believe that she wouldn't object to a match between us."

"I thought the same thing when she was talking about you after dinner," said Florence, simply.

"Well," said I, lifting the little hand under my arm to my mouth, "if I can persuade her to believe me good enough for my treasure as Jack Egerton, may not I hope ultimately to prove myself better as Jack Seymour? Suppose my secret is still ours by the time we reach Sydney; she has invited me to call upon her there, she prolongs my chance of improving her friendship. But suppose I were to go to her now and say, 'Miss Damaris, my name is not Egerton but Seymour; I am the young man whom my darling's papa objects to; I have no noble blood in me whatever, I am respectable, that's all'—what would happen? There'd be the biggest domestic flare-up that ever took place on the ocean. She'd shove herself between us for the rest of the voyage, and barricade her doors against me when we arrived at Sydney. I have a good three months yet to make her love me as a young man; so, my darling Florence, I am sure I had better remain Mr. Egerton for the present."

"Very well, Jack; have your own way. But what are your plans?" said she.

"My plans?" I answered, "do you mean when we reach Australia?"

"Yes."

"Why, I shall live as close to you as I can, and see you as often as you'll let me, and wait for your father's permission."

"Oh, how obstinate and determined you are! Suppose papa orders me to return home?"

"Jack goes with his heart's delight, trust him. Wherever she is, he is. There is only one person in this world of millions who can separate me from you, my own."

"Who is that?" says she, in a whisper of wonder.

"Florence Hawke," said I.

A tightening of her hand upon my arm was her answer to this. I proceeded: "My angel, lovers have no plans. They exist by chance and on chance. We are together at this moment by chance, and you will be my own glorious little wife by chance. Could I have planned Morecombe's sea-sickness, his quitting the ship drunk, your aunt's tears and respect for me because she thinks he told me the story of the conspiracy against your darling heart? No! do not ask me what my plans are. I have none. God, who loves honest young loving hearts, will dispose of us, let me propose as I please. If you will be true to me, my own Florence, my wife you are sure to be in the end. Will you be true? Will you always love me, my darling?"

We were in the deep shadow of the mainsail again, the right place for a holy confirmatory kiss; it was given and taken whilst Captain Jackson and the officer of the watch talked loudly at the other end of the poop, and whilst the helmsman stood black against the stars that slided up and down softly past the taffrail, and whilst the canvas aloft came in to the masts with a kind of sigh against the folds of darkness up there, and the exquisite white chip of new moon swung in the deep indigo of the sky above the topsail yardarm. Presently we were again quietly pacing the deck and talking thus:

"Did you know, Florence, that your aunt is married in heaven?"

"No; who married her there, Jack?"

"She did not say. Probably her husband will be one of those angels who are continually crying. Just before that swab came through the skylight

she was exceedingly sentimental; told me of some
youth who sleeps in Sydney, and whose grave she
has regularly visited once a month for thirteen
years."

"Oh, I know what you mean!" said Florence,
laughing. "There was a poor, sickly, hump-
backed musician named Acorn. Aunt Damaris
got it into her head that he was deeply in love
with her. I never heard that he actually proposed, but they corresponded, and when the poor
creature took to his bed she nursed him. Did she
tell you of that? How strange! It proves how
much she likes you, to be so *very* confidential."

"You have no idea, Florence, how sentimental
she was. She said they were not married until he
was buried, and then they became man and wife.
Queer notions of marriage some people have!
Murphy's swab stopped her from seeing him, I
think, for she stared up through the skylight as
if she expected Acorn to heave in sight. How do
you reconcile her sentimentality with her desire to
force that idiot Morecombe upon you?"

"Oh, she is sentimental for herself, not for
others, Jack. There are more people like her in
the world. . . . Don't talk to me of Mr. Morecombe! It is cruel that such a wound to one's
pride should be dealt with by relatives:" and she
drew herself erect with a note of deep resentment
thrilling through her voice.

However, I was now privileged to humour her
in the manner that pleased me best, and you may
wager I did not long allow my reference to Mr.
Morecombe to keep her resentful. Many a half
hour did I pass with this darling of mine afterwards, but never a sweeter one than this. Did I
say half an hour? It was a mighty long one if
that were all of it. I heard two bells go, and then
three bells; nine o'clock and half-past nine, boys,
and still she was with me. The rim of moon slid
down so far that at last it was looking at us out
of the liquid black over the slip of topmast stunsail
boom on the main yard; the wind had drawn into
a steadier gushing and was striking sparks of green
fire out of the sea as it blew the heads of the
little surges into froth and made a quick glance of
wan light all about over the deep shadow that its
own weight put upon the windward water. The
ship leaned lightly over, and was carrying her
fabric of glimmering canvas through the night as
silently as if a cloud of white vapour rested upon
her hull and was impelling her. It was this
silence aloft and away out in the darkness through
which the stars were shining that seemed to catch
the fancy of my darling, for again and again she
would come to a stand in a kind of listening
posture, though never letting go of my arm, and
I could see the sheen in her eyes—caught from her
soul and nowhere else, for the light was in them

when we stood where no star-beams could fall and where there was no lantern radiance—as she rolled them from the black ocean up to where the marble-like sails melted away into vague spaces, breathing slowly as though she saw more in what she looked at than the water, and the darkness, and the whitish loom of a ship's canvas.

She could not have flattered me more sweetly than she did by appearing to pay no heed to the passage of time. Most of our conversation is not a thing to be repeated, even if I could recall it; for my notion is that what passes between lovers is a sacred matter, no matter how foolish their talk might sound. What right have you to expect me to tell you how often I kissed this girl; whether I put my arm round her waist; the vows and hopes I whispered, and her caresses and answers? Why should young people wait until they are alone to talk and behave as sweethearts, if every squeeze, every sigh, every kiss, every look is to be put down in black and white and given to the world? Would Florence have let me put my lips to her soft cheek, and softer mouth, would she have met as she did all that my love for her had to say, had the sun stood over our mastheads instead of a slip of moon westering fast? No, boys; the darkness hath its secrets, and I'm for letting them be. As much as I choose to tell you you may relish and make the most of, but call me all the loafing land-

lubbers you can put your tongue to if you find me
burning a flare on the *Strathmore's* poop for no
other reason than that all hands may see Jack
Seymour and his Australian pearl making love.
Nor, after all, might you much thank me for
spinning out this yarn by an exact disclosure of
a job in the nice handling of which sailor men
are but clumsy fists. There were spells of silence
between us out and away more poetical and eloquent
than the finest language that was ever spoken,
and who is going to describe them ? When people
make love they never talk it as it is written down
in books. Not they. There's small heed of gram-
mar ; there's too much meaning for long-winded
speeches, and most of the sense that's found goes
out of the words into a squeeze of the hand, a
softening of the eye, the fondling of a wisp of hair
over the ear, a blush, a smile, a coming and going
of the breath that takes the place of purring among
men and women. That's it, boys ; and that's how
it was with us. Oh, of course there were intervals
of sense between us—breakings of fact into our
heaven, like the arrival by balloon of a carful of
commercial gents among the angels. We would
talk of Clifton, of Aunt Damaris, ay, and of Mr.
Alphonso Hawke, and of Emily (very tenderly)
and of my uncle and aunt and cousins ; but the
weight of my passion was always too much for
even the sturdiest of such topics, so that we were

never long upon any one of them before we had it
sloping away under us, and then—plump we would
fall into love-making, until a sudden loud call of
" Lay aft some hands to the weather main braces !
Ease off your bowlines forward ! Look alive,
men ! " startled my darling, who exclaimed, " Oh,
Jack, what time can it be ? "

There was a clock under the skylight. " Twenty
minutes to ten, Florence."

" Is it possible ?—then *indeed* I must say good-
night. What will my aunt think ? " And as the
watch on deck came rumbling aft, sleepily growling
as they stepped up the poop ladder, and flinging
down the coils of braces as if the thunder of the
sound over the heads of the cuddy passengers was
an annoyance that did them good to think of, I
conducted Florence to the companion, and with a
lingering hold of the hand, wished her good-night.

CHAPTER XV.

IN THE NORTH-EAST TRADES.

FLORENCE and I could not be aboard a ship full of people and so manage our behaviour as to escape their detection of the truth. It would have been impossible. We were put down as people who had fallen in love at first sight, but it does not take folks long to get used to things at sea, and our being seen together every day, I was almost writing every hour, soon made us stale as objects of curiosity, though Daniel told me that at the beginning of the voyage some of the passengers were fond of asking questions about us, Mrs. Marmaduke Mortimer and Mrs. O'Brien in particular; but of course he did not choose to know anything beyond that we were going to Australia in his ship, and that I was an old friend of his whom he had lost sight of for years.

But as I have before said, neither Florence nor I allowed the inspection or inquisitiveness of our cuddy companions to trouble us. But for Aunt

Damaris they would have been heartily welcome to the whole story. Yet, although the old lady had not the least imaginable suspicion that I was anybody else but the Mr. John Egerton I represented myself as being, she was not likely to be blinder to what was happening betwixt her niece and me than the others; and this being so it looked uncommonly to me as if matters were drawing up to a head when Florence told me next morning at breakfast that she had informed her it was I and not Captain Thompson whom she had been on deck with during the previous evening. The old lady was breakfasting in her cabin, and Florence took her place between me and Daniel, and that's how it was I happened at that meal to hear what had passed between them after my sweetheart went below.

"Aunt Damaris," said Florence, "was in bed, but wide awake. 'What has been keeping you?' she asked. 'How late you are! It is too bad that Captain Thompson should detain you for more than an hour in the damp night air. You promised not to be longer than twenty minutes.' I answered, 'Mr. Egerton joined me, aunt, and I have been walking with him.' 'And with the captain also?' 'No, the captain went to bed shortly after he had brought me on deck.'" On this. Florence said there was a silence that surprised her, as she expected her aunt would have

angrily rapped out at her for being alone in the
dark on deck with a young man. "Mr. Egerton,"
said she at last, "seems to have fallen in love
with you." "I think he has," replied Florence
in the simple way I could perfectly imagine in
her. "And are you in love with *him?*" asked
Aunt Damaris. "I like him very much," replied
Florence, "and I really don't see why I should not,
considering how warmly you have praised him to
me." "I certainly have praised him," said Aunt
Damaris, "and I think he deserves it. He acted
very nobly in saving Mrs. Joyce's little child, and
his behaviour on that occasion shows that he
possesses some very meritorious qualities. He is
quite a gentleman, at least *I* think him so, and his
manner towards me is full of modesty, respectful-
ness, and good taste. He tells me that his father
is a solicitor, but he is reticent on the subject of
his connections. I do not think he is a relative
of Lord Egerton; he would say so if he were. I
fancy your papa would like him. At all events, he
is the very antipodes of Mr. Morecombe, which,
after my experience of that wretch, is the most
pleasing thing I could desire in a young man.
Are you encouraging him, Florence?" "Well,
aunt, I like him," replied Florence; "and when
one likes a person one can't help enjoying his
company." Here Aunt Damaris fell silent awhile,
and then said, "I don't know what to do, I'm

sure. I'm in your papa's place, and should like to counsel you as he would. I certainly think Mr. Egerton a gentleman and an agreeable young man. But pray don't encourage him too pointedly, please. I want to know more of him, to see into his character and ascertain his true position in society. Perhaps his friend, Captain Thompson, will tell me about him. There is plenty of time; the voyage is only begun, and I have invited him to call upon me at Sydney, you know."

This was the gist of what passed, and my darling's comment upon it to me was, " I was sure, Jack, from a something I cannot describe in her manner, that she was thinking of you—I mean of the *real* you—Jack Seymour, dear. Mr. Morecombe is lost to us, you see, and my aunt will think of course that when I return to England I shall carry with me a heart unchanged for Sophie's sailor cousin; and consequently the genteel and evidently well-conducted Mr. Egerton would be so superior as a lover to the Jack Seymour whom poor Aunt Damaris had been made to think of as a vulgar insulting person, that it is a question for her to consider whether, if I choose to accept his refined attentions and to fall in love with him, she ought to interfere."

This was like a revelation to me, for, to speak the truth, I was so puzzled by my own identity that I would quite forget that one reason Mr. Hawke had in sending his daughter to Australia was to get rid of me, whilst it almost defied me to realize that Aunt Damaris would consider me as Jack Egerton such a substitute for me as Jack Seymour as would be very acceptable to Alphonso, who wanted breeding and name in a man. You see it is hard to think of yourself as two persons; but when my darling, with the sagacity of a clever little woman, had interpreted one idea at least that lay in her aunt's mind, I found on a sudden the old lady's politeness to me and her apparent disregard of my transparent enjoyment of her niece's company vastly more intelligible than when explained merely by the circumstance of my having borrowed an aristocratic name and of knowing all about the plot which had brought her and her niece and Morecombe together in one ship.

We took the north-east trades in twenty-seven and a half degrees north latitude, and carried them down to the parallel of Sierra Leone. In all that while nothing happened outside or inside the ship to call for particular notice. I never lost a chance of being with my darling whether on deck or in the cuddy, and my opportunities were perhaps improved by the circumstance of Aunt Damaris taking a cold that had kept her in her cabin for a week, though I do not know, had she been well, that she would have checked my constant association with Florence. Before she took cold her behaviour to me was quite gracious, and so far as my darling and I were concerned, her attitude gave me the notion that she had made up her mind to let things "slide." Sometimes she would take her place between Daniel and me, sometimes seat herself on Daniel's right, with a capriciousness that indicated a mood not wholly resolved. Whenever she sat next to me she would be constantly making experiments in the shape of carelessly put questions touching my past life. I cannot remember that I fibbed, I hope I didn't; but I was exceedingly cautious in my replies. I gave room for her imagination to tumble about in by artfully importing a certain large ambiguity into my answers, so that she was never in a position to say that I was *not* highly connected, and not in other ways more important than I chose to let her know, though I also took care that she should never afterwards be able to charge me with having told her a real caulker.

A day or two after her talk with Florence in her cabin, she sounded Daniel about me, as my friend made haste to let me know. I was with my darling on deck, looking over the stern at the hollow green seas and the Mother Carey's chickens flashing through the spray in the wake of the ploughing keel. My friend rolled up to us and said : " Jack, Miss Damaris Hawke has been asking me questions about you, my lad. She met me coming out of my cabin, hauled me to the table and fired away. Have you told her that you're the son of a nobleman?"

"Certainly not," I replied, looking from him to Florence, who was watching him with laughing eyes.

"Well, then, she seems to have some notion of that kind in her head," said Thompson. "She says to me, 'Weren't you at school with him, captain?' and I answered 'Yes,' for what is a ship but a school, and a mighty rough one too? and Jack and I were at sea together, Miss Florence, as of course you have heard. 'Did you know his father?' said she. 'No, ma'am,' said I. 'He is a solicitor, he says.' 'Ay, and a first-class solicitor too,' I answered. 'He is a most gentlemanly young man,' says she, kind of sounding me, 'and I wish you could tell me more about him, for his gallant exploit the other day, coupled with his politeness to me, has made me feel very much interested in him.' Well, you may suppose I wasn't going to swallow *that* view of it," said Daniel, with his beaming face turned full upon Florence, who was biting her lip with a look of mingled merriment and confusion; "I quite understood what she was driving at, and if I hadn't been afraid of putting my foot in it by contradicting something you might have told her, I could have spun her on the spot a tiptop yarn about you, Jack—something to make her hair curl.

For, my dear fellow, if she wants you to be a lord's connection, *be* one, man—eh, Miss Florence? Hang it! if it be true that we all come from Adam and Eve, then who's going to call me a liar if I say that the Queen of England's my sister?"

"I am glad you didn't invent," said I, laughing. "If no more passed between you than what you have related, then you gave her no information at all."

"Well, I didn't commit myself," he answered; "I didn't say you *were* a nobleman's eldest son; but as I'm glad to give an old shipmate a hand, I just turned to and gave her my opinion of you, cracking you up in a speech that lasted so long that before I had come to the end of it I had worked a look into her face that was like asking me to hold my jaw. And don't you deserve all the good I can say of you? I am sure Miss Florence thinks so;" and with a comical bow to her, and a loud genial laugh, the large-hearted little fellow stumped off, instantly forgetting all about us no doubt as he rolled his eyes along the ridged horizon to windward and took a skipper's squint at the set of the booming canvas.

But as I have said, I lost sight of Aunt Damaris when the north-east trades began to blow, and heard of her only through Florence, who reported her as very peevish and quarrelsome, her nose of a fiery red, her eyes streaming, and her voice little more than a kind of decayed hoarseness. I was careful to send my respectful compliments and sympathetic inquiries to her again and again, but I will not pretend that I lamented her absence. Hour after hour Florence and I were together, until Mrs. O'Brien would look as if she felt it her duty to come up and congratulate us, whilst Mrs. Marmaduke Mortimer would simper up at us from her book or work as we passed, with an air of languishing encouragement and sympathy that was as comical as it was kind.

The trade wind blew nobly; it swept over us a couple of points abaft the port beam in a swinging torrent that kept the brave fabric humming and roaring day and night. We carried royals and fore-topmast stunsail to it, and with a sort of leaning down of her nose, and heel enough to give her keen stem the slanting leverage it wanted to tear the emerald seas into snowstorms, the *Strathmore* drove along with a thrilling through the length of her that was like the chattering of your teeth, and a noise of thunder aloft as if every ivory-hard rounded sail held a storm in its hollow. I remember one day standing with my darling—who never seemed to tire of the beautiful sight the ship and the sea made, whether in calm or storm— near the wheel, watching the whole length of the vessel sweeping with long floating lurches athwart the surges. I had my eyes on her sweet face, standing out with delicate clearness against the greenish sky over the rail, and was studying with a lover's delight the varying moods in it as she would look from the height of the gleaming royals to the hissing and seething yeast that spread away, from where the lee cathead overhung the water, with a broad swirl of giddy dazzling white.

Suddenly she said, "Does not the ship look grander from the other end there," pointing to the forecastle, "where she would seem to be coming towards you with her noble sails swelling out instead of always being in hollows as we see them here?"

"We can soon satisfy ourselves on that point," said I, "if you'll take my arm and go with me there."

"But the men, Jack——"

"My darling, we're not going aloft: there'll be no footing to pay," said I, laughing and catching up her hand and putting it under my arm. She hung in the wind a bit as if she was afraid; she had never left the poop before, and "Oh, Jack! what would the men say? Would they be rude?" I conquered her timidity at last, and, singing out to Mr. Thornton that I was going to show Miss Hawke what the sea looked like under the bows— for he stared to see me leading her down the poop-ladder—we gained the quarter-deck and went along the waist to the forecastle ladder.

The 'tween-deck passengers were hanging about,

chiefly to leeward out of the way of the wind, smoking and talking, the women nursing babies or watching their youngsters cutting capers in the scuppers. Florence was critically eyed as she passed along, her dress, from the feather in her hat to her little boots, being attentively scanned by those of her own sex amongst the poor people, and I noticed a deal of admiration in the looks of the men, along with a peering past of one another to follow her beautiful figure, whilst they muttered their approval. When we came to the galley and I stopped to show her the ship's kitchen, the boat-swain stood in the lee door taking a few furtive pulls at a sooty pipe, and talking to the cook and the baker, who lounged against a sort of dresser with their bare pale arms crossed upon their shirts.

"How are you, Shilling?" said I. "Cook, beg pardon for intruding. I want to show this lady where all the beautiful dinners you send us aft come from."

The boatswain put his pipe up his sleeve and respectfully flourished his thumb at his mole-skin cap. "Glad to see ye forrard, Mr. Seymour," said he: and then, sucking in his cheeks with a glance of alarm at Florence, "Hegerton I mean, sir. Why, shiver my topsails, as stage sailors say, where's my old memory awandering not to recall that Hegerton's the word, and Hegerton it is."

"We're going to have a look at your ship from

the forecastle, Shilling," said I, winking to him not
to feel distressed. "Meanwhile, Miss Hawke,"
said I, mighty polite before these men, "what do
you think of this sea-kitchen—caboose the old word
is? Do you see those big coppers there? That is
where Jack's pea-soup, and his pork and beef and
duff are boiled. Oh! you should taste those
delicacies. Cook, once upon a time a rough
sailor man pulled the likeness of the hull of a
Chinese junk out of his bosom and asked me what
it was made of. I smelt and peered, and said,
why, it looks like a piece of teak that's been fished
up out of the bed of the ocean. 'Nothing of the
kind,' says he; 'it's a bit of the salt beef that was
served out to the crew in the last ship I was in, and
I'm going to make a will all about this here bit of
beef and nothing else—for it's all I own—and
bequeath it to the British Museum, as the gift of
an English sailor to the people of the United
Kingdom.' What do you think of that, cook?"

"Think?" answered the cook, who had a rather
sour eye; "why, that that rough sailor man was
a-coddin' of you, sir."

"No, no!" exclaimed the boatswain; "coddin'!
why, I've been shipmates with beef that hard ye
might have carved it into bricks and built gentlemen's willas with it."

Here some of the emigrants came shuffling
behind the boatswain and peering over him in

order to see what was going forward; so I made
haste to call Florence's attention to the pots and
pans, and odds and ends of this marine kitchen,
and then, passing my arm through hers, helped her
up the ladder until she stood upon that raised
structure in the bows of a ship called by the name
of top-gallant forecastle, and corresponding with
the elevated after-deck named the poop. There is
all the difference in the world betwixt the fore and
hinder parts of a ship, and the distinction is never
more felt than when the vessel is at sea, sailing
along. Aft, everything is neat and clean and
sparkling: ropes carefully coiled, deck white, and
a glimpse of carpets and fine furniture through the
brilliant skylights. But the forecastle is Jack's
home, and the roof of his tapering habitation has
as rough and coarse a look as the interior. The
great anchors lie stowed behind the rails; the capstan has a rude appearance; maybe you'll find a
pair of dungaree breeches and a shirt or two
swelling out upon the forestay; the giant bowsprit
and jibboom fork far away out, and the landsman's
eye is bewildered by the complication of shrouds,
horses, footropes, bobstays, which come into the
ship from the vast spars.

"What is that hole there?" asked Florence,
pointing with one hand and keeping tight hold of
me with the other.

"A hatch called the forescuttle; one of the doors

which lead into the sailor's parlour and bedroom;" and I conducted her to the edge of it, and we peered into what looked as dark as a pocket, with a streak of light falling down upon a dark-green seaman's chest just below. An instant after a grimy Scandinavian face looked up at us out of a mop of sprawling red curls; whereupon we drew back, for, hard as the shoregoing mind may find this saying to accept, it is nevertheless true that the sailor is a human being, duly endowed with sensitiveness, and that he does not like people to peep and stare at him in his sea-home as if he were a bearded woman in a cage or a Chinese dwarf in a booth. There were one or two seamen at work on the forecastle, but no notice was taken of us beyond the sidelong squint which salts have a knack of throwing at you over the bronzed lump that stands for the outline of a junk of tobacco between the jaws.

"The right place to see the ship is from that spar yonder," said I, pointing to the flying jib-boom; "were there only a lady's saddle aboard, and I could manage to seat you there, you'd enjoy such a dancing gallop through the air, with this great ship thundering after you in your wake, and the sky opening ahead of you to receive your darling form as you come, that you'd have to go back to the time of the Arabian Nights to meet with such another flying steed."

"Oh, I never could get out there!" cried my pet, rounding her beautiful eyes at the distant dancing boom.

"No, and I don't mean that you should try," said I. "But come with me—I'll show you all that is to be seen;" and I took her to the lee rail, just clear of the clew of the topmast staysail, and pointed aloft.

Upon my word it was a noble sight, well worth the journey to the forecastle. The trade wind had settled broad abeam within the past two hours, and the yards were braced far enough forward to enable us to see past the lee leeches as far as the mizen-topsail. The ship under royals and fore-topmast stunsail was flashing her lee channels through the leaping, blowing smother of white; the huge sails went leaning up, one above another, and one yardarm passed another, until the blue sky, along which the trade clouds were driving, seemed to be a vast surface of canvas : the sun was to leeward of the royal-mastheads, and the white light poured down with a sort of blazing gushing upon the bosoms of the sails, leaving the foot of them in shadow against the dazzling azure which swept between the straight black lines of the yards and the rounded bottoms of the cloths ; every staysail was in gloom and stood in superb curves like delicate pencil-drawings ; up behind the heads of the inner and outer jibs you saw the fore-topmast stunsail pulling like an imprisoned cloud at its slender boom; and looking from there to the end of the long, slightly bowed spars which shot out of the forecastle betwixt the knight-heads and soared above the line of the horizon, you ran your eye over the flight of carved-like, steady staysail and jibs pointing one above another, one darkening a space of the brilliant white of the next with the shadow of its clew, whilst, like the swing of a pendulum, these gleaming wings swept and soared over the deep, clear, yeasty ocean blue, that ran away up the dolphin-striker until the horizon stood as high as the junction of the bobstays upon that outrigger. But the wonder and delight of this most beautiful sea-picture lay, not alone in the thunderous heights of canvas; whatever the eye sought yielded a charm; in the sparkling upon the decks, as the slanting heave of the ship shifted the dancing sunshine along her; in the heap of gem-like white water rushing in whirlpools past the line of her bulwark rails; in the play of surges smoothly rolling away to leeward, but coming along on the weather side in curved blue ridges that grew into a transparent green under the bows, every surge with a blowing of crystal smoke about its luminous brow, and here and there a fragment of rainbow that swept along for a breath with the wind, and went out like the flying-fish that sparkled in silver showers from the violet-coloured slant of the seas in a clear leap across the fresh foam of the melting crests, and a vanishing flash into the dark gleaming blue of the billow beyond.

But the best thing of all was to lean over the weather-rail close up at the head, and look down to where you could see the sharp stem with its sheathing of yellow metal, shearing like a hissing hot thing through the water with a liquid slide into the brilliant hollow that would heave the beautiful soft white foam so high as to look almost close to our hands, whilst the rush of the half-buried bows would drive an acre of it creaming ahead faster than the vessel was sailing, until the outer line of the shining swirl seemed a ship's length distant; and then up would float the knife-like cutwater, as if the noble ship meant to bodily leap the space of snow she had hurled forward on her path, the shining water draining down her, and the sea drawing into a hollow beyond, and you felt the glorious buoyant life of the deep-blue surge— oh, how different from the drunken horseplay of narrow waters !—as the vessel poised her beautiful bows on the summit of a long, bright, washing Atlantic sea, looking down as it might be for a breath only into the gleaming shadow, laced with foam, that seemed to be rushing up to meet us, and *then*, with all her sails swelling out their white bosoms for the plunge, swept like an albatross into it, sending a blue wave roaring away on either hand, and filling the great trough with foam.

Man alive! there is no feeling like to what you get from this speeding of a great full-rigged ship athwart the steady trade. A fig for your steamers, say I! The delight, the hope, the sense of liberty, the overwhelming feeling of life that is put into a man by it, makes a boy's heart of the weather-worn organ that beats behind the leather of his breast, and if tears should be in his eyes when he raises them from the windy shining scene to the deeper blue above the mastheads, where the spirit of God looks down on the poor sailor, Jack Seymour would deserve but little mercy if he found anything in those drops to make him grin. And was it wonderful that rainbows should have gleamed in the foam under us, and that every bubble should have shone as if it were an emerald or a ruby or some rich gem of that kind under a crystal cup, when the light of my darling's eyes was upon the sea and the lustre of her wind-swept face, made rosy by the steady blowing, streamed down upon the hurling snow? Well, to be sure, this is a touch beyond nature and a shade too poetical; but I may safely say that never looked she more lovely than on that day when she would turn her brilliant, wondering, admiring eyes from the blue sparkling that raced sweeping by, to me that I might mark her enjoyment, and from me to the leaning towers of canvas above, which she would watch with one hand on mine to support her, and the other to her forehead, whilst the gold of her hair rippled and trembled under her hat, and the pearls betwixt her open red lips shone like the foam-flakes which blew up with every send of the ship's crushing bows. Still too poetical, my lad; but no matter, since this ends my bit of description.

CHAPTER XVI.

ABREAST of Sierra Leone we lost the north-east trades—you may call the longitude nine degrees north. At noon the sun stood almost directly over us, and a man's shadow was so short that it needed half-an-hour's swim of the sun down the ecliptic to persuade him that he had one. You felt the heat when the swinging trade wind ceased to blow. It went out in a breath, the last of its steam-like clouds rolled away over the sea, and the ocean fell into a trance. This was in the afternoon; everybody was on deck, Aunt Damaris among them; but when that wonderful calm came along in the wake of the last soft faint sigh of the wind, the hush of it seemed to fall like the night itself upon the ship. From under the shadow of the awning aft you looked along and saw the light blue of the sky dazzling like silver over the sea betwixt the main and foreshrouds on either hand, and whenever the delicate swell let the ship lie steady for a space on a level keel, then, wherever the sunshine poured, you would see all erect things, the lower masts, the figures of men and women, the galley chimney, the standing rigging, vibrating with the appearance of revolving in the hot steamy atmosphere, like cork-screws slowly turned. The sea went away from the ship's side in a surface of blue oil to the sky, and melted there in a haze that made the distance look immeasurable. The lull was so soothing that in a very short time Captain Jackson was snoring at the top of his pipes out of his wide-open mouth, his wife dozed over a book, Mrs. Marmaduke Mortimer slumbered on the skylight with her head on the ship's ensign—everybody appeared mesme-rized; the hens in their coops muttered as you may hear them in their roosts at midnight: the emi-grants lay about the decks wherever the shadows were; the sailors nodded over their jobs, and an ordinary seaman greasing down the foreroyalmast swung there under the mighty violet dome as though slumbering to the lullaby chanted by the soft white canvas as it gently came into the masts with the heaving of the vessel.

It was desperately hot in the cuddy in spite of windsails and open skylights, and nothing could have taken us to it nor detained us in it but dinner. The passengers were not in a good temper, and Captain Jackson led off at table by exclaiming, as he stirred and looked into his plate,

"What! pea-soup within a stone's throw of the equator!"

"Nothing like hot stuffs in hot weather," said Daniel from his place at the head of the table; "they make you feel cool afterwards."

"I say, captain," cried Mr. Thompson Tucker, "any chance of a breeze, do you know? There are more lively things than being stuck like a buoy in the middle of the ocean."

"Can't say, I'm sure," replied Daniel, turning up his red face to the skylights; "we never hope for much in the way of breezes hereabouts."

"Then what are we to expect?" exclaimed Aunt Damaris, sharply; she was sitting in her old place, leaving Florence to me.

"Why, ma'am, we're to expect what they call catspaws; troublesome currents of air which keep common sailors swearing," answered Daniel.

"We're in the parallels termed the doldrums," said Captain Jackson, with the perspiration standing in globules upon his face. "Scalding pea-soup in the doldrums!" And he wiped his forehead with a large silk pocket-handkerchief.

"Why does he eat it?" whispered Florence to me.

"I don't think it much matters," said Aunt Damaris, snappishly, "whether you call these calms dumdrums or tantrums. They're very annoying, and always make me regret that I am not in a steamer."

"*I* called them doldrums," said Captain Jackson, warmly, "though no doubt they occasionally produce tantrums."

"Of that I am quite sure," exclaimed Aunt Damaris, with a giggle; "and hot pea-soup does the same thing at times, doesn't it, Captain Thompson? Doldrums, indeed!" cried she, suddenly changing her manner; "if sailors give things imbecile names, I wonder sensible people can be found to repeat them."

"Steward!" bawled Captain Thompson, "tumble on deck and see if there's a breath of air, and if so, have the mouth of the windsail slewed to it," while Florence whispered to me, "How pettish aunt is! I hope there won't be a quarrel;" and Mrs. Jackson scowled at the old lady. However, the navy man made no answer, and we were hauled clear of what threatened to be a shindy by Thompson Tucker saying, "I always heard that the sea was monotonous, but never could have guessed what a real bore it is. How can people be sailors? Think of getting up every morning and always seeing the same thing. What have you got at sea? There are no theatres, no concerts, no balls—there's nothing to expect—no letters, no shooting, no hunting, no riding—there's nothing to do except to eat and drink and go to bed. Who'd be a sailor?"

"If there were no sailors you'd get no tea nor

sugar, nor ivory fans and ostrich feathers and
sealskin cloaks, and hundreds of other nice things,"
says mild Mrs. Grant.

"And who'd fight your battles?" said Captain
Jackson, defiantly.

"Yes," said Mrs. Marmaduke Mortimer, "if
there were no sailors, England would be invaded,
and how dreadful that would be;" to which her
husband added, "Dreadful indeed."

"As to fighting my battles," exclaimed Thompson
Tucker, "all that I can say is, if I can't do that
for myself, I don't know who'll do it for me. However, I'm not going to argue that men are not very
kind to put on loose blue trousers or red coats and
go out and shoot my enemies. Whenever I consider how little I am asked to pay in support of the
army and navy, I always feel that it's a cheap
let-off for me. That's why I'm never annoyed
when a military or naval officer gives himself airs.
I say, 'No, let him be proud of being what he is;
he's quite welcome to think himself a finer person
than I; if he didn't, he'd call himself a fool for
venturing his life for a trifle of money and a suit of
livery which he has to pay for himself;' and then,
you see, *I* might have to do it instead."

Aunt Damaris applauded this loudly, no doubt
because it looked to be a kind of slap at Captain
Jackson, whom she detested, while Mrs. Jackson
declared that she had never heard such sentiments,

and Miss Grant piped out, "Oh, I dearly love soldiers!" For my part, I could not help laughing loudly at the stupid creature's reasoning, and Daniel joining in, our volley of mirth set some of the others grinning, and the rest of the dinner-time passed off without any further marked exhibitions of temper.

Aunt Damaris was afraid of dew, but for all that the heat of the cuddy proved too much for her and drove her on deck. It was about eight o'clock, and she found me sitting with Florence, but she said nothing: merely asked me to place a chair for her near her niece, and so joined us.

"Take care you don't catch cold again, aunt," said Florence.

"I must take my chance," she answered; "I cannot stand the atmosphere downstairs—you could bake bread in it."

Here the vessel gently leaned, the mizzen-topsail and top-gallantsail came in sleepily to the mast and shook down a shower of dew that pattered on the deck like a small fall of rain.

"Why, what is that," cried Aunt Damaris, looking up into the breathless black heavens, in which the planets were shining like moons, whilst the myriad orbs behind them seemed to convert the firmament into one vast Milky Way.

"Dew," said I, "and I am afraid it will drop upon you wherever you go, for it collects fast upon

the ropes and rigging as well as the sails and yards.
If you have an umbrella in your cabin, madam——"

"I have, Mr. Egerton ; but I'm not an Indian
princess," said she, "with a retinue of miserable
black slaves to hold umbrellas up over me, and I
really feel too languid to hold up one myself."

"You need not do so, Miss Hawke," said I. "At
all events, after your late bad illness, I am determined not to let you run any risks, so if you will
allow me to get your umbrella—— "

"Oh, Mr. Egerton, you are very kind and attentive," said the old lady, with a perfect gush of
feeling coming out along with her words. "I am
sure I am very sensible of your politeness, sir—I
am, indeed." And another patter of dew draining
down from the swing of the canvas on high, she
started and said, "The steward will find an
umbrella in a bundle under the lower bedstead—tell
him not to open the strap, but to pull the umbrella
out, and to be very careful to—— " and she followed
up with about twenty directions, winding up with,
"Florence, you had better fetch it : the steward is
sure to upset something and pull things about."
Whereupon my darling jumped up, went for the
umbrella, and returned with it.

I stepped up to one of the apprentices and asked
him to get me a couple of rope-yarns, and seized
the handle of the umbrella to the back of the old
lady's chair : and thus sheltered, she pronounced

herself very comfortable and extremely obliged to me for my attention. When the other passengers caught sight of this umbrella, some titters went flying about the shadows along the poop, and I heard Captain Jackson say to somebody he was talking to near the wheel—the navy man never could subdue his voice—" Well, confound me if ever I saw an open umbrella at sea before. Were a squall to come now and blow her overboard, damme if the picture wouldn't be like the flight of a witch on a broomstick ! "

" Did you hear that ? " gasped Aunt Damaris.

" I did," I replied; " it is a very rude remark, but as it was not meant to reach our ears, it will not do to take any notice of it."

It was a wonder that I managed to speak, for I was nearly choked with suppressed laughter, whilst I could see Florence by the clear light of the stars that came slanting fair upon her over the port quarter, shaking with merriment.

" Of all vulgar, horrid ｉpersons," began Aunt Damaris; but Florence put her hand on her arm— " Dear aunt, for goodness sake don't let Captain Jackson's impertinence anger you. Think how uncomfortable it would be for us should there be a quarrel. He cannot be a gentleman to utter such a remark in a loud voice, and therefore you can very well afford to take no notice of him."

" Gentleman ! " cried the old lady, with her face

glimmering under the blackness of the umbrella like the reflection of your countenance in a looking-glass in a dark room, "why, I am beginning to think that word perfectly horrible. If a captain in the Royal Navy isn't a gentleman, if the son of a baronet of ancient family isn't a gentleman, who ought to be, pray? And what excellent samples of gentility the two specimens I mention, prove!" she cried, with a perfect writhe in her voice in the bitterness of the sarcasm she intended; "the one falling drunk and using disgraceful language, and the other shouting out insults to an old lady at the top of his voice, like a costermonger crying fish!"

"He cannot moderate his voice," said I; "he has evidently been used to speaking-trumpets. However, if you wish it, Miss Hawke, I shall be glad to make his affront to you a personal one, and ask him what he meant by his remark."

This seemed to please Aunt Damaris, but Florence exclaimed, "Please do nothing of the kind. We cannot be sure that he is ignorant or has no suspicion of Mr. Morecombe's motive in joining this ship—at all events, it is best to be on the safe side, and consider that the secret may not be *wholly* our own; and I could never forgive you, aunt, if by quarrelling with that man, you caused him to make remarks and hunt about for ideas, and perhaps end in inventing some horrid story about us."

I laughed in my sleeve to hear her talk in this

way; she was not very sincere in her alarm, and Sophie would have called her a sly puss for speaking thus, but to me it was delicious to listen to her, for I could see the meaning that lay behind, and how intimately it concerned her and me. Her words acted like magic on her aunt.

"Well—yes—I think you are right, Florence. It will be more dignified, Mr. Egerton, to leave the man alone. So vulgar a mind is sure to be malicious—and he *might* invent, you know."

"What's that?" suddenly cried Florence, with the shadowy outline of her arm pointing into the east that the swing of the ship in the dead calm had brought broad on the port beam. I fancied she exclaimed in this way to abruptly change the subject, but when I looked, I saw that what had attracted her was a faint reddish light upon the sea-line. The water stretched up to it in a surface of liquid ebony, with here and there the flaking of a star-reflection in the expanding heaving of the deep.

"Is it a ship on fire?" said Aunt Damaris, peering and pecking at it with her face out of the shadow of the umbrella.

"It's the moon rising," I exclaimed.

Just then the low notes of a well-played concertina struck up on the quarter-deck, and three voices joined in—a tenor and two women's. I afterwards heard they were steerage passengers, amongst

those, I mean, who lived under the cuddy; but they
had never sung on deck before, and though I am
not going to tell you that their singing was that of
first-rate artists, nor that in daylight we should
have found it very moving, yet the effect was perfectly thrilling amid the dark deep ocean stillness,
broken only by the moaning wash of waters along
the ship's side and the soft flapping of canvas,
whilst the faint red light in the east grew clearer
and lighter until the arch of the crimson orb stood
up over the horizon, stealthily flashing upon the
black deep a blood-like ray that slowly lengthened
as the orb soared, swiftly changing to orange, then
to pearl, then to silver, with an ice-like rim of the
sea just under her.   In a few minutes she had shot
high and clear, and her light came along in a kind
of flowing silvery sheen that the eye could watch
the approach of until it was rippling full upon the
ship, transforming her canvas into squares of pearl,
whilst every shadow took a deeper shade, and ice-
like sparkles were kindled in the brass-work and
glass.

Oh, it was a sight most beautiful to see the large
tropical stars in her neighbourhood waning in the
blaze of silver she flung over the wonderful indigo
in which they were poised, and to come down from
them to the fan-shaped glow of mild white light
upon the water trembling like a wake of quicksilver
to the very side of the shadowy ship, whilst

in the soft pure radiance every object that the eye rested on took a kind of ethereal delicacy, as if it were a picture that owed its creation to the moon-gleams; the shrouds and standing rigging that were turned towards the light running up into the glimmer overhead like silver wires, the pale shining of the sails waning as they soared, until they looked to dissolve in the airy splendour that was flowing out of the east, the decks appearing like white satin with the gloss and sheen upon them; and a sharp jetty shadow was cast wherever a human figure stood or wherever a rope, a mast, or a yardarm broke the current of light streaming out of the breathless sky and over the tranced deep.

The music ceased on the quarter-deck, and my darling, whose sweet face I had been watching as her eyes followed the ascent of the moon out of the sea, started with a kind of sigh, and exclaimed in a low voice, "How beautiful!—how melancholy!"

"I don't see anything very melancholy in it, if you're talking of the moonrise," said Aunt Damaris; "I consider it very lovely, though I wish it would bring us some wind. What was that they sung down there, Mr. Egerton? A kind of serenade, I think."

"I believe it was," said I, not having the least idea. "They chose the right moment to set off," and I peeped wistfully at Florence, heartily wishing Aunt Damaris and her umbrella were off the poop;

for if ever the melting mood was strong in my heart's delight it was at that moment, when moonlight and music and feeling were combined with that indefinable sadness you feel at sea, when you look along the breathless leagues of water to where the haze of the moonlight seems to fall like a veil from heaven betwixt the watcher and the infinity beyond.

But Aunt Damaris remained fast, and the moonbeams shone in the dew upon the top of her umbrella. Presently the singing was resumed on the quarter-deck; this time by the tenor alone. His song was " Sally in our Alley," as sweet a melody as ever mortal composed, and the plaintive beautiful notes were echoed aloft among the sails and seemed to float away from them in dying tones. Most of the passengers aft went to the break of the poop to listen; and going there myself to take a peep (though I speedily returned to Florence), I spied the quarter-deck crowded with the 'tween-deck and steerage passengers and such of the crew as formed the watch on deck. In the midst of the singing, two bells—nine o'clock—were struck, and the hollow metallic sound rang with curious effect out of the darkness under the mainmast, where the shadow of the folds of the hauled-up mainsail lay dense.

" It is strange," said I, resuming my seat, " how moonlight gives a kind of strangeness to the most familiar objects. Mystical is the only word to express the irradiation. Objects look the mere spectres of themselves in it, catching, I suppose, their vagueness and unreality from what after all is only the ghost or wraith of the light that we live by—I mean the sun."

"It's a very becoming light," said Aunt Damaris. "It confers a chastity on the features which is not imparted by any other kind of illumination, though sperm oil is very soft," and I saw her old eyes fixed on Florence.

"It's a sad light," said my darling: "perhaps because, as you say," she continued, addressing me (she was always trying to shirk calling me Mr. Egerton), "it makes familiar things look unreal, it throws the hue of death over all that lives——"

"Pray don't be dreadful, my dear," exclaimed Aunt Damaris, giving herself a shake. "What sentimental views girls take of life! But cadaverous fancies are not poetical. Dear me! what a fearful calm! Why, if this is to last we shall never—— Gracious mercy! what's that!" she cried: and as she uttered the exclamation, she jumped out of her chair with such force as nearly to drive her bonnet though the umbrella, which with the chair went rolling over to the hencoop.

Many strange and stirring sights had I beheld in my seafaring days; the heavens in the east a bright red at midnight; half-a-dozen waterspouts illuminated by lightning whirling across the ocean in a tempest : fifty leviathans of the deep leaping their black stupendous forms half out of the snow of the rushing surges off the Falkland Islands ; the storm-wave like a white wall rolling out of the pitchy blackness of the horizon ; a cyclone half a mile in diameter racing past the stern of our ship in a smooth sea, making the water boil as it went, but never touching us ; but the like of the sight that had made Aunt Damaris cry out and jump from her chair, that had caused me to spring to my feet as if I had been seared with a red-hot iron, that had carried the passengers in a rush to the side of the ship, that had suspended the singing and all the sounds as if a blight had fallen and paralyzed and withered up the whole company of human beings upon our decks, never before had I encountered.

It was as if the sun had shot out of the dark star-laden sky overhead, and lighted up the sea to the nethermost confines of it. I looked where all the others were looking, and saw a huge flaming body descending from the heavens, within a few degrees from the zenith on our starboard hand ; the brightness of it was the dazzling ardency of molten steel, when maintained at a white and blinding heat by a fan-blast ; it resembled a star falling from its measureless altitude, and growing into a world as big as this as it approached, kept

furiously burning by its own velocity; the moonlight was eclipsed by the splendour; the sea was a
bright gold under the rushing wonder; our ship
stood out as if a noontide effulgence were upon
her, and the consternation and awe and amazement that worked in our faces were as clearly to be
seen as when the tropical sun stood over our mastheads; no noise accompanied its descent; the
horror of it, if I may so speak of any one feature
of a spectacle of matchless, thrilling, breathless,
awful beauty lay in the leagues of wild white light
that it threw out, so that above it not a star was to
be seen, whilst the moon, at which I threw a
hurried glance, had changed into a wan greenish
disk, and the sea under her, even in the far-off
east, gleamed like steel to the amazing radiance of
that flaming descending body. Mates, if you have
never seen such a sight as this, don't think I
exaggerate in my description of it. You know that
God's hand is most visible upon the deep, and that
those who are cradled upon its mighty surface
behold His wonders best there. Here was an in-
comparable manifestation that I see now, after all
these years, as though it were again happening,
and the awe and the spirit of devotion and the
sense of my human littleness visit me anew with
something of the oppressiveness I then felt as I
watched that wondrous fiery body sweeping down
the sky. We held our breath to await the plunge

of it into the sea, and to hear the mighty hissing that we expected would follow; but when it had reached to about six degrees above the horizon, being then, as we were all afterwards agreed, not more than half-a-mile distant from the ship, it exploded with the stinging crash of a burst of thunder that went rolling along past us in a roar and died away out upon the glassy surface in a moan; a thousand glowing fragments leaped for a breath like an outrushing of broken fire from the mouth of a volcano; and then the pained, dazzled, affrighted eye was met by a wave of darkness in the midst of which there was presently to be seen a faint bluish-white luminous smoke that hung in a sort of ring around that part of the air in which the meteor had vanished until the moonlight overpowered the spectral thing with its pearly film, and once more the stars were shining and the sea tenderly flaking the light of them as it softly heaved, whilst the ship melted back into the moonlight phantom she had before resembled, and the ocean-line ran round in a soft black sweep against the distant gloom.

All sorts of exclamations now broke forth from the people on the main and quarter-decks, whilst the passengers aft closed round Daniel and Mr. Thornton to talk about the phenomenon, the sharpest, and apparently the most impressed questioner being Aunt Damaris. I drew off to

where Florence stood near the foremost skylight.

"What do you think of that, my darling, as a
display of fireworks?"

"I never saw anything more terrible and splendid.
What could it have been, Jack?"

"A meteor," said I; "and I should think as
large a one as ever fell."

"Oh, listen to Captain Jackson," she exclaimed,
"he is trying to frighten Aunt Damaris."

The passengers made a block of dark shadow
against the rail in the gloom of the mizzen topsail
that the swing of the ship had brought betwixt
them and the moon, and out of the midst of them
came the loud tones of the navy man: "What I
say is, that if that body had struck this ship fair, it
would have knocked us into a cocked hat, doubled
us up, sent us to the bottom of the sea to add to
the stock of human bones there."

"Oh, how dreadful! how fearfully dangerous the
sea is!" I heard Mrs. Marmaduke Mortimer say.

"It is fearfully dangerous," whispered Aunt
Damaris's saw-like tones; "but I don't believe
that that meteor would have done us much harm
had it struck us. It was soft fire, nothing hard
about it at all; it would have enveloped us like a
flash of lightning, and perhaps have cracked a
mast; but as to splitting the ship—I consider such
ideas nonsense."

" If it was soft fire," said Mrs. Jackson, jeeringly, " pray what made it burst like a bombshell, and with the noise of a thunderbolt, and how came its fragments to fly about ? "

" That don't prove it was hard," said Daniel. " Lightning's soft fire, as Miss Hawke calls it, but it's always followed by noise."

" Whatever it was," observed Mr. Thompson Tucker, " I hope it won't occur again. Those appearances may be interesting to witness from an observatory, but I'm one of those persons who can't swim."

" Had it struck us," cried Captain Jackson, " you wouldn't have wanted to swim. You wouldn't have known what hurt you. It would have smashed us all into jelly-fish, and there'd have been nothing left afloat but a few hats."

" Just now it was to have made bones of us, and now we were to have become jelly-fish," said Aunt Damaris. " Captain Thompson, can't you explain to this gentleman the nature of those fiery bodies, so that if another should fall he need not feel alarmed ? "

" They're like cats and dogs," I whispered to Florence. " It's lucky your aunt isn't a man ; we'd have them fighting in dark corners long before we are up with the Cape."

" Oh, she can protect herself," replied Florence, laughing ; " but it's a thousand pities she should render herself so unpopular. It makes things very uncomfortable for me. Mrs. Jackson is barely civil; you may notice how the others leave aunt and me alone, instead of joining us as they do one another."

"So much the better for *us*, my sweet," said I. "What more could I want than that you and I should be left utterly alone ? "

She put her hand into mine, and thus we stood listening to the voices proceeding from the block of shadow near the quarter-boat. It is needless to say that Captain Jackson had witnessed the fall of a meteor twice the size of the one we had beheld when he had the honour of commanding H.M.S. *Cocksparrow*. "It was in a gale of wind, blowing great guns; we were hove to under the lee clew of the close-reefed main-topsail, making abominable weather of it; it was in the South Atlantic, in longitude about two degrees west. Composants were burning at our yardarms and the air was chokeful of electricity. Just before midnight a meteor of immense size rushed down from out of the clouds " . . . and then he went on to describe the phenomenon we had just seen, greatly exaggerating its dimensions. I knew Daniel too well to suppose that he would let him off.

"That was a wonderful meteor, Captain Jackson, at least eight times larger than the one that dropped close aboard of us north of the Mozambique Channel, the vessel being a small barque in which I was an apprentice. It fell at two bells in the middle watch; it took ten minutes to drop, and the blaze it threw out was so brilliant that it woke up the chief mate, who came on deck with his sextant, thinking he had mistaken the time and that it was just before noon. All the cocks started off a-crowing, and I met the cook coming along to light the galley fire for breakfast."

"Do you believe that, Jack?" whispered Florence.

"It's as true as the navy man's yarn," said I.

"What dreadful fibs sailors tell!" she exclaimed.

"Captain," said Mrs. O'Brien, "is it likely, do you suppose, that mateors are pieces of the sun dhropping off and tumbling upon the earth? The thought's just come into my head, captain."

"No, ma'am," says Daniel, "there are too many meteors to make that theory possible; the sun would have crumbled out long since, and we should all be as blind as the fish which live three thousand fathoms deep under our keel here."

"What makes 'em flame thin?" asked Mrs. O'Brien.

"Friction," replied Mr. Thompson Tucker; "they catch fire by rattling through the air so fast. Why, I suppose now, Captain Jackson, that one of those bodies would travel at the rate of three or four miles a minute."

" Don't know, I'm sure," replied the navy man, " but the fact of their travelling at all proves that they are operated on by the laws of gravity, and consequently have weight in them. Were they soft fire, as Miss Hawke here says, why, damme, they'd go *up* as fire does; they couldn't come *down*."

" Then will you tell me," cried Aunt Damaris, scornfully, " how lightning, that is merely fire without weight in it, falls down out of the clouds ? "

" Oh, that's a convulsion, that's a matter of electricity—another affair altogether," answered Captain Jackson, and probably afraid of being answered by the old lady, he said something to his wife about the dew, and they stalked off.

Aunt Damaris joined Florence and me, exclaiming very audibly, as she approached us, " A convulsion ! No wonder he's given up the sea ! Fancy such an ignorant man as that in charge of a ship of war ! "

Florence begged her not to speak so loud, whilst I went to pick up the capsized chair and umbrella ; but she had had enough of the deck, and after a brief stare round at the beautiful breathless night, she took my darling's arm and went below.

CHAPTER XVII.

ON THE EQUATOR.

If there is one thing that should reconcile a sailor of the old school to steam it is this: it makes calms of no consequence. You cannot fully realize all that that means until you have been hanging about the equator for ten days or so under a frying sun, and on an ocean of molten brass touched here and there with a draught of air that expires in its efforts to reach you. Before I started on this voyage I should have been quite satisfied, for the sake of being with Florence, had I been told that it would consist of nothing but dead calms and headwinds. But a week of the doldrums was too much even for my passion. To look around hour after hour, morning after morning, day after day, and behold always the same eternal placid unruffled heaving, the same deep satin-like blue, dazzling out into a thin tint that was neither green nor azure at the ocean line where the thrilling violet of the sky went down behind it;

the same throbbing, burning, cloudless luminary flashing at noon its tremendous fires right straight down over our heads; became soul-sickening before the week had expired. And yet we had ten days of it!

If you glanced over the side you saw your face there as clear as ever a mirror would give it back. If you gazed along the bulwarks you'd notice the rail of them twisting and writhing along the fore-castle in the giddy breathless atmosphere like the gliding motion of an eel. If you touched a deck-seam, whether in or out of the sunshine, the pitch came up in a string at your finger ends. A bluish haze hung over the vessel as though she were smoking as a manure-heap does. The crew stripped themselves half naked and went about their work with fiery faces and mossy breasts glistening with sweat. There was a constant throwing down of braces and hauling round of yards; for the officer of the watch would be incessantly testing the atmosphere with a moist-ened finger, and if he could detect ever so phantom-like a current of air abroad, whether by the feel of his finger or by the feeble flutter of the vane at the mast-head, he'd fling an order forward from the head of the poop ladder, and the yards would be braced to catch the mockery of a draught. The decks rumbled with curses; the sailors abhorred this boxhauling; what was the good of it, they thought. Shiver the blooming ship! was it right to wring the sweat out of them when the blaze of sunshine on either side the old hooker was just a sheet of burnished silver, and when the heave of the swell never disclosed the faintest wrinkle for leagues and leagues? Better snug the light sails by manning the clewlines and buntlines, haul down the jibs and staysails, and leave nothing but the topsails to dust themselves against the masts and wait for the wind to blow.

But for all that, it was this day and night watchfulness that sneaked us along. Noon would come, and lo! we had crawled out eight miles, ten miles, some such distance, in twenty-four hours, and the deuce knew how it had been done, for all day long the stuff which the cook's mate had hove overboard in the morning, along with an empty bottle, had hung close, sometimes under the counter, sometimes under the bow, sometimes alongside.

I found my account, however, in the deepening and the strengthening of my darling's love for me. As a theatre for the improvement and development of passion a sailing ship may be backed against all the ball-rooms, country lanes, balconies, small dull villages, and fashionable watering-places in the world. In olden times mothers sent their daughters to India, more assured of their finding husbands in the tall glazed castles which carried them round the Cape of Good Hope than on dry land. Steam has put an end to this; passages are too short nowadays to make flirting worth while, as girls say. But you'd have understood what the old voyages tended to had you been with us in the *Strathmore*, hanging for ten days under the sun, with the dead ocean looking like a pavement of silver under the cathedral-dome of the heavens whose violet it reflected. Why, such was the effect of it upon us, that before the week was out there was Thompson Tucker making eyes at modest Miss Grant, whilst her mother sat by with alarm depicted on her countenance, but too mild to frown him down; the Marmaduke Mortimers grew several degrees fonder, and the Joyces carried a more distinctly attached manner in their method of walking about arm-in-arm. Mr. Alphonso Hawke was an old stager, had made the voyage between England and Australia several times, and knew how the monotony of the sea throws people upon one another; and his and Aunt Damaris's scheme for bringing Florence and Mr. Morecombe together never struck me more forcibly as a piece of judgment that might have proved fatal to me had I been left at home and Morecombe taken my place, than it did during those ten days of the doldrums. I remember telling my darling this, and it made her indignant. "The more I saw of Mr. Morecombe the more I disliked him," she exclaimed. "How can you talk such nonsense, Jack?" .

"You undervalue the effect of this calm," said I. "Behold its influence upon Thompson Tucker. Were Captain Jackson a single man, I should not despair of seeing him and Aunt Damaris exchanging locks of hair. This tedium your father foresaw, and as I by being out of sight would have been out of mind——" But an earnest beautiful glance of her deep and speaking eyes brought up this badinage with a round turn, and in a breath I was pouring out repentance, vows, gratitude, love.

All this while her aunt made no sign. I do not say that she believed that Florence and I were deeply in love; when she was present we always threw a sort of reserve into our behaviour and kept the full expression of our devotion for the stars; but she knew we were constantly together, indeed she never came on to the poop if Florence happened to be on deck without finding me with her; and therefore she was perfectly well aware that a very great deal was going on, though she did not know how much. But she made no objection, she showed no uneasiness, her manner towards me was always as full of amiability as her character would allow her to import into her bearing; whenever she found us together she would join us, but say nothing about it either before my face or to

Florence behind my back, behaving, indeed, as if we were sweethearts and recognized as such by her.

I once had a talk with Daniel about this. He found me alone one morning early, fresh from the head pump where I had got an ordinary seaman to play upon me for ten minutes with a sluicing stream of sparkling water out of the blue under the bows. My friend had come up to look for wind, and found me whistling for it over the taffrail. This set us talking of the weather and of old times, and one thing leading to another, "Well, Jack," says he presently, "what's the *Strathmore* going to do for you in the shape of getting you a wife?"

"You see how it goes with us, Daniel," I answered. "I suppose no fonder couple were ever found upon the ocean."

"The aunt seems quite willing, I fancy," said he.

"It looks so. She likes me as Mr. Egerton; the question is, will she like me as Jack Seymour?"

"Any way, among us your secret has been wonderfully well kept. I never thought you'd have been able to maintain your alias long. I reckoned your girl would have split—whipped out with it unconsciously—and smothered the whole blessed job. I suppose if the aunt don't find out the truth for herself, you'll have to tell her who you are some of these days. You can't marry under a false name, can you?"

"Of course I can't," said I. "My policy has been to make Miss Damaris Hawke like me as Mr. Egerton, and I think I've succeeded."

"Is there any chance now of her rounding upon you as Jack Seymour and ordering you to leave her niece alone?" said Daniel.

"I can't tell you. If I knew for certain, I'd heave my alias overboard, for Miss Florence hates to call me Mr. Egerton—she says it makes her feel as if she were telling a story—whilst the masquerading is as little to my taste as to hers."

"There's no doubt," said Daniel, thoughtfully, "that the aunt don't object to you, as Mr. Egerton, making love to her niece. That's as clear as mud in a wineglass. She lets you and Miss Florence be together, and never interferes that I can see. That's a sort of victory, isn't it? If you have the talent to conquer under false colours, can't you do so under true?"

"Well, you see, Daniel," said I, "it's the false colours which have given me the advantage by enabling me to sheer alongside of her without exciting her suspicion as to the real character of the apparently friendly stranger."

"But what are your particular charms as Mr. Egerton?" asked Daniel. "How is it that an alias has allowed you to forge leagues ahead of your rate of sailing when your father's name was written bold on your stern and head ? "

"You're asking me questions," said I, " which are just as much riddles to me as to you. But I'll tell you my notions: first and foremost, Miss Florence was sent away out of England in order to get rid of Jack Seymour. Next, the voyage was likewise planned to bring her and Morecombe together. Keep those points in mind. The plot, so far as Morecombe was concerned, has proved a dead failure. The aunt hates the name of him, and he's as completely out of the running as if he had been sewn up in a hammock and launched through the gangway. But Jack Seymour is still ashore; and the aunt says to herself, ' When my niece returns—and return she must some of these fine days—she'll find that fellow waiting for her. My brother won't like that. He has described the youth as a common, insulting sailor-chap, and I for one never could endure such a family connec-tion as he would make.' So with this thought in her, d'ye see, Daniel, she plumps up against me, Mr. John Egerton, a very gentlemanly, well-bred youth, extraordinarily polite to her, highly compli-mentary, the possessor of a decidedly aristocratic name, and clearly an independent gentleman. She sees that I have fallen in love with Miss Florence, and that Miss Florence very much likes me. So her old mind goes to work, and she says to herself, ' Since Mr. Morecombe is quite out of the question, and since there is very great danger of my niece renewing her affection for that common person, Jack Seymour, when she returns to England, surely I shall be acting with great judgment in encouraging the attentions of this very genteel Mr. Egerton, who, if nothing else comes of it, will at least wholly displace Mr. Jack Seymour from my niece's heart.' "

" You seem to have hit it," said Daniel, grinning at me with a kind of admiration; " hang me if you haven't taken a header into the old maid's mind with a vengeance ! But what on earth can she think of Miss Florence's constancy when she discovers in a few days that she has clean forgotten the Jack Seymour who was one of the causes of her being sent away from home, and fallen in love with the perfect stranger, Mr. John Egerton ? "

" She has said nothing about it," I replied; "and I'm not going to bother myself over her ideas outside those which particularly concern me. If she reasons at all she'll conclude either that her niece is a very impressionable girl, or that Mr. Alphonso Hawke over-emphasized her love for Jack Seymour."

" If the latter's her notion she won't be afraid of your girl's renewing her love for Jack Seymour when she returns home," said Daniel very logically.

"But she can't be sure," said I. " She won't like to think her brother utterly mistaken. What has probably occurred to her is this : that Miss Florence finds Mr. Egerton more fascinating than Mr. Seymour, though if she don't get Mr. Egerton she'll return to the other."

" Well, that's very probable," said Daniel.

" And you must not lose sight," continued I, discussing the thing with some enjoyment of it, for it enabled me to see points which would not occur to me by thinking to myself, " of the marked attention I have paid the old lady, the hold I have on her by professing to have got the story from Mr. Morecombe, her natural liking for me not impaired, I daresay, by my cheap little excursion overboard t'other day, her belief—acquired God knows how—in my social merits."

" Ay," exclaimed Daniel, "and look how *I've* praised you, Jack ! and the Joyces, you know, speak of you as if you were an angel. But I say ! " he whipped out with a kind of groan, slewing his purple face round the sea, "this calm is getting serious. It'll kill my reputation for despatch. Is there no wind left in the world ? " and he dodged over to the compass and flitted restlessly about the deck, and then, after speaking awhile to the second mate, he hove a despairing glance aloft and bundled below.

Letting my thoughts linger a bit over this chat,

I confess .the wonder that he had expressed and that I had all along felt at the manner in which my secret had been kept from Aunt Damaris struck me afresh almost as if it had been new to me. Never did an old maid's face hold a shrewder pair of eyes than Alphonso's sister's, and I could have sworn that her mind was one of the most suspicious in life; and therefore, seeing how quickly Florence had taken to me, and how I had somewhat of a sailorly cut, spite of my clothes and my sham ignorance of everything concerning the sea, and how I was bound to Australia for no reason whatever that she could find out, I say, it was strange that she did not make two and two of all these things, and so guess who I was. But against this you must put, first, that she had never seen me as Jack Seymour; second, that in all probability I had never been described to her outside such general terms as old Hawke's abuse of me conveyed, and which would have nothing to do with my face, figure, or manners; third, that Jack Seymour, being little more than an abstraction to her, she was not nearly so likely to imagine the possibility of his following his sweetheart to sea as would have been the case had she met him in the flesh as Mr. Hawke had; fourth, that the idea of his taking ship with her niece had never in the faintest possible degree occurred to her; fifth, that she would not be aware that Jack

Seymour was unknown by sight, if not more familiarly, to Mr. Morecombe, and the circumstance, therefore, of that young man and Mr. Egerton sharing one berth and conversing as I pretended Mr. Morecombe had conversed with me, would tend almost more than anything else to blind her to the fact that stared her in the face; and finally, that being as I reckoned an extremely suspicious person, she possessed all the qualities which sentence their possessor to the constant mortification of being easily tricked.

But to drop all this problemizing for the plain truth, the calm, as I have said, kept us north of the line for ten days, and all the changes which came were a shifting of the colour of the ocean from the rich azure of the morning to the tin-like glitter of noon, following on with a sullen brassy glare as the sun westered till the flaming luminary sank into a sheet of gold and the darkness came, with the Southern Cross hanging low in the south, and the moon rising later and redder every night, when it became new again and a silver slip in the wake of the sun. But on the afternoon of the tenth day there came a change; you took notice of a staring brightness in the easterly sky against which the white sails showed yellow, a hollower movement of the swell and a rounder sweep in the look of the water from where the ship hung down to the horizon which showed clear against the firmament in a sickly paint-like blue from which the eye recoiled. The sun shone mistily, though the fierceness of his bite was all but insufferable when you stepped clear of the awning. The black fins of half a dozen sharks gleamed out of the oily blue, and had the imagination gone to work for the right kind of embellishment for the glazed, thick, sullen heaving of the swell, it could have hit upon nothing more appropriate.

"They fancy the ship's going to rot through and let us into the water," said Mr. Thornton to me; "they're sagacious beasts, and as patient as the foul fiend himself until what they wait for is within reach of their grinders. But they'll be cheated; there's a squall brewing yonder, and there'll be a breeze of wind behind it if I'm not greatly mistaken."

You needed a sailor's eye for atmospheric effect to understand his meaning when he pointed into the north-west quarter, and I don't fancy that I should have noticed the sign myself but for his indication of it. *Then*, indeed, it was plain enough in the sort of blue film that seemed, so to speak, to be bending the sky down to the sea as if with the weight of it, though the horizon ran in a sharp firm line right through it, and after a minute's gazing one felt it to be the shadow of something drawing up from behind the ocean and that was pressing upon the water in a manner to give the swell a rounder back and a quicker run. By-and-by a streak of haze floated up and looked white enough as it stayed there, but when I turned to take another squint it had changed into a thin brown, and had spread and risen, the fringe of it resembling a smear upon the sky and the sea under it taking a sort of olive tint which brightened out into blue south and north-east.

Aunt Damaris came on deck armed with a large fan; presently Florence arrived. I placed chairs for them, and said with the artlessness of a landsman, "Mr. Thornton thinks we're going to have a squall."

"Thank goodness!" exclaimed Aunt Damaris. "And pray where is it to come from?"

"Yonder, he says," and I pointed to the gathering thickness.

"What is a squall?" asked Mrs. Marmaduke Mortimer who was sitting near, her husband for a wonder not being with her.

"A sudden burst of wind," replied Aunt Damaris in her sharp manner.

"Nothing dangerous, I hope?" said Mrs. Mortimer, looking right up overhead into the sky.

"The burst won't come from there," said Aunt Damaris, "but from the end of the sea yonder;" and she extended her lean hand that sparkled with rings.

" Oh, I see ! " cried the newly-married wife effusively. " Oh, Mr. Egerton, do look at those yellow patches upon the fog there ! Are they not like sunflowers growing in a garden bed."

The sunshine was blazing slantingly upon the rising bodies of vapour, and brightening the brows of them with a sulphur-coloured radiance. The effect was striking, almost wild, for the dark green weltering of the sea under the thickness gave a malignant hint of storm to the look of the heavens there, and the dry yellow gleaming in the van of the coming outburst was just the colour a painter would have chosen for heightening the sullen meaning of the fast rising darkness. In a few minutes this appearance vanished, and the vapour thickened up like the pourings of a factory chimney kept low by the rarefaction of the atmosphere. The swell had increased in volume with amazing rapidity, and the deep ship rolled and wallowed in it as if she had a mind to spring every spar in her. The beating of the canvas was like the continuous discharge of small cannons. You saw the people on the main deck stumbling and lurching, and clinging convulsively as they tried to pass along, and every now and again a flash of smoke-like spray swept on board through a scupper hole as the ship buried her side. During one heavy roll I barely missed stopping Aunt Damaris from tumbling heels over head with her chair ; she was

all but gone when I flung my shoulder against her
and shored her up. This, coupled with the fast
spreading gloom and the wild tumblefication and
the fierce creaking of flapping noises, frightened
her.

"Captain!" she screamed out to Daniel, "what
is the meaning of this? Is it to be a squall or
tempest? Don't deceive me. I know the difference,
sir."

"Nothing to cause you any alarm, Miss Hawke,"
answered the skipper, who stood looking at the
weather past the starboard quarter-boat, and he
then gave some orders to the chief mate. One
might tell he guessed that the worst of whatever
was coming lay in the look of it, for all that Mr.
Thornton sung out was to clew up the royals, haul
down the flying jib, haul up the mainsail and stand
by the topgallant halliards. "When the rain
before the wind, then your topsail halliards mind,"
chants the forecastle poet; and here was the wind
coming first. The swelling vapour rolled up until
it looked all the way to starboard like the loom of
cliffs thousands of feet high, while the scud, like
dust off the floor under the flourishing of a broom,
blew out in pale yellow volumes from under the
compacter masses, and was floating overhead and
dimming the sky into the east, with the sun
amongst it a shapeless sickly blotch of light, before
ever a breath of air could be seen soiling the

polished surface of the mountainous swell. Maybe the wind was waiting for the signal; it came in the shape of a copper-like glare of lightning that more resembled the cloud's reflection of a solid sheet of fire than the whizz of an electric spark; and to the tune of the rumbling of thunder rushed the wind, blowing the gloom left and right, and creating appearance like what they call ox-eyes in it, spaces of light that grew from points into yawning gaps, as though the squall was driving down upon us through tunnels in the sky.

"Look!" cried I to Florence; "how you may see the wind before there is draught enough to extinguish a candle!"

I took her to the rail to watch, whilst Aunt Damaris clawed her way to the companion, on the top steps of which she stood with her sharp nose forking out beyond the hood, and pecking as it might be at the coming squall. It was a fine sight to see the wind rushing along the tops of the swell, flashing white in the hollows, and sweeping with a yell over the brows in a scattering of spray. It looked to advance in the form of an arch, with the legs spreading out from south-west to north-east, and the lifting of the white water under the shearing of it made Daniel reckon there was more in it than he had supposed.

"Let go the topgallant halliards!" he sung out. "Hands by the fore and mizzen topsail halliards!"

And as the yards aloft came running down, with a second brilliant gleam of lightning the squall burst upon the ship and down she leaned to it, motionless for a space, with the smooth water under her lee bubbling and churning half-way up the bulwarks. I had my darling by this time snug under the starboard quarter-boat, for there was no rain in sight as yet, and I wanted her to see the squall, and the boat under which we stood split the wind and sent it screaming clear of us over our heads. Aunt Damaris had vanished, but the other passengers, ladies and gentlemen, held their ground and looked on with interest at a scene full of excitement and commotion, and welcome, God knows, as the first honest break in the ten days of rankling, stewing calm. The helm had been put hard over, and the ship was slowly paying off as she began to stir after the first heavy lean-down: but Lord! the shindy aloft; sails thundering, masts jumping, the gloom as if it were cloud flying through the rigging mingled with a glancing of spume; the crew sprawling about, Mr. Thornton bawling, Daniel excitedly gesticulating at the wheel. Why, I daresay some of the poor 'tween deck folks thought it was all up with us, when, in reality, it was a mere equatorial squall with the worst of it in its teeth, which were soon to leeward of us, and a sprinkling of rain and a fresh breeze to follow.

There is no finer sight, I think, than a full-rigged

ship offers when she is in the act of paying off, heeling over, with a fierce outfly of wind screeching past her. Her lee-rigging hangs slack over the white water; her sails swell out in cloud-like shapes through the buntlines and upon the lowered yards: you note the gradual recovery of the heavy slant of her masts, as with a slow sweep of her jibbooms she settles the wind further and further aft yet, until yielding to the full impulse of the blast, with a long hissing plunge she takes the first of the seas, and like a fleeing madwoman whose tresses stream from her head and whose raiment has the wildness of a witch's as she runs, the ship rushes forward as though she were the very spirit of the storm whose darkness is upon her and whose ravings pierce the ear from her rigging. Several bright flashes of lightning illuminated the heaving snow-like path of the vessel as she headed with the squall and sped for a space on the wings of it. All was flying darkness for awhile, with a roll of thunder playing through as though it would give a tornado-note to the outburst; but in about ten minutes the weight of the wind sensibly diminished, and while the helm was put down to bring the *Strathmore* to her course, I had just time to hand Florence to the companion, when wash came the rain in a bright sheet, crushing out the wind as if by magic, and leaving the ship slapping her wet canvas upon the heavy swell, whilst through the grey deluge to leeward you could catch sight of the white water under the clouds passing away in a whirl of gloom. The rain ceased as suddenly as the wind had expired ; the windward darkness lightened, and a marble-like streak of blue opened betwixt the main and mizzen topsail yardarm ; a wet gleam of sunshine danced along the weltering ocean boundary, and broadening fast flashed up the whole expanse of the deep in the south-west, exposing the glorious blue of it crisping under the breeze that was sure to follow the squall, and making the passing thickness look like a solid shadow upon the sea, shot with a malignant lustre like the bluish tints on battle-smoke, and spanned by a brilliantly rich rainbow through whose exquisitely coloured arch you seemed to gaze on the very darkness of night itself. In a few minutes the welcome breeze was blowing merrily through our rigging, the songs of the sailors rose as they mastheaded the yards, ordinary seamen sprawled about, heavily slapping the decks with swabs, and with her wet planks sparkling in the sunshine and her canvas drying from grey into white, the *Strathmore* rolling heavily and gracefully over the long swell, a line of yeasty foam slipping past her glossy sides, looked to have settled herself fairly down at last for the passage of the equator upon whose northern skirts she had been hanging like a dead thing for ten days.

We crossed the line in nineteen degrees west longitude, carrying a pleasant sailing breeze with us a trifle abaft our starboard beam, and the ship was just a pile of canvas with five stunsails out, the lower stunsail yawning wide over the swinging-boom guyed forward, and every cloth pulling steadily whilst the white trucks swung like silver buttons under the floating clouds which gleamed like the inside of oyster-shells as they sprung sweet and fresh from the deep blue sea and sailed up the azure on the road the sun was taking. In my time, when the equator was crossed on the outward passage to Australia, there would be a stir among the passengers as if they began to consider, at last, that there was a chance some of these fine days of the voyage coming to an end. The running large before the north-east trades is hopeful, but sometimes you will get a dreary sickener betwixt the Channel and the parallel where the steady breeze is picked up; and then perhaps follows the deadly pause upon the glassy equatorial sea, where the water dies out in haze and the sun finds a blazing mirror whereto he combs his flaming beard as he drives on his tour round the world. But the North Atlantic past, hope grows brisk as the south-east trades are approached. The Cape is not very far off now, you think: and then hurrah for an easterly course across the mighty Southern Ocean.

I can answer for the influence of latitude south upon the spirits of the *Strathmore's* passengers. We grew more cordial. If there was any ill-feeling it was betwixt Aunt Damáris and Captain Jackson and his wife. Not that the others liked the old lady very much, but they would come up and talk to her, and she would converse with them more or less politely according to the temper she happened to be in. But she and the Jacksons had nothing to say to one another. This no doubt indirectly helped my case, for the aversion among them made the old lady guess that the navy man and his help-mate would not show her much mercy were they to hear all about the cause of Morecombe's joining the ship; and many a time would I think, as I peered at Aunt Damaris, "If you only knew who *I* was, if you could only conceive the additions the story would gain by the simple disclosure of the truth from *me* to the Jacksons, there'd be no bulk-head in this ship thick enough for you to hide behind."

Friendlier feelings arising with our progress, various amusements were planned. The steerage passenger singers were invited on the poop, and obliged us with a very pretty little concert. Then the 'tween-deck passengers gave a ball upon the main-deck that lasted through the dog watches; a fiddle was brought out of the forecastle, the fellow who played it seated himself on the drum of the quarter-deck capstan, some rum was brought up at the expense of us aft and distributed, diluted, in wineglassfuls amongst the poor people, and we sat at the brake of the poop looking down on as lively a scene as ever kept folks happy and laughing at sea. I see the picture now; Jack Fiddler sawing away with an occasional squirt of tobacco juice over his right shoulder, men and women dancing to his strains, the children frolicking amongst them, the crew looking on from the district of the galley with bronzed grinning faces, till the night fell upon us all with a hurried sweeping embrace of the sea with her shadowy arms and the stars looked down at us through the rope-ladders.

Then the crew would furnish us with some diversion by turning up to dance a little bit of a Dane, a rat of a man, with eyes like a ferret, and a face with an expression upon it such as you'll see sometimes in the gunpowder prickings of sailors upon seamen's arms and breasts. This little fellow was the best hornpipe dancer I ever saw in my life. I never before, and have never since met his equal. He would dress himself up to resemble a man-of-warsman, grass hat on nine hairs, his tawny breast bare to his belt, flowing white pants and low shoes with heels which rattled the planks like castanets. The fiddler would crawl upon the booms, and the Dane take his stand upon the weather side of the forecastle at the head of the ladder, so that we could see him plain under the weather clew of the mainsail that was hauled up; and when all was ready and the fiddle began to squeak, off would go the Dane, footing it as no landsman in this world ever did; no, though he had passed his whole life in doing nothing else; his pace was noble, the twinkling of his feet miraculous, and to see him there with his head floating like a bubble on his shoulders, his arms crossed on his bosom, and a rapping coming from under him like a roll upon a drum, with a graceful leap hear and there, and a sedate march round, and a face all the while as solemn as a mute, was to behold the hornpipe danced as only a sailor knows how.

This delighted Florence more than anything else. Her pulse seemed to keep time to the ocean dance, and I would catch her watching with a glistening eye as you'll see it in people who find more in a thing than it looks to have. You see we had the right kind of setting for that picture; no footlights, no groups of stage mountebanks, nor painted rigging leading heavens know where; but the deep blue white-flecked sea, melting into an evening richness of tint—for these were dog-watch sports, of course—and the fountain-like sound of bubbles and foam coming up over the sides, and the white decks, with the red sunshine lying in pools of light among the shadows, and the groups of rough seamen, simple-hearted as children, smoking and watching on the forecastle, and somehow causing you to raise your eyes from their dark faces to those lofty spars up and down which they were always travelling, where the sails shone like swelling spaces of yellow satin in the hot gleam of the sinking luminary whose radiance touched the greased masts until they looked to be made of amber.

Once we went so far as to shake a foot among ourselves on the poop. The steerage passengers made the music for us, and we got through several quadrilles and a waltz or two capitally. For one of the square dances I had Aunt Damaris as a partner, with Daniel and Mrs. O'Brien to face us. I doubt if the old lady would have consented to dance with anybody else; and on the whole I afterwards considered that I had run a great risk in asking her, as she was more likely than not to fly in my face with the suspicion that I desired to make her ridiculous. But so far from resenting my politeness, she appeared struck and gratified with it. "It's some years now since I have danced," said she, with a sort of simper that would have been exquisitely diverting in some Dresden china comedy of the old school; and you could see that she was remembering the time when she danced often, and when there were partners and to spare for her. She did not hang in the wind

long; I gave her my arm, and then Daniel and
Mrs. O'Brien, and Thompson Tucker and Miss
Grant, and Mr. Joyce and Florence posted themselves, the concertina twanged, and we started.
You'll reckon that the decks were pretty steady, and
that was so. There was the long ocean swell
always hollowing and rounding under our forefoot;
but a steady breeze was in the sails, every sheet
was eased well off, and the ship went along
upright; her curtsies only made our heels the
nimbler. Aunt Damaris and Mrs. O'Brien matched
each other well for airs and graces. The Irish
lady was as stout as my partner was lean; and
they behaved as if they were on the floor of an
amphitheatre with galleries running up to the
sky full of spectators. Their self-consciousness
was something to live in the memory, like the
meteor we had seen, or the sea-serpent. With
slightly lifted dress to give room for their pointed
toes, they went to work as if George III. was on
the throne, curtseying and smirking, though my
partner was the more old-fashioned; she seemed
to bring up a smell of lavender on the poop, and,
to have done her justice, I needed smalls and a
frill. Mrs. O'Brien gave us a taste of Castle airs,
for she had danced at that court I heard her tell
Daniel (who looked as though he did not understand
her by the way), and all that she required to
complete her amazing carriage was a bundle of

feathers. on the top of her head and a bronze-
coloured dress to glisten as her fat form rose and
fell inside it.   To turn from her to Florence! to
glance from that broad homely Irish countenance,
with its long stretch betwixt the nose and the upper
lip, and the small, bright. self-satisfied, black eyes,
to the pet of my heart, lovely always, whether in
sunshine or starlight, flinging a kind of poetry round
her upon the rudest and homeliest details of the
ship's furniture by the magic power of beautifying
with the surpassing grace of her form the gleam
of her deep sweet eyes, the glint of her hair, the
snowlike flash and sparkle of her motioning, un-
gloved hands, whatever was near her, aye, though
it were even Daniel's nor'west face or the lean
acidulated features of her aunt—why, I say, it was
worth keeping your eye fixed for a spell on Mrs.
O'Brien for the delight you found in turning it
afterwards upon Florence Hawke.   You may reckon
I danced with *her ;* one waltz we had—sailors are
noble partners, ladies, in round dances :—and as
we floated round the skylights up to the man at.
the wheel and back again to the break of the poop.
revolving as if we were a couple of angels bent
upon finding Paradise in the strains of a concertina
and upon the white planks of a ship's deck, you
may take it that my hold of her waist was something more than a dancer's grip ; and so well were we
matched in our footing, every movement pairing as

the albatross resting on the wing swings in unison
to the speeding of the surges, that we talked into
one another's ears as we danced as comfortably
and as eloquently as if we were seated and no one
was by.

But these merry-makings did not cover many
evenings.

END OF VOL. II.

LONDON: PRINTED BY WILLIAM CLOWES AND SONS, LIMITED,
STAMFORD STREET AND CHARING CROSS.